G000081437

David Burnell comes from York. He studied maths at Cambridge and taught it for several years to sixth formers in West Africa. After returning to the UK, he applied it to management problems in health, coal mining and the water industry. On "retiring", he completed a PhD at Lancaster University on the deeper meaning of data from London's water meters.

He and his wife split their time between Berkshire and North Cornwall. They have four grown-up children.

By the same author

Cornish Conundrums

Full-length present-day crime stories, featuring industrial mathematician George Gilbert and friends, stemming from projects in different parts of Cornwall.

Doom Watch
Slate Expectations
Looe's Connections
Tunnel Vision
Twisted Limelight
Forever Mine
Crown Dual
Unsettled Score
Brush with Death
Beyond Reach

Tales of Peril and Predicament

A medley of short stories set over the last millennium in locations around the world. They include a few early-life stories of George Gilbert.

Pebbles on the Shore
One Scoop or Two?
Lucky Dip
Hook, Line and Sinker
Tapestry Tangles
Black Hole, Silver Lining

Cornish Conundrum Author Reviews

Doom Watch: "Cornwall and its richly storied coast has a new writer to celebrate in David Burnell. His crafty plotting and engaging characters are sure to please crime fiction fans." Peter Lovesey

"A well-written novel, cleverly structured, with a nicely handled subplot . . ." Rebecca Tope

Slate Expectations: "combines an interesting view of an overlooked side of Cornish history with an engaging pair of sleuths, on the trail from past misdeeds to present murder." Carola Dunn

"An original atmospheric setting which is sure to put Delabole on the map. A many-stranded story keeps the reader guessing, with intriguing local history colouring events up to the present day." Rebecca Tope

Looe's Connections: "A super holiday read set in a super holiday location!" Judith Cutler

Tunnel Vision: "Enjoyable reading for all who love Cornwall and its dramatic history." Ann Granger

Twisted limelight: "The plot twists will keep you guessing up to the last page. A thrilling Cornish mystery." Kim Fleet

"A clever, exciting story of modern-day skulduggery and romance on the beautiful north Cornish coast." Roger Higgs

Forever Mine: "An intriguing mystery set to the backdrop of a wedding in sleepy Cornwall, where all is not as it appears."

Sarah Flint

Crown Dual: "A page-turning contemporary thriller with a deeply compelling narrative." Richard Drysdale

Unsettled Score: "A stack of mysteries to solve, including an unusual murder, all in a wonderful Cornish setting." Stephen Baird

Peter Lovesey holds multiple awards for his crime writing, including a Crime Writers' Cartier Diamond Dagger.

Carola Dunn pens Daisy Dalrymple and Cornish Mysteries.

Rebecca Tope writes the Cotswold and other Mysteries.

Judith Cutler created the DS Fran Harman crime series.

Ann Granger authors the Campbell and Carter Mysteries.

Dr Kim Fleet, poison expert, writes the Eden Grey Mysteries.

Dr Roger Higgs is a Bude geologist and local guide.

Sarah Flint authors the DC Charlotte Stafford series.

Richard Drysdale pens thrillers on Scottish Independence.

Stephen Baird, a Truro Cathedral Guide, is author of "Fire in the straw".

Happy reading!

David Burnell

WELL ABOVE PAR

A Cornish Conundrum

David Burnell

Skein Books

WELL ABOVE PAR

Published by Skein Books, 88, Woodcote Rd, Caversham, Reading, UK

First edition: May 2023.

© Copyright David Burnell 2023
The moral right of the author has been asserted.

This book is a work of fiction but the settings around Fowey, Luxulyan, St Austell and Restormel Castle are real. Joseph Treffry was a pioneering engineer in the nineteenth century; Charles Rashleigh initiated the harbour at Charlestown; Isambard Kingdom Brunel designed the Great Western Railway. The characters and incidents portrayed are from the author's imagination. No character is based on any real person, living or dead; any resemblance is purely coincidental.

ISBN: 9798390964743

The front cover shows the entrance gateway to Restormel Castle near Lostwithiel. In the background is Treffry's Viaduct in the Par Valley. Pictures inside include the main church in Fowey, Charlestown harbour, the China Clay Pit at Wheal Martyn, the Treffry Viaduct and the inside of the Castle doughnut. Thanks to my wife, Marion, for the castle and author cover photos; and to Dr Chris Scruby for photos of Fowey and Charlestown and refinements to various originals.

OUTLINE

Prologue	*November 1808*	*page 3*
Part 1	*February 5th - 12th Commission*	*page 7*
Part 2	*February 6th - 13th Investigation*	*page 65*
Part 3	*February 6th - 13th Altercation*	*page 117*
Part 4	*February 12th - 19th Assignation*	*page 138*
Part 5	*February 12th - 19th Extrapolation*	*page 182*
Part 6	*February 19th - 24th Contention*	*page 222*
Part 7	*February 24th - March 1st Resolution*	*page 273*
Epilogue	*Summer 2023*	*page 329*

x x

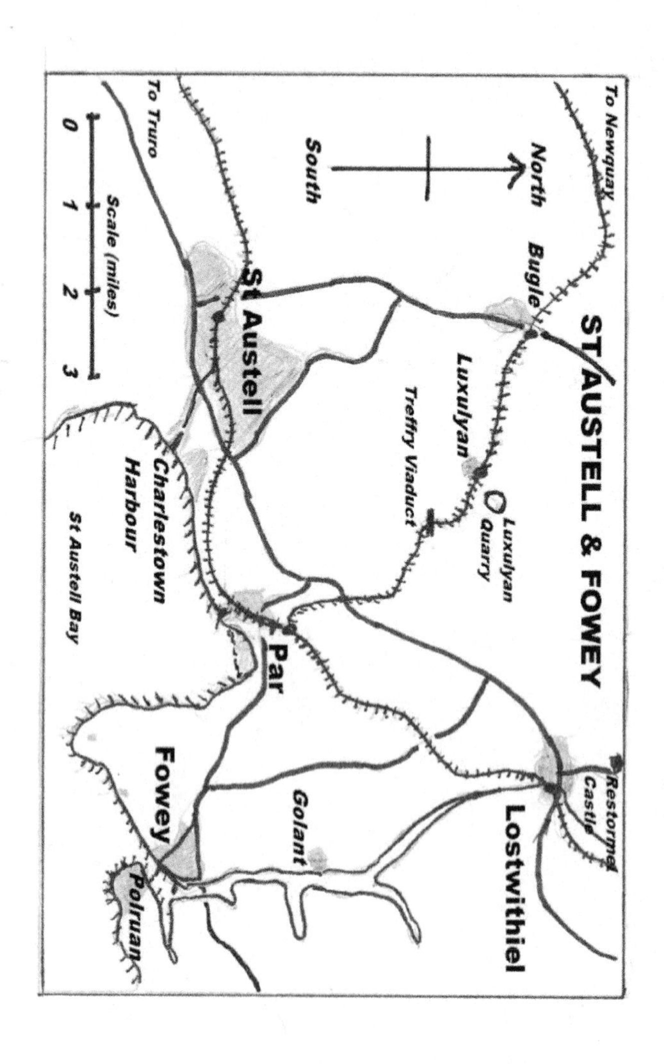
ST AUSTELL & FOWEY
To Newquay
North
South
Bugle
Luxulyan
Treffry Viaduct
Luxulyan Quarry
Lostwithiel
Restormel Castle
Golant
St Austell
Par
Fowey
Polruan
Charlestown Harbour
St Austell Bay
To Truro
Scale (miles)
0
1
2
3

PROLOGUE

It had been a monstrous shock. One moment Joseph was battling with work for the final stage of his degree in his room at Exeter College. The next a servant had come in with tale of a disaster. He was breathing heavily and obviously distraught.

'Sire, I am so sorry to be the bearer of bad news; I bring dreadful tidings from Fowey.'

Joseph laid down the pen from the essay he had just started on ideas for systematic mining, turned in his chair and gestured to his unexpected visitor to sit down.

'Please, Wilbur, settle yourself before you begin.'

Wilbur took a moment to compose himself. 'Sire, your beloved grandfather has passed away; your mother is distraught. The doctor said it was consumption. Three days ago he was in good health. A day later he died. I was sent to find you at once. Your attendance is urgently requested. Right now, the carriage that brought me is being fitted with fresh horses. If you are willing, we can start back within the hour.'

An hour wasn't long to pack his journal, a few textbooks and a bag of clothes but it was enough. Joseph's father had died a long time ago, when he was but six years old; he was his mother's only son. Whatever he was about to discover, a lot would now fall on his shoulders. He had known that might happen one day; he'd never imagined that it would come so soon.

Pausing only to knock at his tutor's door to explain his changed circumstances, Joseph headed for the porters' lodge.

The carriage was waiting in the cobbled street outside. He had one last look at his fine Cotswold-stone college before climbing aboard. Was this the last he would ever see of Oxford and its grandeur?

The first part of the journey was easy enough. The toll road from Oxford to Bristol was adequately maintained, well-travelled and safe – at least for a pair of men. Joseph didn't say much. He was trying to prepare himself for what might lie ahead.

They swapped horses in Bristol while they had a meal, then continued without further delay.

Exeter was the next stop – another toll road but it was judged safe enough – and there they changed horses once more. This time they managed to secure a few hours' sleep. Wilbur was exhausted – he'd been on the go for eighteen hours. Soon Joseph felt impelled to continue. On to Plymouth, then a ferry across the River Tamar and into the Duchy of Cornwall.

Joseph gave a sigh of relief. Oxford had been an amazing experience but this was where he now belonged.

Darkness had fallen. The byways became bumpier as they followed the rugged south Cornwall coast up and down, till they reached the town of Looe – Joseph recalled the aggrieved mutterings in Fowey that here had not just one but two Members of Parliament. Was that why it had a multi-arched bridge across the River Looe? Or was that why it had two MPs?

Finally, they followed the byway – by now little more than a rutted cart track – along the coast until they reached the village of Polruan. Joseph gave thanks for the lamps on his carriage that enabled them to pick out the way. Polruan's dark stone cottages lay up and down the hillside. On the opposite side of the estuary, he knew, was Fowey.

On winter days like this, the river was wide. Murky, fast

moving and tidal, surging up and down the estuary daily: no bridge would ever be built here. But even at this unearthly hour – with no moon to light the way – Joseph hoped they could find a boat to take them to the other side, and maybe a late-night ferryman willing row them over?

Wilbur lived in Fowey and knew where to look. The local ferryman was roused from his slumbers and, despite some barbed muttering, was cajoled into transporting them across the river.

There was no coaching hostel in Polruan. They had to leave the carriage at a simple inn. Soon they found themselves exposed to the elements. It was a wild and stormy night. Their rowing boat bobbed its way unsteadily over the waves, arcing round towards the ancient town of Fowey.

'Tis not the easiest of journeys,' observed Joseph. He could see Wilbur was almost exhausted and he was far gone himself. He gave silent thanks for the man doing the rowing.

'No, sire,' said the servant. 'But the time is not of our choosing.'

Joseph nodded his head sadly. 'True. My grandfather certainly went well before his time.'

The crossing, even with its detours, was only half a mile and by now they were nearing the Fowey landing jetty. Apart from the paraffin lamp at the end of the pier there were few lights visible anywhere.

The darkened town was hardly festive, heightening Joseph's gloom. 'I'm afraid it's long past the time when respectable folk – which includes most of Fowey – are fast asleep.'

'They've no idea when we're coming, sire,' protested Wilbur. 'You can't expect a carriage to meet us at any hour of the day or night.'

'Huh. We'll just have to trudge up the rest of the way on

foot, then. Good job we're travelling light.'

"Light" was a relative term, mused Wilbur. But he said nothing. In those days social and class divisions were frozen.

The ferryman heaved a few more times on the oars, before glancing round to see how close they were to the jetty. By this time Wilbur was feeling lightheaded after his long journey.

Joseph was in his twenties, fit and agile from sport at Oxford. He readied himself as they drew alongside the quay, the boat's rope in his hand. As the next wave reached its peak, he jumped across onto the steps, grabbed the handrail and pulled himself up onto the quay. The sturdy boat rope was quickly wound round the nearest mooring post. Finally, they had arrived.

Wilbur carefully passed up Joseph's baggage and then clambered slowly up alongside him, breathing heavily. He had no fitness regime; youth was not on his side.

Impatiently, Joseph seized the bag from him, turned and headed towards Fore Street. 'Come on, Wilbur, it's not far now.' He tried to sound cheerful but deep down he knew that reaching Fowey was only the start of a very long journey.

Life ahead would involve a great deal more than theoretical engineering.

PART 1

February 5th - 12th

Commission

CHAPTER 1 Sun February 5th Fowey

'So that's how I plan to start it all off,' said Emma Eastham, as she closed her laptop. 'D'you think it'll work?'

Her friend hadn't realised she was supposed to provide criticism and played for time. 'I'm afraid I'm coming at this cold, Emma. I'll get us another drink, then you can explain – but please start your own account from further back.'

She went over to the bar. The Ship Inn was quiet and the landlord was sociable enough. If she was going to be around for a while, he might be a useful person to cultivate.

'Two halves of cider, please. My name's George Gilbert, by the way. I have work down here for a week or two. Are you always this quiet?'

'Hi George, I'm Thomas.' The landlord glanced at the quiet saloon. 'Sunday's always slow, it gets better as the week goes on. It's worse in February, of course. Not many tourists at all.'

George gave him a sympathetic grin and returned to her table with the drinks. 'We'd best make these last, Emma. We might be here for some time. Now, tell me the whole thing.'

Emma took a sip and settled herself. 'Well. You know I'm in Exeter University's Cornish History Outpost at Truro. The Department's grown in the last couple of years. I completed my PhD and I'm now a research associate. But currently the post is only part-time, so I'm always on the lookout for interesting ways for a historian to top up her income.'

'Mm. That's probably even harder for a historian than for a mathematician like me.'

Emma considered. 'I guess that both of us have to be

imaginative on making ourselves useful: no-one owes us a living. Anyway, I saw an advert in a history magazine that was circulating in the Outpost. It was looking for someone to "front up a docudrama around an old Cornish character for a forthcoming BBC4 series".'

George broke in. 'But doesn't Lucy Worsley already do that sort of thing? I watched a series of hers recently. She was talking about Agatha Christie. Going to the places where things happened – the writer's car crash at a pool near Guildford, for example, or the Harrogate hotel she hid away in. Much easier to visualise, I was grabbed. Good television.'

Emma smiled. 'The company that produced Lucy Worsley is after something fresh along those lines. But this time they're after someone less smooth and suave than Worsley – a bit more Cornish.'

George grinned. 'They won't get anyone more Cornish than you, Emma. You were born in Truro. You've even got a Cornish lilt.'

'More to the point, there are not many top historians in this part of the world. Maybe that's why I got the commission.'

'I'd guess most of the competition was grey-haired men in grey suits. A honey blonde in her early forties will impact on a television audience – as long as she knows her stuff. As you do.'

Emma smiled as she took another sip. She needed encouragement. 'I know the background. I've been studying social history for years.'

'So who's the lucky guy we're going to see presented on the television screen?'

Emma looked slightly embarrassed. 'It's not someone I was that familiar with. An industrialist in the early nineteenth century, based here in Fowey. A man called Joseph Treffry.'

George drank some of her cider and pondered. The name

didn't ring any bells. 'To be honest, Emma, that's not a name I know. And I'd say, after working here for ten years, that I know Cornwall fairly well. Treffry might be a hard sell. Your audience might not be too large.'

'Come on, that's the best BBC4 ever hopes for. Even so, I'm up for the challenge. I have to decide how to put it together. In effect I'm the scriptwriter – hence the draft I've just read to you. They seem to think I know a lot more than I do.'

'London-based company. You'll know far more than the rest of 'em,' said George reassuringly. 'You've just got to keep it that way.'

Emma nodded. 'That's why I've based myself here in Fowey for the next two months. I've taken a winter let at Coombe Farm. I want to soak up the local atmosphere while there are no tourists – and find the best camera angles.'

George drank more cider. 'Right. So Fowey was Treffry's main location. What kind of things did he do? Was he some sort of fisherman? You might struggle on that. Hey, was he a boat builder?'

Emma shook her head. The prologue she'd just read to her friend obviously hadn't made much impact.

'No, he was an industrialist. Built things. He constructed an aqueduct in the 1830s that is still standing, in the Par Valley. Way off the beaten track but very impressive. It crosses today's railway line to Newquay, a hundred feet below; and it's six hundred feet across.'

'Sounds impressive. I'm amazed something that old is still standing. So what was it built for?'

'Ah. That's where it gets problematic – and where I need help. Treffry ended up owning a major copper mine near here called Par Consols. Nothing left now but in its heyday it was the "biggest copper producer in Cornwall". What I want is someone to paint the economic background.

'It can't have been all plain sailing. I'd like to be able to talk about why he did the things he did, and the challenges he faced - not just show shots of the end products.'

George took a moment to reflect on this unexpected turn in their conversation.

'So this is a last-but-one century version of a story like Alan Sugar or Richard Branson. The rise of an entrepreneur.

'What might make this series different to Worsley's,' she continued, 'is if it had the numbers behind the story. That's more relevant to an industrialist than it would be to an author – even one as famous as Agatha Christie. I'm certainly intrigued, Emma. But is there any data to work with?'

Emma smiled: she might have found her collaborator. It had been pure chance that she and George had met earlier in Polruan. But the encounter could be fruitful.

'I've been loaned Treffry's journals by his family. They're handwritten, of course, but I can cope with that. In the 1820s, before typewriters, writers were more legible than most of us are today. You've just got to know the lettering differences, which I do.

'I've only skimmed them so far,' she continued, 'but I noticed plenty of numbers in Treffry's plans. After all, he did study engineering at Oxford.'

George, a Cambridge mathematician, nodded. 'Well, that's something. Unusual for the time, I should think. Even so, I don't fancy wrestling for hours with his journals.'

' 'Course not. But there's lots on the internet about mining in Cornwall. The industrial revolution of the 1800s. What if you went back home and built an overall picture?'

'I'm busy right now, Emma, on my own research. I've just had a commission too – improving local traffic.'

'Now there's a challenge. OK. Why don't we meet again in a couple of weeks? Try to fit the local story into the wider picture. There is a second bedroom in my let. You could stay for a few days if it would help.'

CHAPTER 2 Sun February 5th Compatibility

It was mid evening before the women had finished their ciders and left the Ship. Emma had to walk out of Fowey to her farm-house lodgings. They parted company amicably at the hillside car park.

As she drove carefully back up the main road over to her cottage near Tintagel, George had plenty to think about.

Emma's appeal for help didn't take much of her journey. There was plenty she'd be able to do, starting from the internet, but that was for tomorrow. Not tonight.

George had been in Fowey for a purpose. Her new project was to advise on ways on improving traffic flows in the town.

She'd been for a final interview in St Austell on the Friday afternoon. When the contract was awarded, she'd decided to look at the setting for the study before making her way home.

A small piece of interesting work in her own time, even if it was deemed "pro bono" and hardly affected the coffers, could still be fitted in. Her business strategy was never to turn requests down. Especially ones she found intriguing.

On this journey her ongoing dilemma was around Mark.

A year ago it had all seemed so promising. Their reunion, after twelve years apart, had been miraculous. They had even travelled together to meet their long-lost daughter Polly in New Zealand.

It was after that when the problems began.

The trouble was, she and Mark weren't the same people that

they had been a decade earlier. They had both grown older – but not older together. They had diverged in their tastes and their interests.

After Mark had disappeared, George had had twelve years of independent living. She'd moved out of London, bought her own cottage in Treknow, on the edge of Tintagel.

There she had learned to fend for herself, built up a successful consultancy in locations around Cornwall and made a host of new friends. Emma was one of many.

It was only by chance that Mark had not come back and found her happily married. She'd been in a couple of close relationships heading that way, but for various reasons neither had worked out.

The legal complications of restoring a marriage that had ended twelve years earlier, with the husband "dead and buried", were far from straightforward. Some of their legal friends advised that it would be better to get married afresh – or just to stay friends.

Twelve years ago there had been plenty of grief. George had been shown fragmentary burnt human remains from the Iranian air crash, arranged what she had believed to be Mark's funeral, and wept buckets. Her daughter had never fully recovered and emigrated to New Zealand.

But since then George had moved on.

Being a one parent family with a teenage daughter had forced her to rely entirely on herself. With increasing success she had grown to enjoy it. It wasn't easy, maybe not possible, to go back to how things had been.

To be fair, Mark had had a much rougher twelve years than she had. He couldn't – wouldn't? – even speak of his years as a captive in Iran. They were too traumatic.

But his years, once he'd been brought back in the UK,

struggling to restore his memory whilst earning a modest living on routine security, must have been hard as well.

In recent years, as his memory had slowly returned, Mark had pined for the old George. But once he had found her, she was no longer the woman he had remembered.

For one thing she, too, was twelve years older.

They had started to wonder if it would be best to stop trying to be a couple and simply begin a new life as supportive friends.

The complications of roadworks in Bodmin took all her attention for a few minutes. But the topic wouldn't go away.

Mark's problem was that he used to have a well-paid, responsible job that required extensive travel. George grimaced; that was how he'd come to be heading for Iran in the first place.

But he could never go back to that line of work. There were all sorts of complications arising from his long tangle (tango?) with Security. They wouldn't guarantee his safety if he travelled abroard. And Mark certainly wasn't going to risk another spell in an Iranian jail.

Any confidence he'd had in the legendary Foreign Office mandarins – that their deep grasp of power around the world would avoid trouble, or at least lead to rescue if something went wrong – had long since evaporated.

To be fair, while he couldn't remember who he really was, Security had kept him on their books. He hadn't been left to starve. But once he knew the truth it was all a lot harder.

George still recalled the Monday last April when Mark had gone back to London to explain his true identity and challenge his Security bosses.

She had done her best to help him polish his best lines of argument. It had been a tense Sunday, with plenty of disagreement.

George had found his ideas confused. 'Mark, you can't accuse a government agency of "breaking the law". Not in this case, anyway. The facts were never clear. It's been confusion from start to finish. The best you can hope for is the Establishment's instinct for self-protection and the Department's sense of comradeship.'

He hadn't taken that well. Flatly denied the Department had any sense at all. She had tried again.

'Look Mark, there's nothing you can do to force their hand. Threatening to tell your tale to the media won't do you any good. Even if it would sell a few extra papers for the Mirror. Like it or not, you signed the Official Secrets Act when you started security work. OK, I agree it's an outdated Act, passed before the First World War in totally different circumstances, but it still happens to be the law.'

George recalled Mark instancing other cases where the Act had been defied. He'd been doing plenty of research.

'But Mark, this isn't some minor detail, like the government's mates making money out of protective equipment during the worst pandemic for a century. If your case ever went to court, they'd use the Act to gag the media. Stop you getting any publicity at all.

'They can ensure cases are held in camera, you know, so even the Guardian couldn't do that much. You can't take on the whole of the government and expect to win. We're not a banana republic. I'm not sure what "winning" really means here anyway.'

The last remark had provoked further outcry.

'Go on then,' she'd replied, once the tirade had faded away. 'What's the best that you can possibly hope for?'

It seemed Mark still thought he was due compensation for

all that he'd suffered, while being mistaken by the Iranians for a British Security agent.

'But you can't say that was Security's fault. It was just a dreadful, monumental, once-in-a-lifetime mix-up after a plane crash.'

'I could appeal to the court of public opinion.'

'You could. But even if you did that, there's a counter argument. Are you not incredibly lucky still to be alive? Everyone else in that plane was burnt to death. Isn't surviving the best compensation you could ever hope for?'

They'd gone round and round all day.

In the end she had stopped trying to argue and stepped back to give him some coaching. She had appealed to him to stay calm. 'Whatever happens, Mark, losing your temper with officialdom will never help your cause.'

The trouble was, when she had picked him up from Exeter station on that Monday evening, she could see, even before he spoke, that he hadn't stuck to her advice.

After that their occasional bickering had turned into regular arguments.

In the end Mark had been awarded the same kind of settlement as would be given to any other security officer who chose to leave the Secret Service. The only concession was that his time in the service had been backdated to the airline crash in Iran, when he had been interrogated like a security agent by the Iranians, even though he had never intended to be one.

He was awarded a small pension. But that wouldn't start for another decade; and it wasn't a great deal of money.

The award had been accompanied by a fierce reminder – in writing – that he should never speak about his time in Security about anything he had learned in those years, whether in Britain or in Iran.

'How am I supposed to account for the time then?' he had asked. 'I'll be looking for a new job - trying to get back somewhere close to the level I once held. If I can't explain my past, give some sort of reference, they'll suspect I spent those years in prison. Or a mental hospital. Which'll mean I won't get any serious job at all.'

But it turned out they had a standard solution. Mark had been fitted with a new identity and matching paperwork. He was to use the name Mark Renfrew - his middle name - in all circumstances. He even had a matching passport, NHS number and tax reference.

If a potential employer wanted more, he was to explain that he had been working in the North of Scotland as a private detective. He even had been given references which he could cite to prove it.

After this, the magic which had once held Mark and George together gradually lost its grip.

Mark had completed his notice period in Security, continuing to work as a border guard in the GCHQ Listening Station near Bude. Then, free from Security at last, he started to search for another job, somewhere in Cornwall; but that wasn't easy.

There were plenty of low-grade jobs in Cornwall, in the summer months at least. But he was in his early fifties and aspiring for higher responsibility. That sort of job, without the relevant experience, was much harder to find.

And Mark didn't tell her much, even about where he was looking.

George had never been tempted to share any of her consultancy work with anyone: it was private and confidential. She was used to keeping mum. Many of her cases took her away from

Treknow, often for days at a time, so maintaining silence was relatively easy.

But her absences had left Mark to his own devices in Treknow. He had sunk into a dark, lonely place. She had guessed that with nothing much to do, he was probably suffering from renewed depression - or perhaps Post Traumatic Stress Disorder?

They had a close mutual friend in Delabole, Brian, who was the local doctor. He'd been Mark's best man at their wedding, a quarter of a century ago. Those were happier days.

She'd tried hard to persuade Mark to use him for counselling but the men were too close: it wasn't possible to combine medicine and friendship. But when he'd been passed on to a doctor he didn't know, he didn't feel free to tell his long backstory.

The non-communication between Mark and George had grown. It was now on a "need to know" basis. They had continued to share the cottage in Treknow but now had separate bedrooms. They were housemates rather than lovers.

Just before she'd gone off for her project interview in St Austell, George had sensed there was a job he was hoping for. No doubt he would tell her when he was ready.

She was glad of anything that might raise his spirits. Maybe she'd learn more once she was home?

CHAPTER 3 Fri February 3rd Recognition

I'd made it to the final interview, with an organisation called Kernow Lithium Mining – known for short as KLM. The head office was on an industrial estate in a small town called Bugle, five miles north of St Austell.

I'd been surprised to make the earlier phone interview. I'd come across the advert in the Cornish mining section of a recruitment bureau. An interesting job with a respectable salary. The key feature of the salary, as far as I was concerned, was the talk about "real responsibility". I'd done enough time in the last few years as an organisational nonentity.

I'd been even more surprised, two weeks later, when I was called to meet the firm's top managers face to face. I must have hidden my qualms better than I'd feared. Or perhaps researched the area more assiduously? I was desperate to have my strengths recognised and affirmed. I'd felt ignored for much too long.

I went inside and was welcomed at the front desk by a smartly dressed young woman with long dark hair and a big smile. 'I'm Sandra,' she told me. I introduced myself: 'I'm Mark Renfrew'.

She checked for my name on what looked a short list and gave it a tick. Then guided me along the corridor and into the interview room. No extras, just a long table with a window behind. It seemed there were just two interviewers on the panel that morning.

'Good morning, Mark,' said the panel chairman, standing to

greet me. 'My name is Simon Cooke. I'm the managing director of KLM.' He turned to his companion.

'And I'm Rachel, Rachel Tyson I'm the company's personnel director. We were expecting a third senior manager to be with us on the panel, Alexander Price, but he seems not to be here. He sometimes takes his field work too seriously; he might join us later. Let's all sit down.'

'Right,' said Simon. He smiled encouragingly. 'This is the final stage of the selection process. Firstly Rachel and I will each ask you some searching questions. Some of these will seek to expand on what you've already told us or what we've learnt from calls to your various referees. Then we'll move on to what you might contribute to KLM. That'll take an hour.

'After that you'll be free to wander round the office, accompanied by one of my colleagues. Get a sense of whether you'd like to work with us. You can talk to any of our staff who happen to be in today, while we interview the other candidates. One of them will give you a tour of our laboratory; that's housed over the road.'

Rachel took over. 'After that, a few of our staff will take all the candidates out for lunch.' She gave a subdued laugh. 'Bugle is not a tourist hot spot. No Blue Riband restaurant, but there is a decent inn along the road. It's called the Charcoal Grill.'

'I presume there'll be a chance to ask a few questions at some stage?' I hadn't had a face-to-face interview for years, but I remembered it was wise to make it a two-way process.

Privately I was amazed to sense a glimmer of success in my job search.

Through the darkness of the past weeks I'd come to realise that I would never land a senior job in direct competition with others who had more relevant experience.

Then, browsing on the internet, I'd come across a new activity where experience had to be more limited. A company called Cornish Lithium had set itself less than a decade ago to mine lithium in Cornwall.

A new venture. They had plenty on the internet, including a YouTube interview with an impressive Managing Director. I'd watched this several times.

Lithium was a key element in building rechargeable batteries. These batteries powered electric cars. They could also help handle variation in output from solar panels and from wind turbines – the UK weather was never consistent for long.

Achieving "net zero" carbon emissions was a government goal for 2050; the first faltering official response to the notion that the world's fuel habits were about to overheat the planet.

Cornish Lithium was high-powered. I'd never get a job with them. Their team was focussed on science and technology. I'd gritted my teeth, I had no expertise in either.

But it had led me to browse "lithium in Cornwall" further. I'd come across another company with a similar goal: Kernow Lithium Mining, or KLM.

KLM was even younger than Cormish Lithium; but it was recruiting. They wanted someone with an economics background to take charge of security, as part of the leadership team.

I had had a first interview over the phone and been called for a second one face to face. My most promising application to date. Even being called had boosted my morale no end.

Once the questions began, I was comfortable enough to talk about my past, real and imagined.

The early part of my life – childhood in Padstow, an economics degree at Bristol and a business career marketing advanced products in the UK and beyond, was all true – though a long way back.

I had more difficulty with the more recent past, specialising in security.

I'd worked hard on this, of course. Thankfully, George had put me through my paces and I had ended up with a just-about-credible account of how I had become a private detective in Inverness. 'Mark,' she'd reminded me, 'remember: security roles can never be fully disclosed for security reasons.'

Fortunately neither Simon nor Rachel had spent much time in Scotland and the account stood up to their scrutiny. No doubt they had rung the numbers I'd specified and been reassured by the locals (in fact by security folk claiming that role).

My most recent role, helping to guard the GCHQ Camp north of Bude, was true; but now I really couldn't say much because of the Official Secrets Act.

'So, in conclusion, you've had a hugely varied experience,' said Rachel. 'That could be useful if KLM grows as we hope. We might even need hard-knuckle marketing one day. Many of us here - except Simon - haven't been much further than Devon.'

At that point there was a knock at the door and some coffee was brought in. Well organised - and civilised. Now I understood why Sandra had asked about drinks when I first arrived.

'Right,' said Simon, once we'd taken our mugs and resumed our seats. 'Let me tell you a bit about my vision for KLM. Then you can see why we see security as increasingly vital.

'There are two plausible ways of accessing lithium here in Cornwall,' he began. 'One is linked to geothermal energy. Sink two deep boreholes to access very hot water. Pump some of that to the surface, extract the heat and filter out the lithium salts, then return the liquid down the second pipe. If there's enough energy in the hot water, the whole thing could be self-sufficient.'

I was determined to make this interview interactive. 'But boreholes are expensive, so you need to know the geology well enough to know exactly where to drill.' I thanked my lucky stars for what I'd gleaned from the Cornish Lithium video.

Simon nodded. 'Correct. The alternative is drilling directly into selected chunks of granite.'

'Which also needs insight on where there might be lithium in the mica – in sufficient quantities to justify the cost.'

Simon nodded again. 'There are a few places. They were mining one near St Dennis in the 1940s. But there might also be a third way. And that's where KLM hopes to compete.'

He glanced out of the window behind him. 'What d'you see?'

I sensed this was a key question, possibly the crux of the whole interview. Fortunately I had been eying the view during the coffee break.

'That's one of the Cornish Alps, isn't it? The spoil tip from an old China Clay working.'

'That's right.'

There was a pause, then cogs started to whir. 'So is the KLM idea to try and access spoil tips for lithium?'

Simon smiled. 'It sounds like wishful thinking. But there's a lot of wisdom about the old China Clay pits in St Austell. Many lasted till the 1990s – a few are still working today. Many of those workers still live around St Austell. My goal is to harness that knowledge and combine it with careful sampling.'

I was caught up in the account now. 'But it won't be easy,' I protested. 'They didn't care about lithium back then. Spotting it needs the skills of an advanced scientist. Have you got any of those?'

'You'll meet a couple in the laboratory,' responded Rachel.

'Phil and Fiona. Both with PhD's from top universities. Plus solid industrial experience.'

This was starting to sound exciting. I was even more desperate to do well. I tried to fill out the bigger picture in my mind.

'But it can't just be a matter of a few rocks on the surface,' I reflected. 'Surely you'll have to tunnel well inside the spoil tip and take samples from different depths?'

Simon could see I was thinking about the process. 'That's right. Which was why I hired Alex. He used to be Operations Manager at Wheal Richard Clay Pit. He knows the area and most of the key owners like the back of his hand. And he can talk the talk. If anyone can win access for sample digs in the Cornish Alps it's going to be him.'

He'd intrigued me. There was plenty more I could ask but I remembered the job title. What were they expecting of me?

'So why do you need a Security Manager?'

This time it was Rachel who responded. 'KLM has grown rapidly over the last three years. A lot of it is ad hoc. But we are getting some important findings. It's vital we keep them to ourselves until we choose to disclose them.'

'You mean smarter security systems?'

'And plenty more. It's been like the Wild West here. When you hire independent thinkers, they have independent thoughts. We need someone slightly older. Not to bully the staff but to gently lead the way forward.'

For the first time I felt a strong hunger for the job itself. I could do this. It would be an advance on everything I'd done before. But it was within my capability. And there was a worthwhile long-term objective.

Now all I had to do was to convince Simon and Rachel that I was the man they needed.

CHAPTER 4 Fri February 3rd – Sat 4th Luxulyan

It was mid-afternoon by the time I'd finished the interview process at KLM. Finished for the day, anyhow.

I clocked in to the Charcoal Grill, where I'd had a delicious lunch, to stay for a night. I had no idea if I'd be the one chosen, but while I was down this way I might as well have a weekend of relaxation. I was ever so tired of Tintagel.

I'd brought my mountain bike. I'd always had an attachment to bikes, in fact that was how I first met George. It'd be good to stretch my muscles and get some fresh air: it had been a tense day.

I made sure I had my phone with me. Rachel had promised all three candidates that they'd be making a decision that afternoon. For better or worse, I wanted to know what it was.

I looked at my map. I could cycle down to St Austell. But there'd be crowds. Perhaps it would be quieter off the beaten track. I noticed a village called Luxulyan not far away: I was intrigued by the name. Was the village as pretty as it sounded? I decided to take a look.

It didn't take long to get there. The village was pleasant, a collection of stone houses, but it was never going to win the "Prettiest Village in Cornwall" award. Its only unusual feature seemed to be a single-track railway that my map told me led to Bugle.

I'd just started investigating the station, to see if any trains ran at all, when I heard my phone. Hastily I dumped the bike and grabbed a seat on the platform.

'Hello.'

'Is that Mark Renfrew?'

It had to be KLM. They were the only people who had been told my new name. 'It is.'

I swallowed hard. What was the verdict?

'This is Rachel Tyson from KLM. We'd like to offer you a job as Security Manager.'

I knew I was supposed to sound cautious when offered a job, check it all over, but I was too excited. Somebody wanted me!

'That's really exciting, Rachel. Thank you very much. Yes, I'd love to accept.'

There followed a few minutes discussion about starting salary and so on. It was well above what I'd been paid recently and was a long-term commission - not just a short-term contract. Then she said, 'When can you begin?'

'How about Monday morning?' I said it half in jest, but to my surprise the idea was taken seriously.

'That'd be wonderful, Mark. There's plenty for you to do here. Will you commute from Tintagel?'

'I'd like to find somewhere down here as soon as I can. Any suggestion for where I could start looking?'

'If you don't mind being off the beaten track, there's a village called Luxulyan just one stop down the line. A couple of our staff live there and they seem happy enough. The local pub's called the King's Arms: if you're lucky they might even give you a short term let.'

The call ended. I closed the phone and gave a yell. At last, I could start to be a person in my own right.

I would go back to the Charcoal Grill for the night, but I wondered whether the King's Arms might put me up for a night or two from tomorrow. I'd prefer to live a short distance away from the KLM headquarters. It would make it easier to relax when I was off duty. Walking distance was too close.

The King's Arms wasn't hard to find, a stone building on the main road through the village. It was closed for the afternoon but opened at five. I used the intervening half hour to cycle round the rest of the village. Yes, it would be a good place to live. Quiet.

When the door opened I was first in – I hoped they didn't take me for an alcoholic. But it gave me chance to introduce myself to the landlord, before he was swamped by thirsty customers.

The inside of the Arms was pleasant enough and I was their only customer. It wasn't a landlord, though; it was a sturdy looking woman. If she played rugby, she'd be a handy centre three quarter – but she had a welcoming smile.

'Hello,' I said. 'I've just been offered a job in Bugle.'

'Congratulations, sir. And what will you drink to celebrate?'

I peered at her beers. It was a St Austell pub. There was a Hicks, a Proper Job or a Tribute. 'I'd better start with a Proper Job,' I replied. 'In the circumstances. And would you join me?'

There was no-one else here and I guess it would stay quiet until the early evening. We both had just a half. I'd be cycling back to Bugle later.

'So what's the job?' she asked, as she pulled the drinks.

'It's with a company called KLM. They're hoping to mine for lithium.' I'd learned that from their web site: it couldn't be that secret.

'Good to have a worthwhile job these days, sir. Where will you live?'

'I wouldn't mind living in Luxulyan. Just one stop up the line. I assume the trains still operate?'

'When they're not on strike.' She maintained a studied

neutral look, appropriate to her position behind the bar. 'Cheers.'

'I don't suppose you have any information on places to let round here?'

'I could suggest one or two. You could stay here for a week or two if you like, while you check them over.'

'Doesn't it get very noisy in the evenings?'

She laughed. 'You must be joking. 'Cept on Saturdays, of course. That's when we have the karaoke.'

Something different, I thought. 'And is that popular?'

She considered, obviously not wanting to oversell it. 'I think it's a way to socialise. We're too far off the beaten track to attract anyone from outside. If you were living around here, it'd be a good way to meet your neighbours. They're a friendly lot.'

I was still on a high from getting the job. It was my day and I wanted it to continue. Half an hour later I had booked a room for the coming week, seen it, and met the owner less formally. It was her pub; she was the landlord; and she was called Lucy.

After a while I cycled back to Bugle. It was time to see my new place of work on a Friday evening. It was cheerful enough but hardly rowdy.

Next morning I had the Grill's Full English Breakfast. Splendid. Then I loaded my car and came back to Luxulyan, after which I spent the day cycling around the area.

I was back at the King's Arms by nightfall and settling myself in my room. I was the only guest here; the room was a reasonable size. Bigger than my bedroom in Treknow, anyway.

Which reminded me, should I call George? Perhaps if I'd done so this story would have been very different; in fact, it might not have happened at all. The main reason I didn't, looking back, was that I was enjoying my independence – a full-throated life of my own, a job I had won by my own efforts, not under orders from anybody.

No doubt George would be busy on some consultancy remit or other. She was always busy. It was a habit she had acquired in her long years on her own. Now I could be busy too.

Anyway, I decided I would set down my own markers in Luxulyan and Bugle before making contact. She didn't need me; I wanted to prove I didn't need her either.

I had supper in the King's Arms bar – home-cooked shepherd's pie, a sensibly sized portion – and watched the karaoke clientele arrive. Soon I was talking to some of them.

They were friendly enough. Those of working age were based in or around St Austell. When pressed, I admitted I'd just got a job in Bugle, but managed not to say exactly what it was. I was the KLM Security Manager, I was paid not to divulge the firm's secrets. Far better to say too little than too much.

There was someone else running the bar by the time Lucy appeared on the small platform, microphone in hand, to start the karaoke. She no longer looked like the pub's landlord, she was in a swish evening gown. I hoped the bare shoulders wouldn't make her too cold.

To be honest, I hadn't been to a karaoke evening for years and years. It wasn't the sort of thing George would ever do. So I didn't know exactly what to expect. But this was my first evening. I surely couldn't be expected to do anything, except offer generous applause.

In a regular karaoke room, I gather, they have a special machine with a wide range of popular music. The recorded singer can be turned down when required, to allow live performance by a local, singing over the original backing.

Here it was all more low-key. They didn't have a karaoke

box. Instead they had a versatile pianist on a honky-tonk piano, who could play almost anything in the popular canon by ear.

The locals of Luxulyan knew that. Probably that was why they came along week after week. Either that or the limited attraction of Saturday night television.

Without much pressure, the audience shuffled forward in turn to be introduced by Lucy and to offer their version of standards, old and new. From Joan Baez to Oasis.

Shy or confident, they would take the microphone, listen for the opening chords and start to sing. Presumably the pianist would guess what song they were hoping to sing – or perhaps he already knew?

It was better than Saturday night television, anyway.

After an hour there was an interval. For the pianist if no-one else, his fingers must be tingling. There was a rush for the bar. I was surprised to see the glamorous Lucy easing towards my table. She sat down with a mischievous grin.

'Enjoying this, Mark?'

'It's great,' I replied.

'D'you fancy a turn? It'd help you connect to the village.'

If I had ever been asked such a thing before, in my whole life, I swear I'd have run a mile. But somehow my self-confidence had grown with the KLM appointment. And I had to admit, I did sing along to old Beatle tracks when driving.

'If you really think so,' I said. It was another turn on my new road.

Twenty minutes later, when the event resumed, Lucy called me up.

'None of you will know him yet but this is Mark. He's staying here for the next week, hopes to be living here for quite a while.

If any of you've got, or know of, spare accommodation, please approach him afterwards. But right now he's going to sing us "Yesterday".'

The pianist struck an opening chord and I was away. I was so caught up in the moment that I didn't even suffer any nerves. Not as clear as Paul McCartney but it was ok. There were no obvious howlers, I didn't forget the words. Afterwards came wholehearted applause. I sat down quickly before anyone asked for an encore.

But there was an encore of sorts. For I was followed by a gorgeous young lady, Naomi, with another Beatles ballad, "Let it be". That she sang beautifully and received well-deserved applause. No wonder the karaoke was so popular.

After it was all over, I made a point of going over to Naomi to introduce myself. 'So d'you live in the village?' I asked.

'I've been here for years,' she replied. 'I work in Bugle, commute every day up the line.'

'Ah, that's what I'm hoping to do. Perhaps I'll see you at 8.30 on Monday morning?'

CHAPTER 5 Mon February 6th Bugle

Monday morning came soon enough. The start of my new life, where what I did mattered. I was at Luxulyan station in good time, in my suit and tie. I saw Naomi there too, and a couple more aspiring passengers. The train came into view, and to my amazement Naomi stepped to the platform edge and flagged it down.

We all clambered aboard and I took the seat beside her.

'You always need to request trains to stop here,' she explained.

'How about coming back?'

'If you've bought a ticket to Lux, they'll tell the driver at Bugle. You don't need to pull the communication cord - at least, I haven't so far.'

I smiled. The woman had a sense of humour.

It was only ten minutes to Bugle. I came out of the station and turned right. To my surprise Naomi was heading the same way.

'I'm just starting work at KLM,' I said.

'Well, well. That's where I work. Almost since it started, in fact, three years ago. What's your job, then?'

'Security. I only got the job on Friday. I've plenty to learn. What about you?'

'Oh, I run the finance team.'

She made it sound pretty dull. 'Making sure we all get paid every month?'

'That bit's sorted,' she replied. 'Fortunately the payroll is steady. None of us have bonuses. The more difficult part is paying for all the new kit and chemicals for the lab. And funding Alex, of course.'

We walked on a little further as I mused on her reply.

'Is Alex on drugs?' I asked, slightly puzzled.

Naomi smiled. 'I don't think that's where his costs come from. Not most of 'em, anyway.'

I was intrigued. 'What on earth does he do?'

'He's our Acquisition Manager. That's his title, anyway.'

'Which means. . .?'

'Well. You know that KLM is hoping to find lithium in Cornish Clay spoil tips?'

'I've heard that,' I replied. 'Simon told me that at the interview.'

'Finding out if there's any lithium in there is part of the challenge, of course. You need permission even to drill into spoil tips. And finding out who the owners are is not always easy.'

I nodded. 'I can see that.'

'But once you've found lithium, that won't do you any good unless you can buy the tip, or at least negotiate a long-term contract to extract what's inside it. That's where you need an Acquisition Manager.'

To my regret I saw that we had almost reached the KLM office.

'Naomi, that's very interesting. This conversation isn't over. I'm eager to know more. But not right now. We'll have to carry on later.'

I spent the first half of the morning being inducted into KLM by Rachel Tyson. I guess getting a new senior manager on board was a critical activity. The sooner I understood what was really going on, and how that related to the ideal, the faster I could help narrow the gap between the two.

'The biggest clump of work at present happens over in the labs. That's where the money goes. If we have secrets that are worth stealing, they'll be in there.'

'So who are the key staff? It's important we're all on the same page.'

'I think we already said on Friday: we have two with PhDs and relevant industrial experience. Phil is primarily a chemist; Fiona is a geologist. They've each chosen their teams and worked out their research programmes.

'They are looking forward to meeting you. They suggested it might be easiest to chat with them over lunch in the Charcoal Grill.'

So KLM wasn't too hidebound. Strong relationships were crucial and best forged away from the office. I was happy to go along with this philosophy.

Later, we came to the nuts-and-bolts question of where I should sit.

'I'm afraid, Mark, you're here sooner than we dared hope. We are planning to give you an office of your own. You'll have material that needs to be kept under lock and key.'

'Good,' I said. 'But not today?'

She shook her head. 'Right now it's being repainted, refurnished and refitted with new locking mechanisms.'

I gave a rueful smile. 'At least it's happening. What should I do in the meantime?'

'It'll be a bit hand-to-mouth, I'm afraid. Sitting in offices where the staff are known to be out for the day, for example.'

'That's OK. I won't have any secrets worth locking up for a week or two. I want to start by talking to the staff. I see working here as a long-term activity; I want to make it succeed. I need to sell myself to them, and to know where each of 'em stands on security. The Charcoal Grill sounds like a useful temporary office for that; that's if you're happy with staff having a couple of hours off site?'

'Oh we're very relaxed about that sort of thing.'

Her reply rang some sort of bell. 'So is there any sort of log book for KLM that records where everyone is supposed to be day by day? Something I could use to book times when I can see people?'

There was a pause before Rachel gave an answer. 'As I say, Mark, we're very relaxed. Now I think about it, I can see it's far too relaxed. I told you at the interview that security had been given a low priority in KLM. Now you see why we were so keen to find someone to bring more order into chaos.'

I was starting from a low base. But at least Rachel wasn't trying to block me. Not yet, anyway.

'So is there anywhere I can sit today? Just to make notes from the various things you've been telling me. I've got my own laptop. I won't worry about systems issues for the time being.'

Rachel pondered for a moment. Then she had an idea. 'Hold on a minute. I need to check something.' She left the room and returned a few minutes later.

'Alex Price, our Acquisition Manager, isn't in today. I've got a spare key that I can lend you for his office.

A few minutes later, Rachel decided we'd done enough for one day and I was shown Alex's office. The man might be sloppy about telling anyone where he was working, but at least he was tidy enough in his own office.

There was one filing cabinet but it was locked; and Rachel had no key. The white board had been wiped clean. Finally, I saw, his desk was empty. Plenty of space to write but nowhere to store anything.

I tried the desk drawers. Neither were locked but I saw nothing beyond a few highlighter pens and some spare pencils. No sign of a map. I'd been hoping that might have given some clue on Alex's recent movements.

'Isn't anyone here concerned about Alex?' I asked.

'He goes off prospecting, sometimes for weeks at a time,' she replied. 'It's a challenge to find out who owns a spoil tip, you see. He was arrested a couple of times early on for trespass, but never charged. He managed to explain what he was trying to do convincingly enough. Since then he's taken more trouble to find out the name of the current owners; and where they are to be found. Trouble is, that's often not easy.'

'So you don't even know where he's been?'

'Where he's been successful, we know a lot,' said Rachel 'We've sent teams over to the places he tells us, to bore into the tip and take samples. After that there's a whole forest of further work to grapple with. No doubt the lab managers can tell you more.'

I glanced at my watch. I'd almost forgotten about the lab. I saw it was already half past twelve.

'Hey, d'you know what time Phil and Fiona are expecting me? I don't want to keep them waiting.'

'I'd go over there now. We can carry on with this tomorrow.'

CHAPTER 6 Mon February 6th KLM Laboratory

I slipped across to the KLM Laboratory to find the firm's two top scientists, Phil and Fiona. I'd been there on Friday, of course, but then I was an outsider of no special concern; this time I was on the company books. This was a meeting we all wanted to happen.

Phil Williams was a large man, over six foot, with a battered face. I gathered he'd played rugby at university (if "played" is the right word for that bloodthirsty sport). While Fiona Charlton was dainty, as light as a feather. She was a keen cyclist. Both enjoyed surfing in summer months, though not at this time of year.

I told them some of my backstory as we walked up the road to the Charcoal Grill – the most recent stage, when I was helping with GCHQ Security at Bude. The two were both a decade younger than me and obviously sharp. They'd heard of the Bude Listening Station, anyway – even seen its satellite dishes from along the coast near Pentire Head.

The Grill was not busy that Monday but they were still offering a full menu and it sounded delicious. On Phil's recommendation we each ordered steak and chips, with fried mushrooms and tomatoes. Plus a jug of peppercorn sauce.

I hoped I wouldn't have to eat as expansively as this every lunchtime. I didn't like to think how far I'd need to cycle next weekend to keep my weight down. But, hey, this was my first day at a proper job. I took it as part of my celebration.

'I'm afraid I'm no scientist,' I told them, 'but I'd like to learn as much as I can about what you do – in layman's terms. Afterwards, maybe, we can move onto security issues.'

There was obviously going to be some delay in preparing our meals. 'Shall I begin?' asked Phil. I grinned a reply.

'One major strand of our work in KLM is seeing if we can extract lithium in meaningful quantities from old clay spoil tips.'

I nodded: understood so far.

Fiona took over. 'There are geological reasons for thinking that the process which caused granite to degrade into kaolin – that's China Clay – overlap with the processes that give mica containing lithium.

'The spoil tips have already been mashed up in the process of extracting the clay. So if there is anything there, it'll be easier to get at than mining deep down granite.'

They must have told this story before and Phil wasn't going to be left out. 'There's a massive amount of material in these tips, they're all over South Cornwall.'

He paused to collect his thoughts. 'They've been mining clay down here for over a century and it's still being mined on a massive scale. A tenth of what's extracted is converted into clay; the remainder has to be discarded. Hence the Cornish Alps.'

There was a longer pause as lunches arrived. The ribeye steaks came on iron platters, guaranteed to keep meals hot for ages. Plenty of piping hot crinkly chips and all the promised vegetables. Plus three pints of lager.

There was silence as items were shared and the eating began.

I voiced a concern of my own. 'You two make it sound so obvious. But there must be snags or it would have been done long ago. The Cornish have mined practically everything, from tin and copper to tungsten and arsenic. They wouldn't have missed lithium.'

Phil nodded. 'You're right, Mark. There are several problems. For a start, mining into a spoil tip, inserting a bore hole or even a tunnel, is a hazardous business. The tip is solid; but it's not as strong as an identical pile of granite. You need special equipment to reach inside very far.'

He smiled. 'Ours comes from a long way away. I won't tell you where if you don't mind. The "need to know" basis applies here.'

Fiona took over. 'Detecting a low concentration of lithium in a small rock sample is even more of a challenge. Phil is too modest to tell you, but our equipment is state of the art. It came from one of the PhD theses he supervised at Cardiff, but it goes a great deal further.'

'Don't give me all the credit, Fiona. Simon Cooke had a great deal to do with it as well. With his pioneer work, he could easily have earned a PhD of his own, but he preferred to keep it secret.'

We all ate more of our steaks. But silence was a waste of time; there was too much the experts wanted to share. I was keen to learn and they wanted to make the most of me.

'One other innovation within KLM is the ways we go into the spoil tips once we've got access.' This was Fiona.

'How do you mean?'

'Well, the entry point to the tip needs consolidation to make sure it's solid. Concrete surrounds and so on. But once we've got that, we don't just dig one route in. We do a dozen, all at different angles – left and right, up and down. And we travel in as far as we can.'

'Right.'

'Then we take samples along each tunnel.'

'Ah. You mean the start and near the end?'

'No. I mean every few yards, along each line of approach.'

'So that's quite a few.' I was starting to appreciate what it meant to sample a spoil tip in the KLM manner.

'Not just a few, Mark, it's hundreds.

'And then, when we've finally got all our samples and we've analysed the lithium concentration of each, we can project the lithium contours within the tip. There are several more PhDs of research within that.'

'And after that,' added Fiona, 'we can work out if the overall value from the lithium we might recover will more than offset the cost of recovering it. Will it make us a profit?'

'Wow.' I ate the rest of my steak while I tried to consolidate what I'd just been told.

'There's plenty more we could tell you,' said Fiona. 'But I think that's enough for one afternoon.'

We finished the meal not long afterwards. But it was already half past two. We were all too full to have any room for pudding; and we could get coffee back in the office.

'I suggest we have a separate session on security,' I said as we started to walk back to the KLM office. 'I need to do a lot more thinking around what you're just told me.'

Neither scientist seemed overawed by security, or worried that we hadn't got onto it. I feared that around here the subject had been neglected for far too long. But I wasn't going to raise hackles on my first day in the office. I needed all the KLM staff to trust me before I started punching my weight.

CHAPTER 7 Mon February 6th Luxulyan

I sat at Alex's desk for a couple of hours and made notes on what I'd been told. I had to pace myself: this was a marathon, not a sprint.

I was just starting to wonder what time I should leave, to be sure of not missing the train back to Luxulyan, when there was a knock at the door.

'Come in,' I called. And there was Naomi, as bright-eyed as ever. She looked slightly surprised to find me. But she recovered quickly.

'Hi, Mark,' she began. 'If you want the last train tonight, you'd better leave now.'

No point in working late on my first day. I grabbed my sheepskin jacket and followed her to the door. Sandra was no longer manning the reception desk: could anyone just walk in here, late in the day?

Naomi and I strode down the road. I didn't try to converse until we'd reached the station. If this was the last train I didn't want to miss it.

Once we were on board, I saw the train was fuller than the one we'd used this morning. We had adjacent seats, but probably best not to talk about KLM in a crowded carriage. It was only five minutes before it reached Luxulyan. Would it stop without further intervention? To my relief it did. Though Naomi and I were the only two who got out.

'No need to worry about it stopping,' I observed.

She laughed. 'Not on the five thirty, anyway. In rush-hour it stops everywhere. The middle of the day is more of a challenge.'

'So where d'you live?' I asked, as we headed up Station Drive.

'Not far from the King's Arms, I'll show you. Hey, would you like a cup of tea?'

I wasn't going to turn any invitation down. Luxulyan was my home for now and I needed to meet its inhabitants. I'd made a start by singing in the karaoke but that needed to be built on.

'That'd be nice, Naomi. Thank you. You can always get coffee in the office but there's something relaxing about tea in late afternoon.'

Her place, when we reached it, was called "Compton Court". Half a dozen flats set back from the road, built in local stone. They wouldn't let builders defile Luxulyan with common brick.

'Have you lived here long?'

'Several years. Before KLM started, in fact. I was an early recruit.'

She led me into the lounge, went into the kitchen to put the kettle on.

'Make yourself at home, Mark. I'll slip into something less formal.' She disappeared into what I assumed was her bedroom and emerged a few minutes later in jeans and a tropical tee shirt.

'Right, now tea.' She bustled into the kitchen and came back with a tray holding two mugs, a milk jug and a teapot.

'I won't offer you a chocolate biscuit,' she said mischievously. 'I saw you heading out at lunchtime with Phil and Fiona. I assume they forced you to eat at the Charcoal Grill?'

'We ate very well,' I replied. 'In fact, I'm still full. I won't need any more this evening. I'm bushed. It's very tiring, you know, starting to work somewhere new.'

Naomi poured us both some tea. My mind raced through

possible topics of conversation. I wasn't going anywhere near KLM. If I wanted to quiz her on that I could do so in office time.

Then I noticed an acoustic guitar, propped up in the corner.

'Hey, d'you play as well as sing like an angel?'

She blushed: maybe not used to compliments.

'Not very well, though. D'you play, then?'

'Used to. Many years ago. When my daughter was at school and in concerts. It helped her to practice at home.'

Naomi cradled her mug thoughtfully. 'I presume she's left home by now?'

'Not just left home. She's emigrated; gone to New Zealand.'

'But your partner is still around?' She didn't say wife.

'I don't have anyone special at the moment.'

I wasn't going to unpack my tangled relationship with George, least of all to Naomi. I wouldn't phone George or take any message from her until I was more settled here. This was my new life and I didn't want it overshadowed.

In any case, George was used to living on her own. She'd done so for years. She'd hardly notice if I wasn't there. Whereas I needed a period of domestic solitude.

Naomi misunderstood my moment of calm. 'I'm so sorry.' She obviously assumed the worst.

I had to get out of this loop. 'So do you have anyone special?'

Naomi gave a hollow laugh. 'There've been one or two over the years. There was someone special when I used to work in Wheal Richard. That's a clay pit near St Austell. But he died just before the pit was closed down.'

I could see that, for Naomi, the memory of her lost friend was still raw. Best to change the subject.

'So tell me about Luxulyan. What makes up the social life? Or your social life, anyway.'

She took a sip of tea. 'There's a lot of social interaction, but most of it is unstructured. Karaoke night only works because people know one another enough to let their hair down. You did well to join us, by the way.'

I decided not to tell her I had been bounced into it by the King's Arms hostess. For the time being, anyway.

'Does that happen every week?'

'Afraid so. You're committed now. Hey, should you and I work up a duet?'

I hadn't expected that. But I wasn't going to block it. 'We'll need to find a song we both know. One that's still popular today - or at least familiar within the village. That's quite a challenge.'

'D'you still have your guitar?' she asked.

'I hate to admit it, but yes I do.'

'Well,' she said. 'Her's an idea. Would you like to come round for a meal one day this week? And bring your guitar. You can tune the two to match while I prepare the meal. We can see what comes to mind. Remember, you've got to have something to offer on Saturday anyway. Lucy will insist. If we can produce a couple of duets which are roughly in tune, that'd do fine.'

CHAPTER 8 Tues February 7th KLM Security

Naomi was still fizzing with ideas when we met on the platform next morning.

'You game for a meal with me this evening? The only condition, Mark, is that you don't gorge yourself on a banquet over lunch.'

'OK.' I hastened to agree. 'I was up early today. Found the village shop, bought myself a pastie for lunch. So I've no reason to go anywhere. What a friendly little shop. And even better, they've a notice board. It lists Luxulyan flats to let.'

Naomi was a cautious woman. 'Good flats go quickly in Cornwall, Mark. You'd best go and look at them as soon as we're back this evening. I won't have our meal ready till half past seven.'

Then her face softened. 'Doesn't matter if you come a bit earlier, mind. And remember, bring your own guitar.'

At that point the train appeared in the distance and Naomi started her semaphore. Luckily, the driver was able to decipher it and we climbed aboard. Today there were no empty pairs of seats. Our conversation got no further.

Once in the KLM office I was closeted again with Rachel Tyson.

'I had a good time with Phil and Fiona,' I told her. 'They're bright people; very clear in describing a complicated process. But there are valuable secrets inside their heads. Do you have a documents strategy? And if so, where are they kept hidden?'

Rachel looked slightly taken aback by the force of my questions. But she was a senior manager and gave a measured response.

'First of all, Mark, they are both on good salaries,' she began. 'Well above anything they'd earn in academia. Secondly, their contracts include Non-Disclosure Agreements – they can't share anything they learn from working with KLM.'

I waited patiently for point three. There must be more. But it didn't come.

'Rachel, that's all fine as far as it goes,' I said, after a polite pause. 'But what if they do leave? Even if they follow the letter of the law and say nothing to anyone, what happens to KLM? How are we supposed to train up their successors?'

'I don't see why they should,' she protested. 'You've met them. They're as excited as anyone about what we're trying to do. If there is a breakthrough, and a new way to mine lithium, all our shares will be worth a fortune. Yours will rise in value too, by the way.'

I wasn't going to let her wriggle out that easily.

'All those secrets and ideas they told me, they've been discovered in KLM time. So they belong not to them but to KLM. They're a KLM asset – probably, at this moment, its biggest asset. But assets need to be managed. They can't be left to rot in someone's brain – even a latter-day Albert Einstein or Marie Curie.'

Rachel looked shocked. I was propounding a new concept. But to her credit she didn't reject it out of hand.

'Mark, thank you. I'm starting to see why we do really need a security manager. I'm afraid I don't have any answers. But I'm willing to work towards one if you'll be patient with me.'

She picked up her desk diary and looked at forthcoming fixtures. 'I've got meetings all the rest of today and it's my day off tomorrow.' She saw the look of surprise on my face. 'I have to look after my mother,' she explained, 'she's going down with cancer.

'Why don't we meet again, first thing on Thursday morning. We'll both share possible answers to these important issues. I won't sweep this under the carpet, I promise you.'

I continued to use Alex Price's office while he was away. I hadn't been given anywhere else, anyway.

I wondered what sort of a man Alex was. If he burst in and found me in his desk, would he smile tolerantly at the minor incongruities of life or erupt in a towering rage?

My conversation with Rachel, shocking as it was, had left me energised. There really was plenty to do here. I wasn't yet a "man with a mission" but I wasn't out of my depth either. Every pioneering company had to handle its core secrets in a responsible manner. I just needed to be one step ahead of the rest of KLM, in knowing what possible forms that might take.

This would be the time for the Old Boys Network – if I had one. A real one, not just a private detective in a fictional past. I had been sworn to secrecy by my former Security bosses. But they hadn't prohibited me calling them. I still had their contact number etched in my brain.

There was no reason for thinking that Alex's office was bugged. I was as isolated here as I would be anywhere.

I took a deep breath. It might be painful revisiting my previous life but right now it was necessary. Then I dialled the number.

Two hours later I hadn't yet been given a contact number but I was on the trail. As I'd expected, it had been a drawn-out process.

My initial contact had been almost reclusive. I gave her my current name, my last security name and the date of my departure. Then I waited for a return call. There might be further questions.

But I was quietly confident. The number I'd rung was not widely known outside the Security services. There must be someone around who could recognise my voice – even my face on WhatsApp. I was thankful that British Security was so thorough. Though it did test my patience.

In the end I was put through to my old boss. I won't tell you his name, it's probably been changed by now anyway. He was still friendly enough towards me.

I outlined my new job and said I was in Cornwall.

'I'm only on my second day. They're friendly enough but the security is a shambles. Trouble is, it's no use just pointing out the gaps, I need to say how they might be filled.

'So what I really need is a chat with someone who knows the solutions that work. How should you keep track of novel methods, for instance? And how do you restrain wayward geniuses?'

My old boss asked me a few more questions. Then 'Leave it with me,' he said. 'I presume you could travel if necessary?'

'I'd much rather talk to someone face to face than over the phone. Anywhere in the UK. But preferably soon.'

I'd no idea how long it would take to find someone suitable who was also willing to help. But I could wait.

Meanwhile I pondered further on security in KLM. What other weaknesses were waiting to be found?

I had mused with Rachel on the vulnerability of the firm to the loss of their two stars, Phil and Fiona. But had that situation arisen already, with the man who's chair I was now occupying?

No-one else here seemed much concerned at Alex's

absence. But was it more sinister? Ought my top priority to be checking him out?

But that wasn't so easy. If anyone was going to alert the police, it couldn't be a man who'd only been in the office for two days and had never set eyes on him. There were no photographs of a loved one or children around here.

When I next saw Rachel on Thursday, I would ask if they had photos of their staff. But I wasn't hopeful. I hadn't been snapped, anyway.

The best person to go to the police would be the boss, Simon Cooke. But I doubted from what was said at my interview that he was much concerned either. In any case, how secure were the police?

Inviting private enquiries by a discreet police officer was one thing. Having the Daily Mail badgering staff as they left or even bugging the Charcoal Grill would be something else.

I sighed. It would be easier if KLM kept thorough records of staff locations. As Acquisition Manager, Alex would have to travel about a lot. There were plenty of spoil tips around here. It was easier to mine clay from the surface than to dig deep for lithium.

But it would be easier to reassure myself if I knew the locations he had visited. Especially in the last week. Why wasn't he at my interview?

CHAPTER 9 Tues February 7th Supper for two

Naomi was as bouncy as I'd come to expect as we travelled back to Luxulyan. I remembered she worked in Finance: had KLM just received a legacy – an old miner, say, who wanted Cornish mining to last into the future? Then I reflected: old miners would be poor miners; they'd have nothing to leave anyone.

Maybe Naomi was just happy to be having someone for supper?

The train was full and we had no chance to chat until we got out at "Lux", as I noticed Naomi called it. I didn't like the name, sounded like a washing powder. But I wasn't going to argue.

'Right,' I said. 'I'm off to the shop to get the addresses of empty flats. Even visit one or two if possible. But I'll be with you by seven thirty.'

'Good luck,' she replied. We parted; I hoped she was planning something special.

I liked the village shop. The prices were higher than a supermarket's, but not outrageous. You could survive by shopping here if you weren't mobile. As well as in Bugle, anyway.

I bought a bottle of Merlot while I was checking properties, and the shopkeeper gave me her views on each of them (the flats, I mean, not the wines).

She also gave me their addresses, which I translated into distance from the King's Arms. I'd visit the two nearest right away, reserving the third for a visit tomorrow – if I was still looking.

Of course, I hadn't been paying rent to George. The legality of our marriage, with a twelve-year interregnum during which someone from the air crash in Iran, bearing my name, had been dead and buried, was uncertain. But so was the legality of staging a re-wedding without any divorce after the wedding before.

In the end we had shrugged and simply lived together.

It wasn't easy. George had moved on since I disappeared, bought her cottage in Treknow and developed a consultancy around Cornwall. She didn't need to share any of that with me and, for reasons I could understand, she chose not to do so.

But it kept her busy and quite often away from the cottage. We weren't the same people we'd been before I disappeared. She had moved up while I had moved down.

I was desperate to make a success of my new situation.

One immediate result of all that, as I walked round to inspect the flats, was that I wasn't up to date on the latest rents.

Both rents seemed high but not unreachable. I was on a decent salary, I could afford them; but I wouldn't get much for it. One-bedroom flats with miniscule kitchens. Neither really grabbed me. Translating monthly rent into a weekly rate, I'd be no better off than if I stayed on in the King's Arms.

It was a gloomy guitarist who turned up at Naomi's, just after seven.

Was taking two hours to cook a meal a sign of culinary excellence or gross inadequacy? We hadn't discussed what was to be in the meal, or even whether I was vegetarian. But that didn't bother me. After Iran I could eat almost anything – as long as it was properly cooked.

I needn't have worried. Naomi was looking calm, totally in control. I hesitated even to speak – George had sometimes been so focused on her cooking that a casual word had led to a major row. I didn't want that to happen here.

But it didn't. Naomi gave me a radiant smile. 'Mark, so good to see you. Relax. I hope you like Beef Wellington?'

'Sounds delightful. I could tune the guitars if you like?'

'Afterwards, I think. If you really want to help, lay the table. I've avocado to start and a cheesecake to finish.'

Gradually I found my way round the kitchen. Cutlery was easy. 'I brought some wine, Naomi; d'you have glasses?'

'Oh, thank you. Glasses are over there.'

A few minutes later the table was laid and we were seated grappling with our avocados.

'Where did you buy these?' I asked. 'They're not from the village shop.'

'St Austell, last Saturday. That was before I came home to practice for the karaoke. Hey, have you had any ideas on songs?'

I nodded. 'One or two. My old songbook was wrapped up with the guitar. That might give us something.'

Naomi smiled, then went to fetch the main course while I poured out the wine. Piping hot plates and Beef Wellington appeared, then a dish of roast potatoes and a bowl of vegetables.

'Right,' she said. 'Please help yourself.'

'Why don't you serve the beef, Naomi. It looks delicious.'

And it was. A stupendous meal, especially at such short notice. For a few minutes we ate in companionable silence.

'You must have an exercise regime?' I asked, as the meal progressed. How else could she be that slim if she ate like this?

She laughed. 'I'm not in a gym. But I do have my bike. I get out most weekends. It's the hills round here that keep my weight down.'

'I cycle too,' I responded. 'Are you in a cycling club or anything?'

She shook her head. 'I was when I lived in St Austell. But

they were strapping lads that liked to race. To be honest, I couldn't keep up.'

'Which might have been what they intended. I don't go fast, Naomi. I like to enjoy the view.'

She paused for a moment. 'I could introduce you to the area if you liked. We could go for a ride together on Sunday. See if we're compatible on two wheels.'

After the meal I insisted on helping to wash up. 'I'm not leaving you to do all this after I've gone.' It didn't take very long, perhaps because of our animated chatter.

Naomi prepared coffee while I wrestled with the guitars. I don't think I would have bothered if it wasn't for the forthcoming karaoke. I hadn't played mine for ages, I'd been feeling too depressed. But I had a gadget to help tune it. Then I seized Naomi's and applied the same treatment.

Even after a full day at work and lavish cookery, Naomi wasn't a spent force. Indeed, she was a *force majeure*. She brought as much energy to the singing as she had to the meal. It wasn't an optional extra. But it was a new dimension on our relationship. Would it work?

'We obviously both like Beatle songs,' I observed. 'Why don't we start with the ones we did last Saturday?'

'Hey, d'you know the chords? Start playing "Yesterday" and I'll sing along.'

So we did. To my ears it was beautiful. At least, her singing was crystal clear.

Now, though, I'd enthused her. She seized her guitar and gave it a strum. 'Your turn, Mark. "Let it be".'

I stopped strumming and tried to recall the opening words. She knew them and gave me a prompt. Once I'd started they came easily.

We carried on for half an hour. By now Naomi was almost beside herself with delight. While I hadn't enjoyed myself so much for years.

'Naomi,' I said, 'we could go on like this for ages. And I'd love to. But don't you think we should find something different for Saturday?'

'Did you have anything in mind?'

'Well. In my songbook I found some Cornish ballads – with chords attached. The tunes are simple enough. How about one of them?'

'Let me have a look. See if there's anything I know.'

I handed over the songbook. It was an ad-hoc concoction, not intended for public consumption. I'd flagged a couple of possibilities and she selected the first.

'This one was written in 1807,' I said. 'Napoleon was romping across Europe, about to invade Poland. It goes something like this.'

"Come all ye jolly Tinner boys and listen now to me;
I'll tell you of a story, shall make ye for to see,
Concerning Bonaparte, the schemes which he had made
To stop our tin and copper mines, and all our pilchard trade."

Then I came to the chorus. To my delight, Naomi joined in:

"Hurrah for tin and copper, boys, and fisheries likewise!
Hurrah for Cornish maidens - Oh, bless their pretty eyes!
Hurrah for our old gentry, and may they never fail!
Hurrah, hurrah for Cornwall! Hurrah, boys, "one and all!""

'That's a terrific song,' she said. 'I can go with it. Let me try verse two.' There was a pause, then her clear voice rang out.

"He summoned forty thousand men, to Poland they did go,
For to rob and plunder there, you very well do know;
But ten thousand were killed, laid dead in blood and gore,

And thirty thousand ran away - I can't tell where, I'm sure."

We repeated the chorus together, grinning at each other as we did so. Singing together was infectious. I recalled Lennon and McCartney on that roof in their final concert. Then we both moved on to the final verse.

"And should that Bonaparte have forty thousand still
To make into an army, to work his wicked will
And try for to invade us, if he doesn't quickly fly—
Why forty thousand Cornish boys shall know the reason why."

By the time we'd finish, we were high on the song. Not literally but caught up in the emotion.

I suddenly remembered this wasn't a jam session, we were planning to sing this in the karaoke. 'Hey, do you think the pianist at the King's Arms can handle this?'

'I'm sure he will, Mark. But why don't you try playing the chords and I'll sing it again. See how that sounds. If we're taking karaoke off the beaten track, we need to get it right.'

We went round it again and again. Singing alternate verses. Gradually we made better sense of the words. And not being too boastful, my strumming got steadily better.

'Maybe we don't need the pianist at all,' said Naomi. 'Would you be prepared to play in public?'

'With you beside me I'll try anything at all.'

I pondered on these words as I made my way back to the King's Arms at half past eleven. We hadn't intended to go on that long but we'd lost track of time.

The words were spoken spontaneously; but were they really true?

CHAPTER 10 Wed February 9th - 10th Settling in

Wednesday was a quieter day in KLM. Naomi and I met at the station as usual - at least neither of us had overslept - but we were both tired. Not much conversation as we travelled into the office.

I couldn't talk to Rachel today (she was off with her sick mother) and I needed to consult with her before taking any actions. But she had given me a full list of the KLM staff. Looking through it, I realised that I hadn't even seen half of them. There must be other offices - maybe in an adjacent unit? I hadn't seen where Naomi worked, for example.

It would be good to explore the whole office complex further. I needed to check there were no weak points around the back of the building - or down from the loft. Pipes or electric wires might have maintenance access.

More positively, it might give scope for additional security devices. For example, to detect sounds coming from below. I'd no idea what security watch was routinely in place; or whether there was out-of-hours working. There was some sort of security system at the main entrance; but who did it ring through to? Was it operational, or just a fake?

More mundanely, I needed Rachel, when she was back, to inspect the ladies toilet from a security viewpoint. I'd advise her what to look for. But I was still awaiting that phone call from the independent security adviser. I didn't want to receive it in an open office; or worse still, halfway into the loft.

So I sat for the day in Alex's office – I had no idea when he would return, or even where I was supposed to go if he did. I simply sat at his desk and thought hard about exactly what I needed to know; and what might need to be done.

One thing Alex's absence raised (at least for me) was the need for a computerised diary system that kept track of where everyone on KLM's books was – in the office and out on field-work.

We weren't lawyers, charging our customers by the minute. But it had to cover each day. With events like annual leave; and the name and base of each visitor.

But it would have to be kept up to date, with a hundred percent backing from Simon Cooke.

Once a simple desk diary might have sufficed. But these days there must be smarter systems available. KLM certainly needed something.

Alex would be one of the most difficult to bring on board. But might there be half a dozen more like him?

I hoped that the advisor I would eventually meet – there'd been no call yet – would know about the practicality of small companies, especially ones with valuable secrets.

By now I was in need of coffee. There was a filter machine in the main open plan which I'd been told was "easy to operate". Half a dozen staff were working quietly at their computers. One or two smiled at me but they sensed I was busy, didn't choose to break into my thoughts.

I padded back to my desk. And so the day went on.

Naomi came for me at quarter past five, at what was now becoming a tradition. We headed for the station and Luxulyan. It was as we walked up Station Drive that she gave me her news.

'Sorry, can't invite you back this evening, Mark. It's my night out. I'm driving into St Austell for yoga, followed by a simple meal. No Beef Wellington tonight.'

'I'm relaxed on yoga, Naomi. 'I'll have a quiet evening at the King's Arms. Meet a few more locals. I could do with an early night anyway.'

I had one more task I'd lined up for this evening: to inspect the third flat mentioned in the village shop.

Slightly further from the station. No cheaper, but significantly larger. There was a second bedroom and a decent-sized kitchen. The décor was restful: white on most walls, pale green on the rest. Even a couple of pictures.

'We had a couple here,' the landlord said, 'very civilised. But they had to leave suddenly. Her mum was taken ill. That's why they left most of their furniture.'

They'd left enough, anyway. I longed to be settled. This would be better than the King's Arms. I could entertain here – if I had anyone to entertain.

'How long's the tenancy?'

'Minimum six months,' he replied. 'After that stay as long as you like, on a rolling month's notice.'

'Fine. Then can I take it, please.'

We shook hands on the deal and we agreed I'd move in on Sunday week. That'd be something to tell Naomi.

Thursday morning started as usual at Luxulyan station. I decided to keep my news for the return journey.

Rachel was looking wan from her day with her mum, but we knuckled down. We were well into a useful discussion when my phone rang.

'I'm sorry, Rachel. I have to take this.'

'Go back to your office, Mark. I've plenty to get on with.'

I was answering the phone as I reached my door.

'Mark Renfrew?' said a Geordie voice. 'You won't know me but my name's Dougie Huggate. I was asked to call you.'

'I'm Mark,' I replied. 'Seeking wisdom on ways to introduce modern security to a start-up company.'

'Aye. So I was told. I have comparable experience. But could you come to me? First thing tomorrow. I had a review but it's been cancelled. I can give you the whole morning.'

I recalled my promise to my old security boss: "anywhere and anytime". I couldn't back out now.

'I'm starting from mid-Cornwall. You're in the Northeast?'

'That's reet, laddie. Gateshead, to be exact.'

'OK, Dougie. I'll travel up this afternoon and stay overnight. Is there somewhere local you'd recommend?'

We swapped logistics and he rang off. We both knew not to say too much on the phone. It was two days out of the office; but I wouldn't make the necessary dent in KLM without it.

I explained briefly what had happened when I rejoined Rachel. She was immediately practical.

'You'll need to go by car. Luxulyan?' She glanced at the clock. 'The next train's in ten minutes. Go now and you'll just catch it.'

I grabbed my laptop and headed for the door.

Once back at the King's Arms, I hastily packed an overnight bag, set off in my Toyota half an hour later. My satnav predicted arrival at around four o'clock.

I like tight deadlines. I sang my way up the motorways, stopping for a bite at Tamworth services. The Cornish ballad, "Come all ye tinner boys", which I now knew by heart, was a particular favourite. I booked in at the Premier Inn.

It crossed my mind that George might be expecting me to ring her. But my intention was firm: I wouldn't renew contact until I was properly settled with KLM. It was my turn, for once, to be busy.

I was at Dougie's office by eight. He was a bulky man of about my age. If he'd played rugby he'd have been in the scrum. But I doubted he could move fast enough. The Northeast ale had got to him. Mind, his face was cheerful enough. He'd seen plenty of life. I sensed we would get on well.

'This isn't my regular office. It's my safe room for private conversations. No hidden microphones. Our conversation today will remain off the record. Are you happy with that?'

How could I disagree? I only had three days experience of KLM.

'Right,' he went on. 'Just to set your mind at rest, I'll tell you a bit about what I do. Our mutual friend mentioned you were with KLM, so I looked them up on Google: they are hoping, they say, to mine lithium. Now I have an interest in lithium as well.'

He saw a look of horror on my face and hastened to reassure me. 'Don't worry, Mark: I don't want to mine it. My company needs lithium for renewable batteries. You might one day be our supplier. So I'd love to help you if I possibly can.'

'Let me tell you what I've found,' I said, 'and what I fear.' I sketched out my worries and waited for his reaction.

'Most of what you've just told me are the growing pains of a small but ambitious company. The fact they've appointed you means they do want proper security – even if they don't know quite what it looks like. It's not an impossible task.'

He went on to talk about the growth of his own company. 'Bigger than KLM, but it hasn't always been.' Dougie had installed many routine processes. He told me what they'd chosen, and what they'd rejected.

I wrote frantically. This was exactly what I was after. 'Are these hugely expensive?'

'Not really. The real costs are the time spent getting them to bed down properly. The disaster will be if they pay them lip service but then ignore them. Modernising needs effort over several months. Make sure your management buys into it.'

I got him to unpack his advice on the final sentence.

It was a lot of common sense, most of which I knew. But there were one or two gems. 'Sometimes the guys who seem the most awkward, if you're patient, turn into your biggest supporters. I mean, some of these tools are real timesavers. Make sure the refuseniks realise that for themselves. It's well worth it to get them on your side.'

After we'd had a break for coffee, I broached the question of Alex Price. Was that a security matter?

Dougie mused for a while. 'The worst case would be if Alex had taken KLM secrets and sold them to a competitor, perhaps been bribed by a new job at a higher salary.'

'I doubt that could happen, Dougie.'

'Why not?'

'Firstly, not many of KLM's secrets are on paper. A side effect of the current quagmire. Secondly, we don't have local rivals. Cornish Lithium is a major company with government backing, they've plenty of ideas of their own. Lastly, Alex's background was in China Clay. He's no scientist. He'll struggle to get any job based on twenty-year back experience. KLM is probably his last chance.'

Dougie considered for a moment. Then nodded.

'Right. So I don't think you need to worry from a security viewpoint. What if Alex fell down a shaft when meeting a client? Or went for a swim in an old clay lagoon, was poisoned by the residual waste?'

I gave a wry laugh. 'Or he might just be sitting in my office – his office? – this morning, wondering who'd been there earlier.'

Dougie smiled, then was serious. 'But the first of these possibilities, Mark, are maybe matters for the police. It's your Chief Executive that needs to call them. You've enough challenges of your own with the staff on site.'

I left a short time later. It had been an excellent meeting. But now I had a long drive back to Cornwall. With the Friday afternoon traffic I wouldn't be home till mid evening.

PART 2

February 6th - 12th

Investigation

CHAPTER 11 Mon February 6th - 8th Ideas on traffic

George Gibert woke late on Monday to find that Mark was no longer at home. For now, it wasn't something to worry about. She settled herself to start on the Fowey Traffic Study.

The Head of Traffic in St Austell had promised traffic data on Fowey but this was yet to arrive. In the meantime she could turn notes from her walks round Fowey into a coherent document.

George spread a large-scale map of Fowey across the kitchen table. Fowey was perhaps a mile across: the traffic hadn't seemed that bad. The key question was, how might it be improved?

That was a non-question in the depths of winter: she'd seen for herself that traffic wasn't bad. Hopefully the data would pinpoint the summer problems.

There were many yellow lines. Sensible: most streets were narrow enough, even with no cars parked on them. Now, what about parking? She'd seen there could be problems with access to the long-stay car park. But was the parking itself adequate?

She'd counted 250 spaces, with just one way in and out. But if capacity was the issue, could they enlarge this? She peered at the map more carefully.

Buildings weren't distinguished but there was hatching round most of the car park. Another exit would mean purchasing a surrounding property then flattening it. But Fowey was very old. Most buildings would be listed, with legal protection. Did that limit change around the car park? She'd need another visit to check this out.

George made herself a mug of coffee. Open-plan thinking was hard work.

After her break George asked herself, what did visitors do in Fowey? She picked up a leaflet from the Tourist office.

The focus was the jetty. Plenty of rowing and sailing boats and motor launches in high season, though none in February. Two ferries across the river, to Bodinnick and to Polruan. The one to Bodinnick carried a dozen cars. Sufficient, surely? There was no main road on the other side.

Further down the estuary there was a daily boat to Mevagissey, a honey-pot village further down the coast. Maybe that could take fifty passengers? Beyond was Readymoney Cove. Daphne du Maurier had once lived here. Mind, she wasn't as famous as Agatha Christie.

In August there was a regatta. No doubt with masses of visitors and participants, the town decked in flags.

And there was plenty of entertainment for walkers. She'd completed the Hall Walk yesterday: a wooded path above the river from Bodinnick to Polruan. That was where she'd come across Emma. Two ferries, plus a long walk back through Fowey.

Once she had written up her notes, George started a list of ways to improve traffic flows. Traffic lights? Speed humps? One-way streets? Did the few there now point in the right direction?

By now it was time for lunch. Until she had the measured traffic flow data there was little more she could do.

After lunch it was time to educate herself on copper mining in Cornwall. Not just for Emma. It was part of Cornwall's heritage and she was working in the Duchy. She took a deep breath and opened a new notebook.

Tuesday followed a similar pattern. George couldn't investigate traffic without data; and the data hadn't arrived. She spent all day on nineteenth century mining and the economic context.

It was the right century to focus on. The industrial revolution was under way, increasing demand for copper in Britain and around the world. Cornwall, with its turbulent geology, had plenty of it. The British Empire and the United States were hungry for more; and so was the British Navy.

Nelson's victory at Trafalgar in 1805 wasn't just superior seamanship. At the start of the century, George learned, the government decided to install copper sheet under the hulls of the British fleet. This reduced the maintenance needed on rotting planks and spreading barnacles. Best of all, the copper-bottomed vessels could travel through water much faster than their French counterparts.

It was amazing just how much you could learn from the internet once you had clear reason to do so.

Traffic data finally arrived on Wednesday and George transferred it to a spreadsheet. Average traffic flows - vehicles per hour - for every main street in Fowey, for one week in autumn 2022.

Was it early autumn, when there'd still be many tourists? Or the end of November, when there'd be few visitors at all?

The numbers didn't make sense, either on any single day or over the week. For the numbers of vehicles arriving at any street junction must match the number leaving it.

There might be discrepancies - the occasional van halted for a delivery, or the car that managed to park. But the differences between arrivals and departures were huge: they made no sense.

Forget the detail. How was the overall picture?

Equally baffling. There weren't many roads in or out of Fowey. What were the totals like on these?

No data on the car ferry to Bodinnick, which was sloppy. It was part of the overall pattern. But there wasn't a car maker in Fowey, or a scrappers' yard. The number of vehicles coming in to the town must match the number going out – had to be.

But the data implied hundreds of cars were leaving each day for Bodinnick – and none were coming back.

Even if there was some logic behind the flawed numbers, that wouldn't help her study. She needed accurate flows.

George sighed, but she wasn't beaten. A soothing mug of coffee later she started to invent a data collection method of her own.

Counting flows of traffic was not difficult. Not in Fowey. She only wanted one solid week of accurate flows.

She'd been sent "data" from last autumn; she could work with one well-counted week from February. You'd just need traffic counters that were well-motivated and diligent.

Which led her to think of school children. Could they provide what she required?

Older primary school pupils would need supervision: "duty of care" would come into play. Which moved her to older sixth formers. If she'd been approached while at school by a real mathematician, asking for help on a local project, she'd have jumped at it. In the half term holiday, at least. Wouldn't that still be true today?

But wasn't the February half term holiday coming up shortly?

A moment later she was consulting Google, had found the Fimbarrus Academy and learned that it had recently added a sixth form.

George rang them at once. The school secretary was helpful. Yes, the sixth form included maths. Mr Jakes, the senior maths teacher, would be happy to help if he could. He was always interested in real-world applications. He'd had a Registrar from Truro Hospital over, talking on health statistics, only last month.

Then George realised this could be a two-way exchange. She'd love to talk about her work to sixth form maths students. 'Does Mr Jakes have any free periods when I could talk to him?'

An hour later they were conversing profitably over the phone.

CHAPTER 12 Fri February 10th The Fimbarrus Academy

George set out early on Friday for the Fimbarrus Academy.

Peter Jakes had been more than supportive. He was turning over his morning maths lessons so his students had the chance to hear from George on the "Life of an Industrial Mathematician in 2023".

The first part of her talk would be historical. The development of Operational Research in the Second World War; the impact of the subject on new organisations like the National Coal Board and British Steel; the progression from massive computers into today's devices; the spread across Management Science; and her own experience on projects across Cornwall.

After coffee she was to talk about the Fowey Traffic Study. That was her chance to invite volunteers to spend time collecting hard data on the town's current traffic patterns. Their response would show how well her talk had got through.

Next week was the half term break. Peter Jakes had observed that it would do his students good to do something active and useful. 'Better than surfing the internet, anyway.'

George decided to dress as she would to meet a client: an olive-green business suit and lemon shirt. For if she got no volunteers, she'd be back to St Austell, challenging them on the data they'd sent her.

When she got to the Academy, she discovered that there was no school uniform in the sixth form: she'd be the only one in "uniform". But her audience looked tidy enough. Peter Jakes was about her age. She hoped she could match his vigour. His introduction was crisp, then she took over.

The coffee break gave her little chance to relax. She was approached by several students, asking about careers in Management Science. She'd need to bone up on this if she did this sort of thing again.

After the break, the talk was all about her current project. The students seemed surprised that an experienced mathematician should be bothered with traffic jams in Fowey: this stuff was really relevant to everyday life.

This time George contained the interruptions: she had plenty of questions for her audience as well as a few kites to fly.

Finally, she got down to the hard graft of project work in the real world. You could only model what you could measure. She needed reliable traffic data, at hourly intervals, over the whole of next week. 'Would any of you like to help me?'

A show of hands went up. She'd been a hit.

George gave a smile. 'Great. Thanks, guys. That's more volunteers than we have streets in Fowey.'

'Or we could operate in shifts,' suggested Peter Jakes. 'I'm happy to help manage the process; maybe Ms Gilbert and I can do that between us? What time-range should we cover?'

'Well, I doubt there'll be any jams before nine or after five.'

'Talking of time, it's practically lunch time,' said the teacher. 'I'm going to take Ms Gilbert for some light refreshment. But we'll be back by two: can the volunteers meet again here, please. We'll go through the details and work out the shifts.'

He turned to his guest speaker. 'Right, thank you very much, Ms Gilbert. You've given us a fascinating morning.'

There was a hearty round of applause before the students headed off for lunch.

'We're near the town centre,' said the teacher. 'The Ship Inn does a toasty sandwich. Would that do?'

'That'd be fine.'

They strolled down towards the jetty. As they did so, George noticed a gap in the street's housing.

'Don't remember that, Peter. Did it happen recently?'

'Ah. That's the Council's tribute to Ukraine. Started with a few explosions on Monday morning, muffled by thick fog. Then more bangs over the day. Even a skip to pick up the debris. The panels went up yesterday.'

'This week?' George was surprised. No wonder she hadn't noticed it last Sunday. There'd been nothing to notice.

'I'm joking about Ukraine,' Peter admitted. 'No-one knows what's behind it. There's probably no logic at all. There had been odd noises. Maybe they wanted to get rid of the squatters?'

'I hope they gave 'em time to get out before they started. Hey, was anyone hurt?'

'Don't think so,' said Peter. 'They'd got signs up to stop anyone getting too close. Maybe the Council was having a purge on listed buildings? There are far too many here in Fowey. Stops anyone changing anything.'

George didn't say any more, but she wondered if there was something odd going on in the Council. That was two oddities inside a week.

Once at the Ship, George realised she would need to stay the next few nights somewhere: her survey would start tomorrow. She booked herself in while Peter was placing their order.

'Peter, can I get you a drink?' she inquired, as she joined him at the bar.

'I don't usually drink at lunchtime,' he admitted. 'But this is the last day of term. It's my round,' he insisted. 'What'll you have?'

They settled for halves of cider and took their toasties to a table in the corner.

'I've just booked in for the weekend,' said George. 'Once the survey's started, maybe you and I could cover alternate days. Thank you for offering to help, by the way.'

'I'm keen to see the results. And what you make of them. Your talk this morning was really fascinating. I should have looked around harder before I slipped into teaching.'

'Don't rubbish yourself. We need good teachers, especially maths teachers,' said George reassuringly. 'We might need your school's cooperation in the future. Let's see how this works out first.'

CHAPTER 13 Fri February 10th - 11th The Survey

It was four o'clock when George Gilbert finally left the Fimbarrus Academy and walked down to the Ship Inn. She was exhausted.

Young people had so much energy. Wonderfully stimulating but also draining. George hadn't worked with sixth formers for years. Her last survey had been with postgraduates. This was a bit different. She had to try to allow the volunteers to be free-thinking and imaginative, but not to wreck the entire process. She mustn't offend anyone in the town.

Peter had been a tower of strength during the afternoon's briefing, expanding some student ideas while gently blocking others. She could learn a lot from him: he was a wise teacher. Was this a friendship that might grow?

George clocked in and was shown a small room at the top of the Inn. Comfortable enough, would do for a few days. She discarded her business suit and lay on the bed. Five minutes later she was fast asleep.

Next morning George opened the curtains and found she was looking across the town. The Fimbarrus Academy, gleaming cream in the early morning sun, stood high up on the hillside. Closer, further down, was the remains of the demolished building – or at least the builder's boards that had been placed around it. She sensed it might be important, though she had no idea why. It wasn't a problem for today.

She was just finishing breakfast when she was joined by Peter

Jakes. They had agreed it would be better to go round the students together. Peter knew them well while she knew the data she was after. Together they made a good team.

The students had paired off while she had assigned the streets to cover. Two of the pairs were assigned to car parks. One halfway up the hill, the other beside the Bodinnick ferry.

The latter would be asked to measure the operation of the ferry: the timing of a there-and-back crossing? How long were the queues of cars waiting to use it? While she had the team George wanted to know as much as possible.

George and Peter worked their way steadily round the teams. They were all in place, clutching their clip boards.

They wouldn't stay excited for long; but she hoped they'd remain diligent. She'd cross-check later, making sure the net traffic in and out at each street junction was close to zero.

The students were happy to chat.

'Have you done this kind of survey before, Ms Gilbert?'

'Call me George,' she told them. 'Yes, the last one was with students from Imperial College. The first days of the pandemic. We tramped round Delabole, checking who had Covid and where they'd caught it. That was before vaccinations. The Public Health Director for Cornwall wanted to know how it was spreading.'

'Do the students all live in Fowey?' she asked, as they strode along towards Bodinnick ferry.

'Oh no. We take them from as far off as Lostwithiel. Bussed in. Course, there won't be any coming next week, it's the half term break. The two we'll meet next are from out of town.'

George felt guilty. She had assumed her car-counters would all live in Fowey. When they reached the lads at the ferry crossing, Tommy and Wilson, she asked them how they'd travelled in.

'No trouble, miss,' said Tommy. 'We've biked in from Lostwithiel. Only about six miles.'

'What I'd like to understand is how the ferry runs. Is it on a fixed timetable, say three crossings an hour, however many cars are waiting? Or does it wait till it's got a full load? Also, how late in the day can you catch it? Does it run at night?'

There are other things too,' added Peter. 'Can it work at low tide? Is it ever halted by bad weather?'

The lads nodded. There was plenty there to keep them busy. 'We'd best ask the guys running the ferry,' said Tommy. 'They must have discovered all this over the years.'

'They'll probably be pleased someone is taking an interest,' added his partner.

'We'll be back in a couple of hours,' said George. 'Call us if there any problems.'

George and Peter continued to chat as they went round. Everyone seemed fully engaged, adding to the count as each car passed.

'They're fairly streetwise,' she observed, once they'd completed their tour and stopped near the centre for coffee. 'It's cold enough today, but some of 'em have found a way to keep out of the wind.'

One pair had bagged a central window table in their café. 'That's alright for now,' George commented, 'but I bet they won't be allowed to stay there all day.'

'I'll have a word with the manager,' Peter replied. 'Explain what they're doing. I'm sure she'll be glad someone is doing something.'

CHAPTER 14 Sat February 11th Fowey and Golant

The survey went on till five o'clock. Walking round it certainly gave George a better grasp of the town's geography.

She learned that the recently flattened building she could see from her guest room would have backed on to the long-term car park. If she'd been here last Sunday night, she'd have seen or at least heard the explosions to bring it down.

Once they'd taken away the panels and tarmacked over the floor, it could offer a second route in or out. That might reduce traffic congestion, might even make the car park more popular.

It also meant the problem she was addressing was changing beneath her feet. Irritating. She resolved to go over to the Council offices on Monday and ask how she was to proceed.

After their second tour, Peter suggested another coffee. 'They're all doing well, and they're keen to make it work. We don't need to patrol them like a primary school.'

This time they picked a different café. George noticed another pair of car-counters on the table with the best view.

As she fetched drinks George explained to the ladies running the café what the front-table students were doing. She also handed over a twenty-pound note. 'I'm afraid they'll be here most of the day. That's to help cover their drinks. We don't want them sloping off and then making up the numbers.'

'Each tour so far has taken ninety minutes,' observed Peter, glancing at his watch. 'It's nearly one o'clock. Let's have some lunch before we go round again.' It was time, once again, for toasted sandwiches in the Ship.

'We'll do just two more tours today,' declared George, as they munched their toasties. 'The youngsters are doing well. The problem will be keeping them keen through next week.'

The experienced teacher had a suggestion. Combatting student boredom was a perennial problem.

'Why don't we widen the inquiry? Get the students to collect local views on the traffic. Especially shopkeepers, they'll know as well as anyone. Can't that be part of your study?'

'You're right, Peter. We could concoct a second survey. With multiple-choice answers and scope to widen these out. That could be really useful. Mind, what we need most is suggestions for improvement. It would be horrible to finish and miss out something the locals thought was obvious.'

They mulled over the idea during the afternoon tours. Bounced it off the counting pairs and got an enthusiastic response. George could see another working evening ahead, to get something ready for tomorrow.

'Right, Peter,' said George when they'd done with their students for the day. 'Thank you so much. You've been a real help.'

'I've enjoyed it. And our conversations.'

'So what are you plans for this evening?'

'Nothing special. I live on the far side of the Gribbin. On my own, I'm afraid. My wife died of cancer five years ago.'

'Peter, I'm so sorry.' There was a short pause. Then they both started to speak simultaneously.

'I don't suppose . . .,' said George.

'I'd be happy to help . . .,' said Peter.

They laughed at their linguistic collision. 'Right. You go first,' said George.

'I was thinking, you'd be spending time this evening drafting out the second survey. I'd be happy to help with that if you wanted. I mean, I've thought about Fowey traffic as much as anyone. I've lived near here most of my life.'

'Peter, that would be terrific. I know Fowey far less well than places in North Cornwall. But I have one caveat: I insist on a couple of hours off before we start.'

'I agree. Why don't we go out for a meal, somewhere away from central Fowey? My only condition that we don't mention surveys of any sort. If either of us do, we'll pay some sort of forfeit.'

George laughed. 'Agreed. First though, I'm going back to the Ship Inn for a shower. I don't have a vast range of going-out dresses with me but I'll do my best.'

'Right. I'll drive home, my car's up at the Academy. I'll book somewhere to eat and pick you up from the Ship at . . .?'

'Six thirty. For a meal at seven. We'll take a couple of hours over it then come back and knock out another survey.'

When Peter turned up at the Ship an hour later, he'd obviously made an effort: dark red jacket, cobalt blue shirt and cream chinos. The combination made him look rather smart.

George had only one dress in her suitcase, mid-blue, so she didn't have much choice. But the shower had refreshed her and made her short, dark hair especially curly. She looked ready to go out. It was a long time since she'd been out anywhere.

'Tonight's meal is on me,' said Peter, as she got into the car.

'It certainly isn't. We'll go Dutch or not go at all.'

He smiled. 'If you insist, George. I'm not going to argue.'

'So where are we going? Or is it a closely guarded secret?'

He laughed. 'I thought we could try the Fisherman's Arms in Golant. It's said to be "small and friendly". Out of Fowey, anyway.'

'Have you been there before?'

'To be honest, George, I haven't. In the years before Annie died, she was too ill to go anywhere. Since then, I haven't had anyone to go with.' He laughed. 'Sounds pathetic. I'm really not a hermit - honest.'

'I never thought you were. Had you been married long?'

'Twenty years. Annie and I were both local to Fowey – she was from Polruan. How about you?'

The question was asked casually but it wasn't casual at all. George was glad it had come in a darkened car, not a well-lit restaurant. She took a moment to fashion her response.

'I was married for fifteen years,' she said. 'But my husband was declared dead in a dreadful air crash in Iran in 2009. After that I bought a small cottage in Cornwall, near Tintagel and started looking for work down here. I've been an independent Cornish consultant ever since.'

It was all true, though not the whole truth. But her reconnection with Mark was too bizarre, too complicated to share with anyone this early in a new friendship.

Her recent relationship with her one-time husband had left her wondering if there was any life left there at all. They'd been out of touch now for over a week; she had no idea where he was. She had tried to contact him but the call had been blocked – maybe he'd got a new phone? He'd made no attempt to contact her.

'We can't live in the past,' Peter observed, as he drove towards Golant. 'We can only try our best to live life to the full each day. You're doing that, anyway. From what I saw today.'

It was a generous compliment but George hadn't worked out how best to respond before they came to Golant and saw the Fisherman's Arms lit up before them.

The restaurant was pleasantly full but not overcrowded. Good job Peter had booked ahead.

They studied the menu and decided to give themselves a treat. Peter chose Peking Duck, while George ordered a lamb shank plus dauphinoise potatoes. They each had a half of cider, they wouldn't get through a whole bottle of wine. Peter was aware he was driving.

'It's unusual to come out,' observed George. 'I haven't been anywhere like this for ages.'

Their table was by the window. The River Fowey was flowing outside, they could hear water gushing past. They could see nothing at this time of night.

'It's been a long day.' She remembered just in time not to mention the word "survey", wondered what Peter had in mind as a forfeit. 'But I'd say it's gone pretty well.'

Peter nodded. 'Both days have. It was fascinating to hear about your consultancy. Is it all as interesting as this?'

'I'm not sure this one's going that well. There's something odd about that flattened building close to your school.'

'What's that?'

'I saw it from my guestroom this morning. The old building was next to the long stay car park. Which is a brute to get in or out of – even if you don't meet someone coming the other way.'

Peter nodded; he knew what she meant. 'Yes. Giving the main park a second exit might make a lot of difference.'

'That's exactly the sort of conclusion I'd hope you might read in my final report.'

He frowned. 'What's wrong with that?'

'It's the timing, Peter. It's odd. They shouldn't be starting to implement my findings before I've even started the study. As it happens, I was over here last weekend, straight after I'd won the project. So I've seen the change. But if I'd started a week later, I'd never have seen the old layout at all. It's all in the wrong order.'

A young waitress in a demure black dress arrived with their meals at that point, causing a break in conversation.

When they resumed Peter forced himself to handle George's concerns from a teaching perspective.

He took four cards from his pocket, then wrote one word on each: Commission; Findings; Implementation; Response. Then he laid them out on the table.

'George, can I put it like this? If the order had been: a) commission a study; b) await the findings; c) start the implementation, that would have been fine. But doing a), then c), then b) doesn't make sense.'

He laid the cards out in two different orders as he spoke.

'There is another way.' He seized the cards again. 'a) Carry out some long-planned change; b) commission a study around the changed layout; c) respond to its recommendations.

'That would also be OK. But it isn't what happened.'

The cards lay on the table challenging them as they continued their meal. But they moved on to other topics.

The waitress came a while later to ask about desserts. They consulted the dessert menu and decided to each have some pavlova.

As they were deciding the waitress was eyeing the cards on the table.

'Still using your prompt cards, sir?'

Peter looked up and smiled. 'Hey, Isobel. I didn't recognise you, looking so smart.'

'I could say the same about you, sir.'

Her eyes travelled on to George. 'And if you don't mind my saying, ma'm, you look like a film star. Fame comes at last to the Fisherman's Arms.'

The girl realised she'd overreached herself. 'I'll get your desserts right away.'

As she went, George turned to Peter. 'D'you know every waitress around here? Or just the prettiest ones?'

But he wasn't embarrassed. 'Isobel is our star student. She's just won a place to do maths at Cambridge.'

'Pity she's not on the survey.' George had used the banned word before she'd even realised.

But Peter chose not to notice. 'Ask her why when she comes back.' So she did.

'I'd love to help on the survey, Ms Gilbert, but I'm working full-time here all next week.'

'Which college are you hoping to go to, Isobel?'

'Kings. Where the Christmas Carols comes from.'

'I was at Trinity Hall – almost next door. Make the most of it, it's a very special place. And don't work all the time.'

'You didn't say that yesterday.'

George laughed. 'Time and place, my dear. My outlet was night hikes. I had to climb out of college over a ten-foot wall, climb back in later. An old bike was carefully parked beneath the spike. Not so easy, though, if you were small like me.'

'My mate Wilson's a night climber. But he's going to Oxford.' She spoke disparagingly.

'Oxford has produced our last five Prime Ministers,' observed Peter.

'I'm not sure that's something to boast about,' retorted Isobel. She giggled. 'I'd better leave you two to eat.'

CHAPTER 15 Sat February 11th - 12th The Tavern

It was much later than they had planned by the time they left the Fisherman's Arms.

Coffee had been served in a mostly empty lounge; and they'd invited Isobel to join them. She had checked with the manager before doing so and brought back an extra cup and saucer.

Isobel was very keen to quiz a Cornwall-based maths graduate from the place she'd be going. George was happy to encourage a young woman who would be following, thirty years later, in her footsteps. Her own talk yesterday had broken the ice.

For a while Peter was happy to listen. Eventually the conversation came round to Wilson.

'So which buildings does your mate Wilson climb?' asked George. Peter was pretending not to listen; better if he didn't know this.

'All the old ones around Fowey. The best bit, he says, is getting from one to another. Their roofs are all different heights.'

'That's 'cos they were all built at different times,' said George. 'I hope he doesn't try to climb in. That'd be criminal.'

'I told him that. He won't go into any that are occupied,' replied Isobel. 'Just the vacant ones. Like the one near the long-stay car park. That was empty for ages. He wanted to know what was inside.'

'And what was there?'

'"It was really empty," he said. "No furniture or anything." But he thought someone else had been staying there - with a sleeping bag or something. Hey, didn't they pull it down quickly?'

'We'll be talking to Wilson tomorrow,' said Peter. 'He and Tommy are counting the cars at the Bodinnick ferry.'

'Talking of which,' added George, 'it's half past ten. Don't you think we should be going?'

'I hope Isobel doesn't read too much into seeing us having a meal together,' said George as they travelled back into Fowey.

'It's been a fun evening, anyway,' replied Peter. 'Be thankful she didn't photograph us. Once on Facebook it could have started a rumour.'

'If I'm ever going to hug you, Peter, it'll be in private, not in public.'

'There are various ways that remark could be taken, George. Let's not go too fast.' His response was almost too quick.

Then he sighed. 'You know, George, I don't think we should draft anything this evening. We're probably not in the mood for questions. It could wait another day, couldn't it?'

Back in the Ship guestroom, George slept like a proverbial log. The previous evening had been calming as well as thoroughly enjoyable. Peter was someone that she could imagine growing fond of. But she was fifty, she told herself, too old for a shallow relationship.

On Sunday morning she woke early. But though it was light it was also cold. She sat up in bed, drafting ideas for questions. Asking both what locals made of the current situation; and what things they would like to change. Having spent Saturday walking round Fowey she had plenty of ideas of her own. That was good; they'd need to offer survey participants a sensible range of options.

She was eating in the Ship breakfast room by the time Peter

arrived. He was looking chirpy, like the cat that had collared the cream. She gave him a welcoming grin. 'Have you had breakfast?'

'I'm into porridge, thank you. But if I'm going to be here all next week, I might switch to bacon and egg. It looks delicious.'

'I need all the energy I can find. You know, the students have got the hang of this. Do they need us around so much? Hey, could you keep an eye on them for me tomorrow?'

'Sure.' He looked slightly puzzled.

'I want to confront my client in St Austell Council over that flattened building. Do they intend to knock through another entrance for the car park?'

'You know, I was thinking about it when I took the cards out of my jacket. It couldn't be some sort of scam, could it?'

'How d'you mean?'

'Well, they might not intend to take any notice of your survey, whatever it says. It might be just a smokescreen for something they're going to do anyway.'

'Or have done already,' she replied. 'Yes, that thought had crossed my mind. Not very motivating, I was trying to ignore it. But why would they need a smokescreen?'

Peter mused as George continued her breakfast. 'It might have been hard to get official permission to knock down that building. Say, if it was listed. Most of 'em are, you know, in the middle of Fowey.'

When they set off they were faster now, they knew where to find the pairs and there weren't many outstanding issues.

Eventually they reached the Bodinnick ferry. Wilson was there but not Tommy.

'Where's your mate?' asked George. She hoped he hadn't given up.

Wilson gave her a grin. 'Oh, he's over in Bodinnick. Recording the queue size as it grows or shrinks, also chatting to the drivers. I'm doing the same thing over here.'

'That's great,' said George. 'Have you time for one or two questions on a different matter?'

'Fire away,' he said cheerfully.

'Well. Mr Jakes and I were having a meal at the Fisherman's Arms last night and we met Isobel – she was our waitress. I gather she's off to Cambridge next October. She mentioned that you were heading for Oxford.'

'Subject to A-levels, of course. But maths is easier than anything else, as I'm sure you two learned years and years ago?'

George nodded. 'I was telling her about my night time escapades in Cambridge. Shinning over a ten-foot wall. Somehow or other Isobel told me you were already a night climber, here in Fowey.'

Wilson looked surprised that his mate had shared his secret but didn't try to deny it.

'It's safer than climbing the cliffs, anyway,' he declared. 'You're never far from help if something dreadful happens.'

'Whereas, if you fell on the cliffs, you might not be found for days.' Peter was doing his best to set the young man's mind at rest. 'I'm not saying anything, Wilson. Don't worry, my duty of care stops at the Academy gate.'

Wilson noticed another car coming down the hill and added a mark on his clipboard. Then he turned back to his supervisors.

'Anyway, what's your question?'

George took over. 'Mr Jakes and I are interested in the old building next to the long stay car park, the one that was knocked down early last week. D'you know the one I mean?'

'The Old Tavern. Yeah, that was one of my favourites.'

'Was that its proper name, or just your private nickname?'

The "Tavern" bit was real enough. Over the doorway, very faded. But I asked the Museum keeper. He couldn't recall it selling beer in his lifetime. He's well old, must be in his seventies. So the Tavern could have closed much earlier – maybe the century before last. That's why I added the "Old".'

George gave him a grin. 'How did you get in?'

Wilson smiled. 'From the roof, via the roof next door. There was a skylight but for some reason it wasn't locked, so I just climbed in. It was easy enough. I even got Izzy in there a couple of times.'

This was new information; George wanted to extract all she could. Fortunately Wilson recorded another car, giving her a few seconds to think.

'So what did Isobel make of it?'

'She said it was creepy. And the toilet wasn't up to much. But she's a tidy girl. Next time she brought a brush and swept the whole floor.' He smiled as he recalled the female housekeeping instincts, aroused even on a two-hundred-year-old building.

'It was the time after that when I realised Izzy and I weren't the only visitors.'

'What?'

'No. Because Izzy had swept so well, you could see fresh dirty footprints across the floor. A bigger sized print than mine, so I assumed it was a man. I followed them down from the skylight into the old Tavern bar; then across to the entrance to the cellar.'

George and Peter were agog. 'And what was down there?'

He sighed. 'I couldn't get in. There was a padlock. But that wasn't two hundred years old, it was brand new. Of course, I didn't have a key. Or know who might have one.'

There was a thoughtful silence, then George asked, 'So what happened after that?'

'I didn't go in again. Didn't fancy meeting someone bigger than me who was up to no good. I crept back to the skylight and then out to safety. There's no point in making night climbing harder than it need be.'

Suddenly we heard a call from the returning ferry. It was Tommy, coming back to report his findings to his partner.

'I think we'll leave you to it,' said Peter. 'We'll be back later. Thank you for sharing so clearly.'

CHAPTER 16 Mon February 13th St Austell

On Monday morning George Gilbert phoned the St Austell Council and arranged for a visit to her client, Head of Traffic Clive Nicholls, later that morning.

She used the intervening time to put her thoughts in order, with a couple of PowerPoint slides based on Peter's cards. She also took a picture of the flattened building, the Old Tavern, from her guestroom window. She managed to zoom the image so the building made up most of the picture.

For completeness she also took a picture from the long-stay car park, showing the shell from a different angle. There was no doubt that, when the demolition was finished, it would be easy to build a separate entry to the car park through the gap that had been created – if that was what was intended.

Nicholls was alone in his office when the meeting began. Fair enough, this was for guidance, not to present results.

'I want to tell you briefly what I've been doing so far, then move on to a potentially serious obstacle.'

Clive nodded his acceptance of her agenda.

George didn't waste time on details. She unfolded her large-scale map of Fowey and laid it on his desk. 'I'll explain the extra symbols as we go along.'

Briefly she told how the traffic data she'd been sent made no sense. She illustrated the hourly flows at one road junction, with twice as many vehicles arriving as departing. 'That's happening all over. The good news is that I haven't let bad data snooker me. I've set up a traffic monitoring survey of my own.'

Clive looked upset. 'How on earth have you done that? And how much will it cost? I'm warning you, Ms Gilbert, I'll need higher approval before you breach your expense limits.'

'Please, let me explain.'

George outlined her visit to the Fimbarrus Academy, the news that this week was the half term holiday, and sixth formers volunteering to count traffic flows over the coming week.

She pointed out where each was pair was stationed; then told him the Academy was treating it as useful work experience. It wouldn't cost the Council anything.

Clive was stunned. In his mind traffic surveys took weeks to organise, cost thousands to run and even more to analyse. But he was a senior manager. He had the wisdom not to interfere in an ongoing project - at least, while the project manager was looking confident.

Fifteen minutes had gone. George reckoned she'd probably had half her time.

'Right, Clive. I'd like to move onto a possible obstacle.'

'Go on.' He looked like a rabbit in the headlights.

'These are two pictures of the Old Tavern, it's located here.' She pointed to the Fowey map.

'So you can see, Clive, its demolition would make it much easier to add a new entrance to the main car park.'

He smiled. 'Great. Doesn't sound like an obstacle to me.'

George sighed. 'The thing is, Clive, the problem - the layout of Fowey - has changed. After I was awarded the contract.'

'Come, come. Does that matter, Ms Gilbert? I didn't have you down as a nit-picker. If we were starting the whole thing a month later, you'd still be happy to accept it, wouldn't you?'

George tried again. 'It doesn't matter at all if the streets of Fowey were altered in the past. But right now, the building's been demolished but there's no new car park entrance. I can only model what's there. Which, I'm afraid, is ill-defined.'

Clive was looking confused.

'You told me, when I started, to complete this study quickly: it was urgent. That's why I've been giving it top priority.

'If you want a full study of Fowey traffic as it is right now, I can do that. But it'll be out of date once the new entrance is completed. I don't want the Council to waste its money. So what should I do?'

There was silence. The truth, thought George, was that what Clive really wanted was for her to stop bothering him.

He didn't care about the study's accuracy; he just wanted it to happen. He would be judged on the process, not the result. Value for money was low on his priorities.

George had one last idea. 'Clive, could you tell me who chose to flatten the Tavern last week? Which department would it come under?'

'How would that help?' He wanted to expend as little effort as possible.

'Well. If we knew that, we'd also know when it's due to be completed. The hardest part's already been done. Finishing it quickly would mean I could simply postpone the whole study, start again once the change had been completed.'

She could see he didn't like the word "postpone".

'The thing is, Clive,' she concluded, 'I'd need to know when to begin. I do have other projects. Or do you want me to carry on right away? Not to worry about the flattened Tavern at all. It's up to you.'

George came out the meeting five minutes later feeling highly frustrated. She hadn't got through. Hadn't even got a clear ruling.

It didn't make sense to ignore the change in Fowey that was about to happen – an improved car park. But she'd been given no remit to do anything else.

What she needed was to pour out her woes to an old friend. Peter was shaping up for the role but he didn't know her well enough. She needed to talk to someone who'd seen her in action through trials and tribulations.

The person that could do that best in South Cornwall was Frances Cober. In contrast to her, Frances was tall, slender and blonde. When they'd last been together, she was a police sergeant in Helston. Not a million miles from St Austell. If she was around today, George could drive over for lunch and an off-the-record consultation.

Ten seconds later she'd pulled out her phone. The call was ringing, anyway.

'Hi Frances. It's George.'

'George, I've got some news for you,' said Frances. 'I've just been promoted. As of next week I'll be an inspector in the St Austell police.'

'Hey. Congratulations! Inspector, eh! Smashed through the glass ceiling at last. Well done. When do you start?'

'Next Monday's my first day on duty.'

'So where are you right now?'

'I'm over in St Austell, looking at flats. I've got an appointment to see one this afternoon. When I've got something, I'll put my cottage in Gweek on the market. After all, it's a fisherman's cottage in a tourist hot spot.' She giggled. 'As long as the rent I gain is more than the amount I'll be paying, it'll be fine. And where are you, George?'

'You won't believe this, but I'm in St Austell too.'

'We must have lunch together. Today? Might be our last chance before I'm sucked into the police maelstrom.'

'Where d'you fancy?

'Well, I was given a few tips on places to eat by my predecessor. She's lived here for years.'

Ten minutes later the two friends were giving each other a long-time-no-see hug in the "Bengal Beekeeper".

'I've been told I must try the Madras curry,' said Frances.

'OK by me,' George replied. 'With a drink to celebrate your appointment?'

A few minutes later the meal had ordered and they had been seated at a secluded table, tucked in beside the wall.

For a while George gave Frances the floor. The last few weeks had been traumatic; she was glad to share some of it with a non-police friend.

'I suspect the fact that Geraldine had held the women's side of policing in St Austell together made it easier to appoint another woman – though that wasn't explicit in the advert.'

George nodded. Female promotion was far from easy – though not as bad as it used to be.

'They even put the candidates through a physical, George. Imagine it! A couple of beefy, overweight policemen and me. I mean, I'm not at Olympic swimmer or anything but I do a lot of walking on the cliffs.'

She grinned and then continued. 'If they were after someone to stand in the middle of a busy traffic junction and control the cars for hours on end, the two would have stood a chance. But you might need to chase a drug dealer or tackle a rapist: they'd never do that.'

Their curries were brought at that point, disrupting Frances' flow. Once they'd sorted the mango chutney and the poppadom's, George took her chance.

'Talking of traffic, Frances, I'm down in Fowey doing a traffic study for the Council. But I've just had a hell of a meeting. Made me thoroughly discouraged.'

'Would it help to share it?'

George needed no second bidding. She launched forth into the tale so far. It was a long story, but fortunately she was more succinct than the suspects Frances was used to grilling in the interview room.

'So let me get this straight,' said Frances, breaking off another piece of poppadom: this curry was hot. 'Your client started making the changes before the study had even got started? If you hadn't been true George Gilbert, dead keen to get going, you might never have known.'

She grinned and gave her verdict. 'They must know the answer they want. You're in some sort of Council skulduggery.'

'Would that be illegal?'

'It's hardly crime of the century, is it? Bureaucratic banshee, I'd call it. Take the money and give 'em an answer. You can only answer the question you've been set, George. Even you can't solve everything.'

They both grappled with their curries. The Madras sauce was extremely hot, even with lashings of mango chutney to soften the taste. Not a meal to eat in a hurry.

Frances stopped eating to give her tongue a break. It felt like it was on fire. She sipped more of her glass of water.

'You used to say, George, that the virtue of a computer model was that once calibrated it would help you look at alternatives.'

The comment gave her friend a jolt. Yes, she was right. "The value of a good model is not just to explain the present but also to explore the future." Her words to the sixth formers of Fimbarrus Academy only last Friday.

How much of Fowey's alleged traffic problem was linked to that long-stay car park? An interesting question, whatever the Head of Traffic thought of it.

'That's really helpful, Frances. I've been feeling far too sorry for myself. There is something I can do after all. Thank you.'

They ate more of their curries and took remedial action. Frances asked for more water. This wasn't just a battle, it was a campaign.

'If you are talking about crime,' she said, 'I'd have more hope of it in this flattened building you keep talking about. Tell me about it.'

George was glad of an excuse to stop eating.

'It was called the Tavern. Been there since the nineteenth century – if not earlier. It wasn't occupied. Been empty for ages.'

'How d'you know that? What are your sources?' The career police officer was always after hard evidence.

'Well, turns out one of our survey lads is a night climber in Fowey. One night he got onto the roof of the Tavern and found the skylight open, so he climbed in to have a look. There was nothing inside at all.'

George felt a sudden anxiety. 'You're not going to arrest him for trespass, are you?'

Frances laughed. 'You haven't told me his name, for a start. And the building's been knocked down; I doubt we'd find the fingerprints. Perhaps I'd better not be told his full name, though.'

George wasn't sure if she was serious or joking. But the comment led her on to the rest of Wilson's story.

'The lad took his mate in there. She swept the place clean. On his next visit he saw fresh footprints. They led to a strong padlock, on what he presumed was the cellar entrance.'

'Mm. That might have been something criminal. Was the Tavern always a pub?'

'I've no idea. How could you tell?'

'How about the Land Registry?' Then doubts flooded in. 'But that didn't start till 1862. If it became the Tavern after that date, it should have been recorded. The padlock suggests there was something down there. It'd be good to know just what it was.'

CHAPTER 17 Mon February 13th Tavern inquiries

The Bengal Beekeeper's red-hot Madras Curry made their meal last longer than they'd intended. Frances had to rush off for an appointment at three, to look at a flat on the edge of St Austell.

George needed to be back in Fowey. She wanted to see the survey team in action. It couldn't all be left to Peter.

This time she made use of the long-stay car park, booked herself a ticket for the week. She couldn't be an Academy visitor the whole time. The pair of students assigned here were still diligently recording, though they looked bored. The car park itself was half empty.

George took the chance to examine the old Tavern remnants more carefully. Would it really allow a separate exit? Was there anything else that would block the way?

She clambered round outside the builder's panels, reached the road that she had walked down on Friday from the Academy to central Fowey. A through route looked highly feasible.

George stood out in the road to see over the ten-foot panels. The Tavern had been the end of the row. The wall common to the next building along was smooth enough – no sticking out chimney breast, anyway - but looked a bit battered. As a minimum it would need complete re-rendering, followed by several coats of external paint. Though probably not magnolia.

George set out to visit all her team in turn. She'd leave the Bodinnick pair till last, that might be a longer conversation.

All seemed pleased to see her. Face-to-face contact was far better than emails. She'd need to talk to Peter this evening about how to organise the rest of the week. The team were dutiful but not exactly buzzing. How much data did she really need?

When she got to the Bodinnick ferry, Tommy and Wilson were still there. They'd expanded their role to working out the maximum capacity of the ferry, if it always turned round straight away. What was the optimal queuing mechanism?

They'd also considered whether a faster ferry might make much difference.

Fortunately Tommy had to be home for a weekly trumpet lesson, so it was easy to have time with Wilson on his own. She noticed a café close to the car park and took him for a drink and a piece of cake.

The place was not busy. They found a table in the corner; cake and drinks of hot chocolate were brought over.

'I had a good look at the long-stay car park this afternoon,' George began. 'The Old Tavern is in a key location. The route offers a second exit to Academy Rd. I saw the client this morning, in St Austell. Our study needs to include ideas on what difference to traffic such a new entrance might make.'

Wilson nodded. He appreciated being part of the project thinking.

'That's the main road into the town,' he replied. 'Would it really make sense to have more cars coming out onto it?'

'Good point.' George took a sip of her chocolate. At least it was hot. 'It might mean making Academy Rd one way. That'd complicate the traffic flows around Fowey. There'd need to be a matching one-way route back again.'

Wilson was a bright lad. He'd not considered such thing before but he was starting to realise that the real world was a complicated place.

'Are you sure it'd be easy to make a passage through?'

'That's a very good question. It all depends on what happened to the cellar when the building was brought down. It might need to be filled in. You'd need to assess whether its ceiling supports could cope with regular traffic – all sorts of vehicles. It's not just cars which use the car park. There'll be plenty of buses in the summer.'

There was a pause. Wilson started to munch his chocolate brownie. It was time, thought George, to be radical.

'What I was wondering was, is there any way we could get inside the Tavern and have a fresh look at that cellar?'

Wilson grinned. 'You're not exactly a hidebound woman, are you, George.'

'I can think outside the box if I need to. Or in this case, inside the box. But I'd say it's part of the traffic study.'

Now Wilson laughed. 'You mean, that's what you would say if you were caught on the site?'

George didn't answer. It was an unanswerable question. But she continued to advance her ideas. 'Now you told me yesterday that you got into the Tavern via the roof next door. But, of course, the Tavern roof is no longer there. So would it work if you took a long rope, looped it round next door's chimney, then abseiled down onto the Tavern floor?'

Wilson looked at her hard. Blinked. Yes, this really was the Cambridge graduate that had lectured them only three days earlier.

'Good job Mr Jakes isn't here,' he observed. 'Trouble is, I'd say you've overthought the problem.'

'How d'you mean?'

'Well, there's only a ten-foot wooden board round the Tavern at present. You'd be doing this at night, I assume. All you'd need is a climbing rope with a strong hook on one end. You'd throw it up to catch on the panel top. Then you'd pull yourself up, sit astride it and jump down the other side. When I'm night climbing, that's one of my standard ways in. I've got the rope that we'd need at home.'

There was a pause. 'Would you like another mug of chocolate, Wilson?'

'I think I need something stronger,' he replied. 'Are you being serious or is this just a wild thought experiment?'

George went to the counter to order more chocolate before she answered his question. And waited till the waitress had brought them and departed.

She took a deep breath. 'I'm not saying I want to break down the cellar door, Wilson. But it would be good to know if it's still there. And you've been there, you'd know exactly where to look.

'We could work out the size of the problem with an hour's quiet inspection. Mind, I'm a bit scared of going in there on my own. Even if you had lent me your special rope.'

Wilson was quiet for a moment. Then he looked up.

'Despite Izzy's comments, George, I'm cautious about my night climbing. For instance, I never go out on a night in term time: I don't want to fall asleep in any of my lessons.'

George waited for him to continue.

'We don't have lessons this week, of course. If I wasn't on the survey, I'd have been going out at least once. It's my dose of freedom, you see. So the question for me is, how can we conduct this expedition without losing too much sleep?'

It seemed they were inching towards a plan.

'When you go night climbing, do you cycle over here?'

'I do. Takes half an hour each way.'

'Well, I have a car. What if I fetched you and took you home again afterwards? That'd save you an hour.'

He nodded. 'That's a good idea. OK, then. I don't mind losing, say, an hour's sleep. There's no moon at present. So how about tonight?'

CHAPTER 18 Mon February 13th Night climb

George found Peter Jakes waiting in the lounge bar when she got back to the Ship Inn. She could get his roundup of the day before she had to negotiate a light supper. It had been a busy day. She needed a rest before tonight's adventures.

'So how's it gone today, Peter?'

'No crises, thank goodness. But I've got a suggestion for the rest of the week.'

'Fire away. Then I'll tell you my ideas.'

He took a deep breath. 'The students are bored. There's not enough work for lively minds. The winter traffic here isn't bad. So I made one or two changes. I hope you'll approve.'

George silently rejoiced at an independent initiative. 'Go on.'

'I reckoned it would help if the students were together at some point in the day. To reinforce the collective effort and cheer one another up. So I took the executive decision of declaring a half-hour lunch break, in the café beside the main church of St Fimbarrus. From 12.45 to 1.15.'

He paused, glanced at her. George hadn't blown up so far.

'Then I got each pair to pick the one who would arrive for lunch a bit late; and the other who would leave a bit early. That narrowed the time left uncovered by them both. They also recorded the start and end of the time no-one was there. I reckoned we could scale up the forty-five minutes we had tracked by four-thirds to get an estimate for the whole hour. Not exact but it won't be far off.'

'I've only one question,' said George, after a moment's musing.

'Yes?'

'Who paid for the lunches?'

Peter looked slightly embarrassed. 'I did, actually. It was about sixty quid. It wasn't that big a lunch.'

'Right. That's a survey expense. Tell me your bank account and I'll refund it. And we'll do the same for the rest of the week. It's the least we can do for all this free effort. I'm very grateful.'

There was a pause for a few minutes then George gave him her feedback She stuck to the edited highlights. Peter didn't need to know all the ups and downs.

'I had a fairly abortive meeting with my client in St Austell,' she began. 'Quite short. I told him the data he'd sent me was useless. Then I tried to explain the four-card sequence you showed me in the Fisherman's Arms. But he wouldn't give a clear response.'

Peter broke in. 'I had an idea last night about the dud data, by the way. While I was in the bath.'

'Go on, then. I hope I won't have to watch this on video.'

He smiled. 'Not this time. You know we were asking ourselves if the whole study might be a Council smokescreen. Well, suppose they'd collected some data but it showed the traffic problems in Fowey were negligible. Then you ask them for Fowey traffic data. It wouldn't cross their minds that you'd collect you own; or know what to expect. So what if they took their valid data and added, say, a hundred vehicles to each value?'

'That's an interesting suggestion,' said George with a smile. 'I can give you the dud data, if you like, to put alongside our own data so far. See if you can decode it.'

It might not work but it was worth a try. George resumed.

'On the odd sequence within the project, I was quite disheartened. But now I'm on a resurgence. If we can collect the data to build the right sort of model, it should be possible, first, to show it fits with what we observe; and second to predict the effects if things changed.'

'How d'you mean?' asked Peter.

'What I was thinking of is the effect of creating a second entrance to the car park. What difference might that make? Would it be worth doing at all?'

Peter frowned, puzzled. 'Surely a second entrance must make things better? It's an awkward turn.'

'That's what I thought. But I had a closer look when I parked this afternoon. A new opening would mean cars exiting onto Academy Rd.'

Peter intervened. 'But that's already got a twenty miles per hour speed limit. Our school is halfway up it.'

'Right. But if the traffic's going to increase, you might need to turn Academy Rd into a one-way street.

'Mm. That might not go down well with our teachers,' observed Peter thoughtfully. 'Or the parents bringing their kids.'

'But if you did that, Peter, you'd need another one-way street somewhere to balance the flows, going the opposite way. It's not straightforward. Our simple traffic model, based on the data you're collecting, might really come into its own.'

They talked around the problem for a while. Peter was taken by the idea but was obviously feeling tired.

She looked him in the eye. 'Look, Peter. You've held the fort today. Why don't you take a day off tomorrow? I'll see you again, here, on Wednesday morning. Maybe it'll be your turn to see what changes I've made.'

George and Wilson had agreed that they would try to break into the Tavern soon after midnight.

'That'll be late enough,' advised Wilson. 'No-one is awake in Fowey much after eleven. Then, if all goes well, we should both get a fair night's sleep from one o'clock onwards. Pick me up at midnight.' He gave her his address in Lostwithiel and marked its position on her map.

George made sure her phone was fully charged. She wanted some pictures of the cellar door, at least – if it was still there.

She managed to negotiate a light supper from the bar and retired to her room by nine, setting her alarm for half past eleven. Her professional life had made her used to all sorts of odd deadlines; she slept soundly for a couple of hours before the alarm dinged.

She couldn't dress completely in black but she did her best: dark-blue jeans, a purple jumper and dark trainers. She'd also got her charcoal beanie.

Ten minutes later she was up at the car park, easing her car out of the main exit. Wilson's address was already in her satnav. She was outside his house just after midnight.

Wilson was waiting in the porch, clutching his rucksack. She presumed it must hold the hooked rope. With a grunt of acknowledgement but scarcely a word, they set off back for Fowey.

The long stay car park was the best start for this adventure. The Tavern's boards were just visible from the glow of a distant streetlight. There was no-one else around.

'We'll get in from this side,' Wilson muttered. 'Better than doing anything on the road. There are still a few cars about.'

He pulled out a rope with a hook on the end. George gave a nod. Then he coiled the rope in one hand and lobbed the hook with the other. It caught on the top on the first attempt.

He'd done this sort of thing before. 'D'you want to go first?' he whispered.

George swallowed hard then gave a nod. "Women and children first" was a fair policy when filling a lifeboat, but harder when you were breaking in.

She knew she was fairly fit – she went on regular early morning jogs – but was she fit enough? It was time to find out.

Then she saw that Wilson had refined the rope by tying knots in it every two feet, all the way up. It made climbing it (relatively) easy.

George reached up the rope as far as she could. Then she arranged her feet on either side of the lowest knot and heaved herself slowly up. No need to rush darling, she told herself. She hung by her arms until her feet had found the next knot, then pushed up again till she could grasp the next handhold.

Five long minutes later she was sitting astride the narrow top of the builder's panel, waiting for Wilson to follow her. It wasn't the most comfortable of positions.

She was glad he wasn't too long. It suddenly looked a long way down.

'Could we use the rope again?' she whispered. Quickly, he reversed the hook then dropped the other end down inside the Tavern.

'You go first,' he whispered.

Turning herself round needed some care. She dangled by her arms until her feet wrapped round a knot. Then, slowly, she worked her way down the rope. It wasn't that hard. At least, it wouldn't have been if it wasn't pitch dark inside someone else's building.

She wasn't used to this. Wilson didn't find it hard at all. He was well used to it, she told herself.

Now they were inside the Tavern. Wilson reached into his pack and produced a pair of torches. 'You'd better have your own, George. Make sure you point it downwards. We don't want to arouse any attention outside.'

George's eyes were getting used to the dark now and she could make out the shape and size of the Tavern. The floor-space wasn't very large, perhaps seven metres square. (Was the small capacity why it had gone bust?) She shone her torch round briefly. There was no furniture, the floor was clear.

Wilson nodded towards one of the corners. Then he walked slowly towards it. She followed him, every sense on full alert. Her heart was pounding; no doubt adrenalin was flowing.

'It's still here,' he whispered.

George moved forward, stood beside him, looked down and shone her torch. There was a square hatch, perhaps a metre across. The door itself was wooden and old. It was hard to be sure of the colour in the torchlight, but it was probably a dingy green. George mused: would a forensic historian have been able to estimate the age from the paint?

Most significant of all, there was no padlock in view. Just a flange where it had once been positioned.

Wilson turned slowly towards her. 'If you want to see what's down there, George, now's your chance.'

George gave a gulp. How curious was she? And how brave?

PART 3

February 6th - 13th

Altercation

CHAPTER 19 Mon February 6th – 7th Emma in Place

Emma Eastham felt she was making headway. On Monday she had talked at length to the elderly curator of Fowey Museum and been given a rather garbled account of Joseph Treffry. But she had learned that there were descendants of the Treffry family still living in "Place", the Treffry home, located close to the centre of Fowey.

A tentative phone call had followed. After which Emma had been invited by the current owner, Susannah, to call round for coffee on the Tuesday morning.

'I can't tell you anything about Joseph's copper mines or his transport ventures,' Susannah had said, 'but we do know the family history - or at least, the version that's been handed down.'

Emma was starting to realise that developing a docudrama for the BBC opened many doors. It was up to her to make the most of the opportunity.

Susannah Treffry opened the Place door herself. Emma recognised her from the photograph on the internet. A smartly dressed woman in her forties, possibly enticed to share her angle on the story by the distant prospect of TV recognition. The same sort of pull as was used regularly by the Antiques Roadshow.

'So you're the budding new Lucy Worsley,' Susannah said, as she led her visitor into a spacious lounge with what she assumed were paintings of ancestors on the walls.

'I hope so, the Cornish version. I've been given the chance

to make it work. Thank you for seeing me so quickly.'

'I'm never that busy in February. My husband's gone up to London for a few days. So I'm all yours. Would you like to start with coffee or shall we keep that as our end-of-chat treat?'

'Let's talk first. What made me aware of you was a conversation I had yesterday with the man in the Museum.'

Susannah smiled. 'Ah yes. Rufus. He knows a lot about boats, rather less about Fowey families – except Daphne du Maurier, of course.'

'Yes. What surprised me was when he was scathing about Joseph Treffry. Said he wasn't really a Treffry at all. Can you enlighten me?'

Susannah sighed. 'You've plunged right into nineteenth century scandal, my dear. I'm not sure your viewers will like it.'

'I'm sure most of 'em will cope. They'll have been hardened by current politics.'

There was a pause. Perhaps Susannah was wondering where to start. Then she began.

'The Treffrys have been in Fowey for centuries. They're one of the town's oldest families. Kept out of politics, by and large, and not too enthusiastic to fight for or against the monarch of the day. Their great failing was the inability to produce male heirs.'

'That's one way that present-day society has improved, don't you think?' observed Emma. 'Women's equality has made some headway. Though the House of Windsor seems proficient enough at producing male descendants. Charles, then William, then another George. . .'

'For better or worse,' muttered Susannah. Probably best not to mention the "Spare". Then she got back to her own family.

'The Treffry who lived here in the late seventeen hundreds could only produce a daughter. She in turn married a man called Austen, who was also distinguished – he was once Lord Mayor of Plymouth.

'They had one son, Joseph – Joseph Austen. But his father died when he was six years old. In due course, his mother came back here. Then the old Treffry died. Joseph was called back to Place from Oxford University, where he'd been studying Engineering – he never completed the course. When the old man's will was read out, it turned out that Joseph was to inherit the Treffry land – the whole Place estate – but only if he changed his name to Treffry. He did so by deed poll. His full name became Joseph Austen Treffry.'

Emma had been scribbling notes as Susannah spoke. There was a moment of silence.

'So that's why the museum man was a bit sniffy about him. Not fair really, he was part of the Treffry family. Hey, did the business of name changing happen very often in those times?'

'It happened to Joseph's own descendant in 1850. He had no children of his own – too busy, I guess, making money from his assorted copper mines. So he spent a lot on this building, which had been neglected for years and needed a great deal of maintenance; then in his will he bequeathed what was left to his cousin, who lived, would you believe it, on the Isles of Scilly. But only provided the man changed his name to Treffry too. There have been Treffrys here ever since.'

Emma was scribbling away. She'd read some of this in her background research on the internet but hearing it face to face from a relative made it much easier to grasp. She wondered what else she might learn.

'Susannah, you say Joseph had no children of his own. Was he ever married?'

'Not that's been recorded. There was no mention of a wife in his will, anyway. That was signed in 1840, when he was 58.

I'm sure plenty of women would have liked the chance: he was handsome, well-educated, well-connected and wealthy. But all his energies seemed to go into maximising profit from his mining ventures.'

'No rumours of dalliances on the side?'

Susannah shook her head. 'We can't say. No record, anyway. But newspapers were less intrusive in those days. Even if there was anything it might not have made the headlines.'

'That's a pity from a programme point of view,' said Emma judicially. 'A juicy romance would boost the audience, give the show an extra dimension.'

'Well, if you want that, Emma, you should be looking elsewhere in Fowey.'

Emma knew she had to stay focussed. 'That would only work if it could be linked fairly closely to Joseph's story.'

The hostess smiled. 'Well, there was someone. But why don't I make us some coffee before I tell you.'

Fifteen minutes later, after a short detour to the Treffry kitchen – well laid out, thought Emma, but not too large or ostentatious – and a conversation around the difficulties they'd each experienced on buying provisions in these straitened times, they were back in the lounge.

Susannah sipped her coffee before she began. 'The person you really need, if you want a horrible personal disaster, is a man called Charles Rashleigh.'

'Will this give me some romance?'

'There are plenty of feelings; but I'm not sure if I'd call them romance.'

'I've come across the name, anyway. Though not associated with Fowey. Please, tell me more.'

Susannah took a deep breath. 'Charles was a younger son in

the Rashleigh family. They've been in Fowey as long as we have. But they've been more involved in national politics. Several have been Members of Parliament.'

'Fowey was a "rotten borough", though. It was the days before real elections.'

'Huh. You think we have real elections now?' asked Susannah provocatively. It was an interesting question but not one Emma wanted to pursue at this moment.

'So, anyway, there's a Rashleigh home that's similar to Place?'

'There is. It's called Menabilly, out towards the Gribbin. Not as grand as Place, though.'

'So what was the link between Rashleigh and Treffry?' Emma wanted to remind her source that she was meant to be preparing a programme about the latter.

'Rashleigh was thirty years older. He owned a mine or two on the west side of Par. He needed a way to export the copper ore so it could be smelted in South Wales. But there was no port near enough, not one with enough deep water to take the schooners that he intended to use. We've a deep river here, of course, but he wasn't going to haul his ore all the way over to Fowey. No lorries in those days.'

'Or railways,' added Emma. 'Or even decent roads.'

'So, in the last decade of the 1700s, Charles Rashleigh built himself the brand new port of Charlestown. A mile out of St Austell.'

'Which he named after himself?' suggested Emma.

'No, he didn't. That'd be far too arrogant. But once it was working, and a small township had built up around it, the occupants of the town named it after him.'

'That'd certainly be a good visual image on television,' said Emma. 'Viewers will no doubt have seen the harbour on Poldark, but they probably don't know its history. What's the link to Treffry?'

'This where it gets interesting,' chuckled Susannah. 'You see, Treffry had an interest in copper mines just above Par, much closer to the River Fowey. So he wanted to take his copper ore across to Fowey.'

'Yes?'

'He had plans to build a horse-drawn tramway – the steam engine, running on a railway line, hadn't yet been invented. The trouble was, to reach Fowey, he would need to cross land owned by Rashleigh. And Rashleigh refused. Refused to let him buy it, or even to travel over it.'

'Must have been a smashing row,' said Emma. 'I wonder if we could re-enact it. Alright, Susannah, you've convinced me. I have to include Charles Rashleigh in this programme. He's a stark contrast to Treffry.'

'There's a lot more I could tell you about Charles Rashleigh, Emma. But it might be best to do that on a separate occasion. I'm seeing one of my friends for lunch in half an hour. What's your diary like? Could you possibly come back again tomorrow?'

CHAPTER 20 Tues February 7th- 8th Place

Emma used Tuesday afternoon to tidy her notes and extend her enquiries to include Charles Rashleigh. There was plenty about him on the internet once you knew to look. Susannah might tell her much the same story tomorrow; but if she was prepared, she'd be able to ask more searching questions.

She thought harder about the notion of enacting his row with Treffry. Done well, that would certainly make good television. It could even be set in a local pub - the Ship Inn, for example, where she'd met George on Sunday. That had probably been here in the eighteen hundreds - it looked old enough. You wouldn't want a large audience, but the place had been almost empty on Sunday evening.

Which meant she just needed a couple of local actors. St Austell was the largest town nearby. Quickly she googled "theatres in St Austell" and found the St Austell Arts Centre on Truro Road. It hosted the StormBox Theatre Company. With a contact number.

Soon Emma was talking to the StormBox secretary, Donna. It was her job, Donna declared, to unearth opportunities for her "gang". Ideally, significant events with a large cast and a decent audience. They had a booking for a church event at Easter, but not much else. She had to agree, February was a pretty dead month. Even a small gig for two or three of her actors would break up the monotony.

'So, d'you meet in the winter?'

'We've a fortnightly catch up on Wednesday evenings. Half

past seven in the Arts Centre. Join us tomorrow if you like.'

Nothing might come of it, but she had to try. It gave her a motive for thinking harder about Rashleigh and his tussles. She suddenly realised that, if this idea was going to work, she would need to turn herself into a playwright. That was a step beyond merely writing her own script. But she was up for the challenge.

Susannah looked as keen as before when Emma returned to Place on Wednesday morning. They agreed to leave the coffee for a while and sat once more in the lounge.

Emma took out her notebook. 'So I'm interested, Susannah, in all you can remember about Charles Rashleigh.'

'Let's go back to 1790. Charles, aged forty-three, had decided to build a harbour in what was to become Charlestown. By now he had moved away from Menabilly and was living in Duporth Manor, overlooking the intended site. I think he owned a copper mine in nearby Holmbush.'

'And was he a wealthy man at this point?'

'Certainly. Though none was inherited. He was the tenth child, with six older brothers. He wouldn't be left much directly, even if it was all shared equally. Which of course it wasn't.'

'So what did he do?'

'He became a property developer. Not a fantastically successful one. But then he married an heiress from Heligan, a bit further down the coast.' The name caused Susannah to digress.

'Have you ever been to the Gardens of Heligan, Emma?'

'Near Mevagissey? A couple of times. They're very attractive. You can get a boat there from Fowey, I believe.'

Susannah shook her head. 'Not in the winter. And I doubt it operated at all in the eighteenth century. Anyway, all that matters for this story is that, at this point, 1790, Charles was wealthy. There weren't many banks in those days – or, at least, not ones you could trust. So he kept most of his money in a huge, locked chest in his bedroom.'

'He'd need a great deal of money to build a harbour,' mused Emma. 'Even if the basic design was very simple.'

'Oh, the design was clever enough. It was done by John Smeaton, the man who designed the Eddystone Lighthouse.'

'But he'd still need money. . .'

'Of course. Rashleigh was never going to supervise the construction himself. He was above that sort of thing, he was landed gentry. There were umpteen contractors needed to dig the harbour channel and lay the quayside. They all had to be chosen; and to be regularly paid.'

'Right. Exactly how was that achieved?'

'Well. Charles had recently taken on a young footman called Joseph Dingley. It was said that he was very pretty.'

Emma looked up from her notes. 'You mean, handsome?'

'No, I mean pretty.' She paused. 'After all, Charles hadn't married the Heligan heiress out of passion, had he?'

There was a thoughtful silence and then she resumed.

'Dingley was appointed superintendent and deputed to hire the contractors and pay their wages, from the chest in the bedroom. He was given the key. He must have been in there quite a lot. Occasionally there would be left an I.O.U. But Rashleigh trusted him, trusted him implicitly; left all the detail to his footman. Over nearly ten years.'

'At the end of which. . .?'

'It turned out the chest was empty. Dingley had paid the workers and embezzled the rest. That was reckoned to be around £32,000 in the currency of the time, which would be worth, say, two or three million today.'

'Wow.'

Emma paused for a moment, considering.

'So I presume Rashleigh fired Dingley and then tried to get his money back?'

'He certainly took Dingley to court. But courts weren't very detached in those days and Dingley was very plausible. Said Rashleigh knew all about it. He'd given him the chest key. And after all, there was now the splendid harbour he could look at from his manor, which we can see even today.'

'D'you think it's time for coffee, Susannah? My brain is starting to hurt.'

The two women went into the kitchen; the hostess brought out her coffee machine and put on the kettle.

Emma decided she could risk a compliment. 'You've certainly got an attractive home, Susannah.'

'It was modernised with Treffry's mining profits and then his legacy. Been steadily improved by Treffrys ever since. Both home-grown and imported. No, I don't want to move anywhere else.'

Once they were seated again, they returned to the Rashleigh saga.

Emma wanted to firm up the link with Treffry. 'So at what point did Treffry cross swords with Rashleigh?'

'That's a good question, Emma. It must have been after 1808. Treffry was at Oxford before then. And I guess it was before 1811, when Rashleigh finished battling with the courts. He wouldn't argue with anyone after that. So maybe 1810?'

Emma nodded. 'Right. I was just thinking about that conversation. Rashleigh wasn't very wise, was he? I mean, he could have had a regular income from Treffry for years and years, just by leasing him some land.'

'Yes. I don't think Rashleigh was ever wise. He was a hot-headed man, driven by impulse. Let his heart rule his brain, shall we say.'

'You can't say that just from one swindle.'

'But, Emma, it wasn't the only one.'

'How d'you mean?'

'Well, after Dingley's trial was over and the man had disappeared with his loot, Rashleigh stayed on in Duporth Manor. But he still needed a footman.'

'Paid for, no doubt, by the long-suffering wife.'

'Probably. But you wouldn't believe it, he took on another pretty young man. Also called Joseph. And much the same thing happened again.'

'You mean, in the bedroom?'

Susannah shook her head. 'That's not recorded. No, I mean Rashleigh was swindled again. He lost all his remaining money. Died a pauper in 1826.'

There was a shocked silence as Emma noted down the details.

'Gosh. If it wasn't so very sad it sounds like a script for the next edition of Fawlty Towers.' Only that morning she'd seen, to her horror, reports that John Cleese was planning a follow-up series.

'If you are going to enact Rashleigh's tumultuous meeting with Treffry, Emma, there's plenty of backstory. Trouble is, the BBC might not want to handle it.'

CHAPTER 21 Wed February 7th Charlestown

Emma decided it would be best to stay on the trail of Charles Rashleigh for the afternoon. She needed the story – or stories? – as clear as possible in her mind before she visited the theatre group in St Austell.

Also, she wanted to hear the man's story from another viewpoint. Multiple sources, as long as they broadly agreed, made for a more secure history. And where they differed was a starting point for further research. Accuracy was important if she was to be a BBC4 historian. She'd looked up Lucy Worsley: she was a professional historian based at Hampton Court, not just a persuasive face.

So after leaving Place, she walked back to her lodging at Coombe, picked up her car and drove over to Charlestown. Five miles as the crow flew, visible across the sea from Menabilly. But the ten miles by road was hardly direct. She swept down the road from St Austell. There was a carpark, barely 50 yards from the harbour – one even offering free parking in winter months.

She noted the Rashleigh Arms just up the road. That'd be a good place for lunch. But first she had to walk round the harbour.

Emma was Truro born and bred; she'd been here many times. But this was different. Now she wasn't just enjoying the location but imagining it as the background for retelling the tale of Charles Rashleigh.

The quay looked much as it must have done in 1800. No

road round it. Just various stalls, selling – or at least hoping to sell – much the same kind of goods as two hundred years ago: different sorts of snacks and drinks, alongside the occasional trinket.

There were a couple of sailing vessels moored alongside the jetty of the inner harbour, even their lower sails had been fitted. They didn't carry the flag of the Jolly Roger, mind, just the Kernow black cross.

For a small fee, paid in one of the huts, you could get on board and explore them. But that wasn't for today. She'd heard no mention of either Treffry or Rashleigh being sailors. She had to stay focussed. Whatever else there was to be discovered was on land.

She wandered round, soaking in the atmosphere. Thought about unusual camera angles and took various photographs. She'd browse these afterwards. She'd have to come back here again.

But right now Emma was feeling hungry. What had the Rashleigh Arms to offer? And whom might she meet?

One benefit of being a single woman in a less than crowded pub, thought the historian, was that it would be easy to start up a conversation. Better a promising source than being captured by the pub bore.

There weren't many customers, but she was happy to talk to the landlord, a burly man in his fifties with dragon tattoos down both arms. He could have lived in Charlestown for ages. She claimed a stool and studied the chalked-up menu behind him.

'Can I have a Cornish pastie, please? And a half of bitter – the St Austell, I think.'

'Right miss. I'll get your drink then go and order the pastie. You're not in any hurry, I hope?'

Emma wondered what made her look like one of the idle rich. Then realised she still had her smart camera hanging round her neck: horror of horror, she had been mistaken for a tourist.

'No hurry at all.'

The beer was handed over, then the man disappeared. She hoped they had some pasties on the premises and weren't having to fetch one from a stall on the harbour.

Then he returned.

'Is this your first visit to Charlestown, miss?'

'Oh no, I'm from Truro. Been here lots of times.'

'It's a cold day to come 'ere.'

'True. But I have a special reason.'

An intriguing observation, and the landlord was hooked.

'So what's that?'

'Well. I've been asked to produce a programme for the BBC about a Cornish hero – a real one, not just Poldark.'

'Someone present day?' Perhaps he hoped for fame at last.

'Nope.'

He thought for a moment. 'Nineteenth century?'

'Died then, actually born the century before.'

The man thought further. 'There's only one man around here who fits them dates that you'd make a film of. Is it Charles Rashleigh?'

'The creator of Charlestown. Yes, it's him.'

He grinned. He was, after all, the landlord of the Rashleigh Arms. 'Right. So's you've got the key fact already.'

'But I'm sure there's plenty more.' She smiled. 'I've been asked to generate a whole program, not just a snippet. Can you help me?'

The landlord tidied a few returned glasses as he considered. 'Any programme centred round Charlestown must be good for business. But the best person to talk to would be Alfie.'

'And where might I find him?'

'He's over in yon corner. If you wants to take your drink over, I'll bring the pastie to you when it's ready.'

This was as good as she could have hoped for. Assuming the man would let her ask questions and wasn't just the pub bore.

Alfie was drinking on his own. He looked a similar age to the landlord, they presumably knew each other well.

'Hi,' Emma said, as she approached his table. 'The landlord suggested I should talk to you. My name's Emma.'

He wasn't often accosted by attractive blondes and nodded. 'Pleased to meet you, Emma. I'm Alfie. What d'you want to talk about?'

'I'm trying to produce a programme for the BBC about Charles Rashleigh. I know a few basic facts but I'd love to know more. Can you help me?'

'I can try.' He eyed his nearly empty glass. 'What's it worth?'

Emma smiled as she sat down. 'I'm happy to buy your next drink, anyway. More if you can keep talking. So what sort of a man was this Rashleigh?'

He mused on where to start. 'Well. You know he came from one of the poshest families in Fowey?'

'I'd heard that. But he wasn't the oldest child?'

'By no means.' Alfie laughed. 'He was about the tenth. One or two older ones might die young but not the whole lot. So he had largely to fend for himself.'

'And what did that mean?'

'He became the eighteenth-century equivalent of an estate agent. In other words, m'dear, he was a property developer.'

'Not a mine owner?' asked Emma. 'I noticed plenty of old shafts around here, marked on my map.'

'I don't think so. But he realised that these mines were struggling to find markets. They needed to get their copper ore over to South Wales for smelting – they'd got the coal there, you see.'

'But there was no suitable port here in the 1790s?'

Alfie grinned. 'Rashleigh was a shrewd man in some ways. He was perhaps the first to realise that ports didn't have to be God-given. They could be constructed. Got his mate John Smeaton to design a brand-new harbour. Then he set about building it. It was ready for use by the turn of the century.'

'So Poldark could have used it – if he'd been a real person, that is?'

'Well, it's the only port in Cornwall that looks like it did back then, so it's an obvious place to film. Lots of films made here – not just Poldark.'

'Even so, if it took a decade to build, that's ten years before it could make any profit. So how was it paid for?'

At that point there was an interruption as Emma's Cornish pastie was brought to the table. 'Can you bring another pint for Alfie, please. And another half of St Austell's for myself? I'll settle up at the end.' She assumed the landlord would know which beer his friend was drinking.

The drinks were brought a minute later.

Alfie had a slurp and then started to answer the question.

'All estate agents have to travel, you see. No telephones in those days. On his travels, Rashleigh came across a wealthy woman from Heligan called Grace. She was an heiress – and a widow. So he snapped her up.' Alfie shook his head. 'Poor woman. She probably didn't realise what she was getting into.'

Emma made sure she understood where his tale was going. 'You mean that Grace's wealth was what funded the development?'

'Must 've done. Rashleigh couldn't afford it. Mind, he made

it look like it was his money. Kept it locked in a chest in his chamber.'

'Women weren't as money-minded in those days,' observed Emma. 'Or, at least, they expected to it to be handled by their husband.'

'Oh it wasn't that.' He shook his head. 'Grace wasn't given a chance. Rashleigh didn't touch the money himself, he made his servant the intermediary, do all the deals. That was a man called Joseph Dingley.'

He said the name in a hostile tone of voice.

'I gather, Alfie, that you don't approve.'

'Well. Nobody knows the whole story. It was said that Rashleigh was more taken by Dingley than he was by Grace. He was probably much younger, maybe prettier. Anyway, Rashleigh didn't ask many questions about what was being spent. And over the years of neglect, Dingley took the whole lot. Left the developer of Charlestown harbour, living in Duporth Manor, almost penniless.'

CHAPTER 22 Wed February 8th Drama in St Austell

Emma used the afternoon to explore the hamlet of Duporth, close to Charlestown. She could find no sign of Duporth Manor, Rashleigh's long-term abode. It must have been flattened and built over. She wondered how quickly after Rashleigh's death that had occurred. And what motive lay behind it.

Late in the afternoon she headed into St Austell and found an Italian restaurant offering early evening meals. It wasn't a fast service, but she used the time between courses to organise her notes on her two heroes, Rashleigh and Treffry. If all went well, she might have a chance to sketch out the row between them to the drama team.

Soon after seven she retrieved her car and set out for the St Austell Arts Centre, home of the StormBox drama group. There was plenty going on when she arrived. She saw she could have had a more economical meal from the Centre café - she'd do that next time. There were also several rooms being used for meetings. She was told the drama group was in a small room towards the rear.

The lady in charge was chatting to a few early arrivals when she saw Emma and came over to welcome her.

'Hello. I'm Donna. And I assume you're Emma?'

Emma smiled. 'That's right. I'm pleased to meet you. And this is your space?'

'It is until we're gearing up for a production. Then we're allowed to rehearse on the main stage. But that won't happen till near Easter. This time of year the meeting is mostly a means to hold the group together – or the core members, anyway.'

'How many are you expecting?'

'A dozen. We'll start with informal chat over coffee, then we have notices – if any.' Donna smiled. 'There won't be any reviews to dissect, anyway. Finally we'll have an acting exercise. I do have something to offer, but I'd be happy to hand over to you if you like. Hey, would you like some coffee?'

Emma moved round and introduced herself to the various actors as she sipped her coffee. They mostly lived in St Austell, though there was a couple from Charlestown. No-one from as far away as Fowey. (Emma noted she must check there was nothing like this happening over there. Based around the St Fimbarrus Church, for example?)

Here there was a mixture of ages and gender and a discernible, warm camaraderie. Folk obviously knew each other well.

As Donna had predicted, once they were all sitting down, the notices were brief. Obviously, nothing moved fast in St Austell, at least in the depths of winter. Then the leader turned to Emma.

'Emma, would you like to explain the commission you've been given and how we might be able to help you.'

Emma smiled and took a breath. 'Thank you, Donna. It's a privilege to meet you all. It's like this. The BBC has decided it would like to put on a series about less well-known Cornish heroes from the past. Real-life Poldarks, as it were. The sort of thing Lucy Worsley is so good at with her docudramas on BBC4.

'But Lucy was much too posh for this. They wanted someone from Cornwall; and I was lucky enough to win the commission.

'Now, I'm a professional historian, based in Truro. I don't have any broadcasting experience, but I'm happy to give it a go. I'm sure I can produce a viable script. I've written and read out enough essays on complex subjects in the past.'

Emma paused to draw breath. The group were following her, anyway.

'What makes all Lucy Worsley's series so good, I believe, is that she tells a reasonably accurate story, with key scenes acted out in real locations as she goes along. I don't know if Cornwall can offer anything that's remotely as good. The series may never be filmed; or even if it makes a film, it may still never be shown.

'My challenge,' she concluded, 'is to make sure neither of those things happens. So tonight, if you are all game, I want to see how we might re-enact one of the scenes that did happen, which is a row between two of my leading subjects.'

There was a positive response. The group had more appetite for trying something that might be filmed – might even, one day, be broadcast – than for carrying out yet another exercise. Donna was a lively leader but even she couldn't make up scenes to play out every fortnight that really gripped their imaginations.

'So please, Emma, tell us about your subjects; and especially this altercation.'

Emma introduced them to Joseph Treffry and Charles Rashleigh. Charles was the better known here because of Charlestown. Not many had heard of Treffry. But they were local, all had a good grasp of mining.

Then the historian went on to outline the row between the two men over copper ore access from the mine to the coast.

'I don't know many of the details,' she continued. 'But it's a key part of both their stories – could bring them to life. At least it could in the version I'm hoping to present.'

'Right,' said Donna decisively. 'I think Emma has told us enough. We'll have to make a lot of things up. Not just the row itself but how these two local giants of the nineteenth century might have felt about one another – both before their big argument and afterwards.

'So I suggest we divide into two teams. Half will try to unpack Joseph Treffry: what sort of a man was he, what were his goals? The rest will wrestle with Charles Rashleigh. Meanwhile Emma and I will float between you, listening hard and providing facts where these are known.'

Emma didn't want to leave the Centre with their musings uncaptured. 'At the end of the evening would it be possible for each team to elect a couple to play the role of the two subjects as they now see it? Then we'll have two embryonic versions of the row. With your permission, I'll record them on my laptop to reflect on later.'

'That'd be good,' responded Donna. 'Improvisation is a vital skill for every actor. But it's also good to listen back on what we actually said and how it might be improved. We might even try to play the row more often, using different actors. Give it half an hour, anyway. But remember, folks, we have to be out of the Centre by ten o'clock. If at the end the topic has grabbed you, we can continue with it next time.'

The next hour was lively. The room buzzed. Emma felt stretched in all directions. Better than she'd ever dared hope.

She'd been coming at the row from the viewpoint of a serious historian, collecting hard evidence – which going back two hundred years was almost non-existent. But the actors weren't so burdened by what they knew: it was more what they could imagine, within the outline they'd been given. This could be very useful to give her programme life.

'So when's this row supposed to have happened?' asked someone in Team A, when Emma joined them.

'Around 1810,' said Emma. 'After Treffry came back from his studies in Oxford, which was 1808.'

'But at that point,' observed one of the team, 'Charlestown harbour had already been operating for a decade. So this was hardly a conversation between equals.'

This raised some discussion, then someone asked, 'So Rashleigh was older than Treffry?'

'A lot,' Emma replied. He was born in 1747. That's 35 years before Treffry.'

'But Treffry had received a top-class education,' one of the team remarked. 'He wouldn't feel in awe of anyone.'

'So you can imagine a jostling for power between them. No wonder it turned nasty.'

Emma left Team A and moved onto Team B. They were considering the exact arrangement Treffry might be hoping for, and how Rashleigh, with his brand-new harbour, might feel about it.

'I've been told the mine which Treffry owned was near Par,' advised Emma. 'Nearer to the Fowey estuary than to Charlestown.'

'So how would the copper ore be transported to the boat?'

'Were there any railways in 1810?'

'Not for another half century,' Emma told them. 'The line from Plymouth to Turo wasn't completed till 1858.'

'So all they'd have was a horse and cart?'

Emma thought she'd better give them more information. 'We know that Treffry was interested in trams. That's why he built his famous viaduct up at Luxulyan. That might be his method of choice.'

One of Team B was into technology. 'But trams also run on

rails, even if they're horse drawn. There'd be plenty of new infrastructure needed. Maybe Rashleigh was an early Friend of the Earth? Didn't want rails built across his land?'

There was plenty of free thinking going on, thought Emma. This could turn into a very profitable evening.

CHAPTER 23 Thurs February 9th Coombe Farm

Emma awoke late on Thursday morning. She had returned close to midnight from the St Austell Arts Centre, worn out but very happy. There was a lot of thinking to process.

She made herself porridge and a mug of coffee, then sat down to listen to the recordings of the two teams' "row replays".

Team A had focussed on the potential power struggle between Treffry and Rashleigh when the two had met.

Treffry was pictured as supremely confident: Oxford-educated, the newly installed lord of the manor in Place, now wanting to make his mark as a man of power, within the mining community. He could see the need for long-term markets for the ore being mined – without that the whole business was doomed. He also knew the potential of his home port of Fowey for the purpose, with its deep harbour.

Rashleigh was the more vulnerable, the tenth child of a notable family with little education, making his own way through life with the aid of a wealthy woman. His best achievement had been to catch her straight after her previous husband had passed on. And he'd translated that windfall into the new harbour at West Porthmear. It was a stupendous achievement. The place wasn't yet called Charlestown. But he had some sense of business. He knew it needed regular customers to recoup the costs.

There was nothing impossible in this scenario. But Emma wondered where it might lead, once the two men had reached an impasse? What would Treffry do if he couldn't have easy access to Fowey; but wouldn't commit himself to regular use of

Charlestown?

Emma turned to Team B's offering.

This team had included the couple from Charlestown, who had some inside knowledge. Possibly they shared Alfie's reservations about Rashleigh's tastes, or maybe his financial acumen?

Their response had been a scenario in which Grace, Rashleigh's wife, accompanied him to the negotiations. That had given a role for one of the female actors in the team.

So although Rashleigh was less impressive than Treffry, his maturity no match for the driving force of youth, the numbers were two to one in his favour.

On this basis, the blocking of Treffry's plan had not been a triumph for environmental reasons. More it was the determination of a forceful woman not to be bullied or ignored. Maybe she had already suffered too much?

Emma broke off to make herself a mug of coffee and pondered the A and B scenarios.

She had seen several actors who would make plausible Treffrys or Rashleighs. They all had the mandatory Cornish accents but spoke clearly enough for a wider audience. No doubt they'd be just as good working to a script as ad-libbing the parts after a short discussion.

She hadn't planned it but the demos had also been a valid form of interview. Even that was progress of a sort.

Emma wondered about the suggested involvement of Grace alongside Charles. As several female StormBox actors had told her, if she was to capture a female audience for the BBC, it was important that women were part of the story. Not so easy in nineteenth century Cornwall: feminism was in its infancy.

Emma sighed. As far as she knew, there really was no written record of this meeting. So if she wanted to present a vibrant history, she'd have to make something up.

Grace had really existed. Had indeed funded the port of Charlestown. That deserved some recognition. This would be one belated way for her to do so.

But Emma wasn't altogether convinced by the Team B scenario. If Grace had been there, if maybe she had invited Treffry to their home for a meal, surely he'd be expected to bring a female companion with him?

That was a bigger challenge. Not impossible. But there had been no mention in her research of Treffry having any interest in the opposite sex. He'd been driven primarily by building infrastructure and making money. Maybe he hadn't had time for much else?

Emma let her imagination loose. Suppose she wasn't presenting history but was writing a nineteenth century drama? How might this evening have gone then? It sounded like the start of a play by Alan Bennett.

Treffry would probably have taken a female acquaintance from Place. Someone younger and attractive. The invitation would be couched as a friendly request; and would no doubt be willingly accepted.

As she thought around the problem, Emma realised that this wouldn't be the only time a female companion would be required. Treffry had a social position to maintain. Would he be careful not to take the same companion twice? Or maybe he wouldn't care, would stick on the first girl he felt any affinity with? For the time being, she decided, she'd call her Hester.

So how might the evening at Duporth Manor have gone? She'd already given some thought to the power-pushing chemistry between the men. What might be happening between the women?

It was a pity she had no hard data on Grace's age. Was she

even older than Charles; or a young flame, younger perhaps than Treffry himself?

Might there be some light flirting between Treffry and Grace? Emma could imagine a young Grace, dressed in a slightly suggestive manner at the prospect of a visit by a younger man, wiping the floor with the luckless Hester. Was that why Rashleigh had turned down the business?

Or had the whole thing happened the other way round? Had Rashleigh felt the draw of a young Hester – perhaps in contrast to his older, more boring Grace? Had he started the gentle flirting? Was that why Treffry lost interest in any deal and rejected the option of using Charlestown harbour as his outlet?

The St Austell acting group could improvise all sorts of scenarios along such lines. She must attend the next gathering.

After another mug of coffee Emma went back to an earlier question.

For whatever reason the meeting had led nowhere. What might Treffry have done next?

She unfolded her St Austell Explorer map for inspiration. There was Par. No trace of it now, but apparently Treffry had shares in a pit there. In that case, what else might he do?

Then came a thought. What if the impact between the two wasn't over funding? Treffry might have been challenged, even inspired, by Rashleigh's example. For if the older man could build a new harbour, why couldn't young Treffry?

Today there was a harbour at Par. It wasn't open to visitors and she had never seen inside. Next to it she saw the name "China Clay Dries.'

Emma knew the China Clay industry had impacted the landscape north of St Austell; the waste from clay mining had become vast spoil heaps. It had looked a complete mess for most of her life, though now the worst tips were greened over. But she'd never had reason to study it in detail.

Everyone had told her that Treffry had dealt in copper, not China Clay. That came much later. Maybe she needed to learn more about this harbour at Par? Had it always been used for clay? Or had there been a time when it shipped out copper ore?

If Treffry had gone from trying to hire an existing port at Charlestown to building a new one for himself, that would be a worthwhile outcome of his meeting with Charles Rashleigh, however rumbustious.

If so, the meeting - the altercation - might make a suitable hinge point to carry her programme forward.

PART 4

February 13th - 18th

Assignation

CHAPTER 24 Mon February 13th KLM

My second week in Kernow Lithium Mining. Already it was starting to feel like home. More than I'd ever felt as a lowly border watcher with Security.

I started the day with Rachel Tyson. I wanted to report back on my trip to the Northeast. There were plenty of issues to raise back here. But this is a marathon not a sprint, I reminded myself.

'Morning, Mark,' she greeted me. 'Had a good weekend?'

I could have filled half the morning answering that. My heart was still singing with joy.

I could have told her about singing a duet alongside Naomi in the King's Arms karaoke. "Come all you jolly tinner boys. . .". Naomi had sung beautifully and it had gone down a storm. We'd even been pressured to perform an encore; fortunately, we had a second Cornish ballad in reserve.

Or I could have told Rachel about my cycle ride on Sunday with my new friend. It was one of those crisp cold starts: bracing, sharp and clear, great as long as you kept moving. Naomi turned up in what I assumed must be her regular cycling gear - black lycra shorts and a tee shirt with a Greenpeace slogan, with an unzipped fleece over the top.

I'd dressed more warmly, of course. My knees had never been a feature I wanted to flaunt. We both had cycling helmets; I mean, I was a Security officer.

We'd cycled along the back lanes to Lanlivery, an even

smaller village than Luxulyan. Then over to Lostwithiel – Naomi told me 'this was the capital of Cornwall in its heyday'. We'd stopped there for coffee. Then along more lanes and paths down to the village of Golant. Its pub, the Fisherman's Arms, stood beside the River Fowey.

Naomi had cooked me Beef Wellington last week. It was my turn; I treated her to a traditional Sunday lunch.

After that we'd made our way – more slowly, it was a good lunch – over to Par. Then, following what Naomi said was the River Par, we travelled all the way back to Luxulyan. On route we'd passed underneath the Treffry Viaduct, a hundred feet above us. "The finest feature of the village", Naomi had boasted. It was certainly well above par. I had no idea then who Treffry was, or what the viaduct was supposed to carry.

I didn't tell Rachel all this. She didn't need to know who I was cycling with. Though she must have known Naomi lived in Luxulyan; and had probably heard of the karaoke.

'On Friday I went to see someone involved in new security arrangements for a growing firm in the northeast.'

Rachel looked more interested than I had feared. At least her eyes hadn't glazed over.

'Dougie was a sensible chap,' I continued. 'But he made it clear that installing good security was a long-term project, couldn't be done on the cheap.'

I went on to summarise my Friday's conversation.

'Some of what needs to be done is technical: buying the right security and so on. Assuming KLM approves the funding, I can do that. But what is more critical, Dougie said, is "bringing the people with you". Without that, security will be just an expensive white elephant. It'll trample over everything and achieve nothing – except alienate the staff.'

'Wow.' Rachel looked a bit stunned. 'This is all a bit heavy for Monday morning.'

I gave her a reassuring grin. 'Look, Rachel. I'm here for the long haul. I love this part of Cornwall; you've built up a great team that are highly motivated. I buy into the goal. I don't want to disrupt any of that. But over time, if I'm allowed, I do want to improve it.

'It doesn't need to be rushed,' I went on. 'It's work over months, not just weeks. But if we're going to do it, it does need to be planned. And most of all it needs the support of senior management.'

'Why don't we have a coffee?' she asked. 'Then let's go through Dougie's ideas in more detail. After all, that's what we're paying you for. It would be wise for me to listen.'

Rachel and I had a long chat after that. But the chemistry was good. I voiced all sorts of observations on my first few days in KLM. Some were misunderstandings. There was much more going on than I had supposed. Even an adjacent office I'd not yet been in. But others were legitimate concerns.

'One more thing that's bothered me,' I said, 'is Alex Price. At the trivial end of the scale, I'm squatting in his office. He might burst in at any moment and be incandescent to see me. Well, I can cope with that.

'But more seriously, Rachel, is it OK for a senior KLM manager to be wandering the countryside off piste, with no-one here knowing where he is – or at least, when he'll be back?'

There was a thoughtful pause.

'I think you may be right, Mark. It needs an outsider to give us a fresh perspective. We've got his home address, of course. I believe he lives in St Austell. And we have his phone number. But I tried ringing him just before your interview, and he wasn't answering.'

I wasn't satisfied. 'So that's over a week since anyone heard from him? Is he often out of touch for that long?'

Rachel gave a rueful grin. 'Alex makes the case for a proper diary system irresistible. To be honest, I don't know. I don't explicitly track people in KLM.' She mused for a moment.

'I'd say, Alex used to be around the office once or twice a month. He'd come in to file his expenses, if nothing else. This "distant relationship" phase only started happening recently. Even then, he might have appeared on a Wednesday. I wouldn't see him then, I'd be off with my mother.'

Rachel wasn't the only pair of eyes round here. 'Well, might someone else know? Sandra on reception, for example?'

With a sigh, Rachel gave way. 'Well, Mark, why don't you take a few hours going round the office, asking everyone when Alex was last seen or is next expected. Use the fact that you're in his office as an excuse; you "need to know how long you've got".

'It is really poor actually. We shouldn't be expecting you to squat at all. If you do that, it'll give you a chance to introduce yourself, and to see the rest of the firm's offices.'

CHAPTER 25 Tues February 14th Naomi's Tale

I had hoped to see the head of KLM, Simon Cooke, sometime on that Monday, but his secretary told me he'd be out till Wednesday. He was 'up in London, doing something with lithium lovers'. Possibly he was pushing government ministers to move from sloganizing on to action?

Obviously, Alex wasn't the only one who was out of the office for days on end. But at least, for Simon, someone here knew when he'd be back. I booked a session with him for Wednesday afternoon.

Then I went round the office, seeking traces of Alex. Without much success. He didn't seem to be very close to other staff, they'd hardly missed him. The most authoritative source was the receptionist, Sandra. But she said she hadn't seen him come in for two weeks.

Half way through the afternoon I found Naomi's hideaway. She was in the unit next door; their door even had its own lock. This was the Finance Den. I found only two women in there, Naomi and Gwynneth. It was afternoon tea time and they found me a spare mug.

I'd never met Gwynneth at all. I introduced myself and my role in the company. Then I explained that today I was searching for more details on a senior manager called Alex Price – not least, I said, because I was camped out in his room, but only till he returned.

The women agreed they could break from the ever-present

demands of finance to give me half an hour talking about Alex.

Gwynneth was the younger, presumably Naomi's co-worker and junior. Two was better than one, a lot safer than having no backup in this key Department. Keeping on top of finance was vital to KLM.

I had made a point of not talking about KLM with Naomi while we were socialising in Luxulyan. So I was able to explain to them both how no-one in the main office had heard from Alex, the Acquisition Manager, for a couple of weeks. Could these two tell me anything?

Gwynneth went first, her attention all on me. 'I hardly knew Alex at all, Mark. I joined KLM only recently.'

She'd occasionally seen him when she was in the main office but had no special reason to connect with him. 'He was a lot older than me,' she explained, 'well above my paygrade.'

Another blank. I turned to Naomi. It was a surprise to discover that Naomi had a lot more to say.

'Before I say anything, Mark, can I check: is this a private conversation? I wouldn't want any of it to get back to Alex.'

I did my best to reassure her. 'I'm here as security guru. I'm not planning to broadcast what I hear to anyone.'

'Hey, Naomi,' said Gwynneth, 'd'you want me to go and collect some files from the main office? I can take as long as you want.'

Naomi considered for a second, then shook her head. 'Stay here, Gwynneth. Probably be good for you to hear the full story as well.'

I had no idea what was coming next. I sipped my tea, made sure I was sitting comfortably, took out my notebook. At least I was going to have something to put on the missing man's profile.

Naomi took a deep breath. 'If you want to sum Alex up in

one phrase, Mark, I'd say he's a rampant bully.'

'That's a strong statement. Could you expand it, please? Have there been incidents here – anything you'd be willing to share?'

She shook her head. 'Nothing since I came to KLM, I've kept out of the man's way. What I'm thinking of happened nearly thirty years ago.'

I didn't say anything. I hadn't asked Naomi her age but I reckoned she was in her forties. Was this going to be a tale of child molestation?

'Please go on,' I said.

'There was a China Clay pit north of St Austell called Wheal Richard. A younger Alex ruled the roost. He'd just been made Operations Manager at the tender age of twenty-eight.

'I was the newest recruit to admin – just eighteen. Straight from school. An innocent, slightly overweight girl in a largely man's world. I guess I stood out in an office of middle-aged women, mostly partners of the male workforce. It didn't take him long to notice me.'

Naomi paused. These were obviously painful memories.

'One day Alex came into the office. Demanded someone to walk round the works with him, taking note of all the things he intended to fix. Right now, he said, the whole place was a mess. There was no way they would close Wheal Richard by the time he'd got it sorted. I volunteered; hadn't even seen the further reaches of the pit before.'

There was a longer paused, then she asked me, 'You've not met Alex, have you?'

'Not yet. He was supposed to be on the interview panel but he didn't appear. He doesn't keep self-portraits on his desk.'

Naomi nodded. 'He's a strong, heavily built man. If he was a rugby player he'd have played in the scrum. All those years ago he was very fit. Though his curly hair was starting to thin, even then. And like anyone who did play in the second row, he had huge, sticking out ears – even more than our new King.'

I couldn't help but smile. 'That's the best description I've heard in a long time. Vivid. Thank you.' I hastily scribbled it down.

Naomi finished drinking her tea before she nerved herself to continue.

'Alex said he was taking me to the far end of the works. Up the hill and through the wood. It was early spring, the daffodils were just coming out. I even pointed them out to him but got no response. . . It was late afternoon, there was no-one else around. Then, without warning, he grabbed my arm, pulled me off the path into the bushes, and started peeling off my clothes. It was horrible.'

For a minute she couldn't go on. Gwynneth stood up and got her some more tea. I kept silent, waiting for whatever came next.

'I'm sure he would have gone all the way with me. There was a gloating, lustful look on his face. But I was incredibly lucky. As I stepped back, I happened to stand on one of the fallen pieces of the fence. It was lying on the ground, nails still sticking out – a small part of the bigger mess the works had got itself into. My end went down; the other end came up. Right between Alex's legs. One of the nails caught him smack in the goolies.'

She stopped to take a drink from her tea mug.

'I didn't know that much about male anatomy in those days. I didn't know exactly what damage I'd done. But as sure as heck I wasn't going to stay to find out. Alex was doubled up, groaning in agony.

'I headed away through the woods. Didn't stop running till I got to the pit forecourt. The afternoon bus to take the workers back to St Austell happened to be there, about to set off. I threw myself on board and collapsed onto the front passenger seat. That was how I got away.'

There was a long silence. It seemed Naomi had finished her tale but Gwynneth and I didn't dare say anything.

In the end Gwynneth spoke. 'So did you go to the police? What happened next?'

Naomi snorted. 'I was eighteen, remember. I wasn't going to relive the whole bloody nightmare in front of a bunch of coppers. Who was going to believe my story anyway? I was up against the authority of the Operations Manager.'

'But you couldn't just go back to the works next morning?'

'I never went back at all, Gwynneth. Left 'em all to it. I managed to get a job with the Council. Slowly pulled my life back together. They were very good to me over the years, sent me on all sorts of training courses. That's how I got into Finance.'

There was another pause. It was time I spoke. 'Thank you so much for sharing all that with us, Naomi. It was very brave of you. I'm so sorry to have caused you to rake up an old nightmare. But can I ask a more up to date question. Why on earth did you come to KLM, where Alex was once again one of the managers?'

She smiled. 'That's simple, Mark. It was thirty years ago, remember. I'd changed a lot in that time. Lost the excess weight and got some glasses. I'd taken up cycling to keep fit and the guitar to keep me entertained. Moved out of St Austell. I didn't think that, after all this time, Alex would recognise me at all. I'm not sure he even knew my name. And I'm far from being the youngest female on the payroll.'

I kept my eyes on Naomi but I hoped Gwynneth was taking note. My friend continued.

'But once I saw his name on the payroll sheet, I went to see

Rachel, told her I needed to be kept away from Alex. She didn't ask for details but took me at my word. She managed to hire this second unit for KLM and got the extra lock fitted. Gwynneth and I have our own keys. We feel perfectly safe in here, don't we?'

'Safe enough, anyway.' Gwynneth had obviously been shaken by the story. I hoped it wouldn't do lasting damage.

CHAPTER 26 Wed February 15th Simon Cooke, KLM

Neither Naomi nor I referred to her story as we travelled back to Luxulyan. I hoped it wouldn't spoil our friendship. I was only a few years older than her and not too bulky; I hope I didn't remind her of Alex Price. I was grateful when she suggested cooking us another meal together, later in the week. Even if it was only to find a new ballad for the next karaoke.

I did my best to prepare for my meeting with Simon Cooke. I'd been given plenty of sources of smarter systems and rang as many as I could. Before I met the managing director, I wanted to turn Dougie's generalities into specifics. I needed Simon's support on the whole process.

'Welcome, Mark,' said Simon, as I entered his office on Wednesday afternoon. 'I'm sorry we haven't had chance to talk since you joined us last week. I had several unavoidable meetings. A large part of my role here is maintaining KLM's place in the wider community. The "need for lithium" conversation seems to be warming up. But this afternoon the diary has given me a break. The floor is yours; take as long as you need.'

He noticed, belatedly, that I was still standing. 'Hey, take one of the comfortable chairs. I don't need to face you over a desk. Not on our first chat.'

His office was larger than Alex's or Rachel's. Like the interview room, its window faced out onto the Cornish Alps. We sat facing one another in a pair of easy chairs with a coffee table between us. Simon was a real "people person".

'I'm really enjoying KLM,' I began. 'The staff I've met have been as friendly as you could ever hope for. I haven't come across Alex yet, though I've been using his office until mine is ready. But Rachel has been great. So were Phil and Fiona, over in the lab, as well as in the Charcoal Grill.'

He smiled. 'So where are you living?'

'I've found a flat over in Luxulyan, one stop down the line. I'll be moving in at the end of next week.' I decided not to mention the karaoke nights at the King's Arms. News would travel back here eventually. I was in no hurry yet to talk about Naomi.

There was a knock at the door. Sandra appeared with a cafetiere and a pair of mugs. You couldn't fault the boss's hosting skills.

Mug in hand, I gave Simon a summary of the data I had gathered on KLM security. I'd thought hard on how to present this. I didn't want to sound aggressive towards my new boss, but it wouldn't do to be too gentle.

There was a challenge here and I'd been brought in to meet it. I needed to know if he was going to join me on the journey. If he wasn't, I'd be best moving on.

'Everyone I've met has agreed,' I began. 'The core administrative systems in KLM haven't kept up with the pace of new ideas. They are never the most exciting parts of any start-up company, least of all one that's grappling with big new ideas.'

'That's why you're here, Mark.' He wasn't fazed so far.

I nodded. 'So at the end of last week, I went to see a person I had found through my old Security links. A chap called Dougie. He'd been carefully chosen for me; he was also into lithium. Not the mining side,' I hastened to add, 'but using the stuff. Dougie was security manager in a new firm, set up to produce lithium batteries.'

Why talk so much about Dougie? I had decided to

introduce the new ideas via a named external source. If Simon was offended, I wasn't the immediate source of the offence. It could all be blamed on faraway Dougie.

But Simon wasn't offended at all. 'Gosh. He sounds like a useful person to know. Well done for finding him. You know, business is always about knowing the right people. And then being on good terms with them. So what did he have to say?'

'He gave me a lot of advice on software systems. He'd had to go through the whole slog himself. I can tell you much more about that later. He was also insistent: the key ideas had to be written down and kept somewhere safe, offsite. They were a KLM asset and needed protection.

'His core message, though, was that good security wasn't primarily a matter of technology. It all depended on bringing people with you.'

There was a short, reflective silence. I drank some of my coffee.

'Let's leave the technology for now,' said Simon. 'I'm more interested in his ideas on getting whole-hearted buy-in. Inside KLM, I guess the key idea-holders are the scientists: Phil and Fiona. What d'you think they'd make of being asked to write everything down?'

I was silent for a moment. 'It's not just the day-by-day activities, of course – any scientist would do that. It's the core ideas behind them, written out as if for an academic paper. If the idea was presented cold, Simon, I could image them being rather disturbed. Perhaps they'd suspect the firm was trying to do away with their services; avoid going on paying their high salaries. It might even make them want to get out before they're pushed. Which isn't the intention at all.'

Simon didn't like the sound of this. But before he could speak, I pressed on.

'But as I understand it, they've both been paid handsomely to work here as those ideas were developing. The ideas might have come from them, but they now belong to KLM. We'd be stupid as a company not to make sure they're kept totally secure.'

'So how should we approach it?'

'How about this?' I paused to polish my logic. 'Their ideas only came about because of even more clever starting ideas from you. You provided the context and the overall framework; you gave them a reason to take it all seriously. All worthwhile scientific achievements are team productions. These two are both top scientists, I'm sure they understand that.'

Simon thought about my comments. Then he nodded. 'So this is a task for the team leader. Me. It needs an informal session with the pair of them. You wouldn't need to be there, Mark, in fact it might be better if you weren't. I can blame you for the need for the three of us to take corporate action. I mean, it would be awful if we were all killed in a traffic accident.'

'Or even a plane crash.' I'd spoken the words without deep thought but it was the backstory of my life. Fortunately the event wasn't on the CV I'd provided of Mark Renfrew. Simon glanced at me but had no easy way of enquiring further.

We'd reached a break point and he called Sandra for more coffee.

After the break, while the going was good, I moved on to another topic that I'd discussed with Dougie: the disappearance of Alex Price.

'With everyone coming and going, Simon, you might not have noticed that Alex Price isn't around at the moment. But I have: he hasn't been here at all since I came. I have the privilege of occupying his office and I've never even met him.

'I talked about it with Rachel on Monday. She suggested I went round the office, talking to everyone, asking when they'd last seen Alex. Turned out, no-one had seen him since the week before I joined – that's over two weeks ago. Isn't that a long time for anyone to be out of the office, without anyone here knowing when he'll be back?'

Simon was not particularly defensive. 'Do you think I should know? I mean, he's a senior manager. Doesn't need to be mollycoddled.'

'There's not necessarily anything wrong at all, Simon. But he is on the KLM payroll. Shouldn't we have some idea what he's doing? If he's going round trying to negotiate access to old China Clay tips, I can imagine that finding the right person to talk to is far from easy: most of the pits owning the spoil tips are no longer in business. They'd have closed years ago. No, you wouldn't want him on a tight rein. But can he be left to roam entirely free for weeks on end?'

Simon looked thoughtful now. 'Mm. Is your concern based around security, Mark?'

'Well. Having a senior manager who knows a lot about KLM's hopes and dreams being out of touch with the office is not great for security. Presumably you were the one who recruited him? Is he here for technical know-how or for his practical drive on getting things done?'

Simon considered. 'The latter, I'd say. Alex was the Operations Manager of a major China Clay pit. But that was nearly thirty years ago. Knowledge fades. No, Alex's contribution to KLM is to connect the clever thinking in our labs with the real world of spoil tips. And to negotiate an affordable leasing rate, once a suitable tip is found.

'Making a deal with other former clay-pit managers is what I hope is his forte. We haven't got that far yet though.'

I thought for a moment. What else could I say?

'As well as security, Simon, there's a basic duty of care. Alex is your employee. How long can you leave it before you talk to the police, possibly register him as a missing person? A month? He's already been away over a fortnight. If you are going to report him, isn't it best done sooner rather than later?'

I could see Simon wasn't used to being told what to do. KLM was his baby; he was, after all, the managing director.

I was smiling, speaking gently, making sure I wouldn't come over as aggressive. But I was going out on a limb. How would he react?

'I've thought of alerting the police, of course. When he failed to show up for your interview was when I had a good excuse to do so. He knew he was meant to be here; I told him so myself.

'But involving outsiders would have caused us a lot of stress. No doubt the police would send someone competent; they would want to see our records. Which, as you know, are somewhat patchy.

'They'd also want to visit Alex's office to collect his fingerprints and so on. But you've been living in it for over a week: it'd be a forensic quagmire.

'I don't even have a picture of Alex. The worst thing would be if the police set up a wider appeal, and I had to appear with them, beseeching the public for help. It's not the image KLM is after. It wouldn't do us any favours in the lithium community.'

It was a real problem. Simon was not making this up. Admitting on television that he had lost one of his senior managers was hardly an endorsement of KLM competence.

'I've got one suggestion,' I remarked, after we'd gone round the problem for some time.

'Yes?' Simon's face was gloomy.

'The fact that I only arrived here after Alex went missing, have never met him, gives me an outsider status. If anything happened it can't have anything to do with me. And I have dealt with the police from time to time, I know something of their ways.'

'So. . .?'

'What if I were to drop security matters for a day or two? Pull together the kind of report on Alex in KLM that would make sense to an intelligent police officer – there are still a few around, I believe.'

'What kind of things?'

'I'd tell staff that you had personally asked me to pull it together. Gently interview them and record anything of value. Also I'd see if I can find any traces in Alex's office that would help a future search.

'We should give ourselves a hard deadline. Say, the end of next week. Alex might return before then of his own accord. But if/when we did call them, we'd have done the first stage of the inquiry ourselves. If we did, I'd be happy to present it and to be the lead interface on whatever came next.'

CHAPTER 27 Thurs February 16th The Detective

On Thursday morning, I went into my office (still no sign of Alex) and tried to view it with a policeman's eyes.

I'd started the day with Rachel Tyson. Wanted to make sure she understood what I was doing and supported it; and knew that it was being done at Simon Cooke's request.

There were also a few questions I had to ask. Did she have any next-of-kin data? Or any photograph of Alex? She had neither; they weren't part of their standard application form. She admitted that, with hindsight, this was a defect on the KLM system. Nor could she give me anything on his friends. 'He was a bit of a loner,' she declared.

I got her to tell me Alex's address. It was in St Austell. 'Course, I don't know if he still lives there.'

'Don't worry, Rachel, I'm planning to check. So how long had Alex been with KLM?'

Rachel checked back through the interview schedules to find when he had first appeared. 'He joined us three years ago. And always had the same office.'

'Ah,' I asked, 'and how often was the office cleaned?'

'We have twice-a-week cleaning. Wednesday and Friday evenings, seven till nine, after all the staff have left. I've checked their references. They've been given skeleton keys.'

Finally, I asked Rachel about Alex's office. 'I recall, when you first led me to it, there were no books in the bookshelf. Did that happen recently or did he used to have plenty of books?

Can you remember what any of them were?'

She confirmed that there had been a few books. 'Though I can't tell you what they were. I never got the feeling Alex was much of a reader.'

I felt I'd learned all I could and strode along to what was becoming my own office.

This used to be Alex's den. I was glad Naomi had spoken to me so frankly three days before. It gave me a completely different perspective on the previous occupant and what might have happened to him. He was – or at least used to be – capable of being very wild indeed. Had he tried to molest anyone else more recently?

How should I behave from now on if this was some sort of crime scene? I'd a collection of items in my rucksack. Should I put on the new latex gloves, or crocs over my shoes?

It would be daft. I'd been in here for over a week, touching everything. Bit late to stop now.

Whatever might be gleaned from dusting the office chair for DNA had long since been overshadowed by my own robust backside. I felt like the Rowan Atkinson of detection, "Johnny English at your service". Hopefully I wasn't that bad. I sat at my desk and studied the space around me.

What was I really after? At a minimum, it would be good to collect Alex's fingerprints, maybe even his DNA. Had he ever featured on the police crime database? It could be useful, say, if his body was found. Was that still possible?

No chance on the desk or chair. I'd corrupted anything that might once have been there. I had no idea when I started that Alex might have gone missing.

But was there anything else? I tried to remember. I'd not touched the filing cabinet, once Rachel had told me she had no key.

I wandered over to the cabinet and examined the top carefully. But it didn't look hopeful. The zealous cleaners had dusted it too carefully.

I meandered over to the window. No view of the Cornish Alps from here. I was about to return to the desk when something caught my eye. A small key, on a hook beside the window. I certainly hadn't used that – I wasn't opening the window in February.

But I remembered, Alex had been here all last summer. He'd probably have opened the window at some stage.

I went back to my rucksack, took out latex gloves and a clear plastic evidence bag, photographed the setting. A moment later I'd tucked the key inside the bag, with a label saying where I'd found it.

Might there be anything in the desk drawers? I pulled both open, took a photograph of each and stared at the contents. The minutiae of office life. Paper clips, two rubbers, a ruler, a box of drawing pins, a few highlighter pens. I'd certainly not used those. A moment later they had a labelled evidence bag of their own.

I was about to shut the drawers when something occurred to me. A lack of symmetry. Why hadn't they pulled out equally?

I tried pulling the shorter drawer harder. Peered inside for something catching, that stopped it coming further. There was nothing obvious. I'd never have noticed anything if I hadn't been on a deliberate search. But now I was interested.

I took the ruler and poked the drawer's back wall. To my surprise there was a small amount of movement, as if it was hinged on a horizontal axis.

I moved the ruler down and tried again. This time the movement was substantial. The wall tilted until it was completely horizontal. I took another photograph, then fetched my torch from the rucksack: what could I see now? There was a space beyond the back wall – and something else inside it.

Suddenly, I realised that, with the fake back wall now horizontal, I could pull the drawer out just as far as its neighbour. And, of course, see what was hidden at the rear.

It was a thirty cm wide roll of clear plastic.

My brain was doing cartwheels but now I needed to think clearly. I left my office, carefully locking the door. Then headed out for a walk around the industrial estate.

I found it impossible to believe that the secret drawer space was not linked in some way with Alex's disappearance. But why use it to hide a roll of clear plastic? What on earth was it for?

As I strode around rather aimlessly, I noticed a sign at the estate entrance. Below the name was a map, showing all the units currently in occupation. But these changed all the time. The map couldn't be reprinted every time there was a new occupant. That was handled by a clear plastic sheet overlaying the original. It even had one or two new arrivals handwritten in.

Then it clicked. My newly found plastic roll would probably show new information, if placed in front of the correct map.

But if so, where was the map? Most plausibly it must be in Alex's possession. In that case, I deduced, it was probably a standard map – like, for example, the Explorer map of the St Austell area. A well-thumbed copy of that was nestling in my rucksack. The next step in my research now beckoned.

Back in my office I sat once more at the desk. Did either of the drawers offer any more clues? I peered in one more time.

Then it came to me. You wouldn't just "place" the plastic over the map. Getting it positioned precisely would be vital. But you could use something like drawing pins to hold it in place.

Slowly, carefully, I unfolded the plastic roll and laid it across the desk. It was half a metre long and thirty centimetres wide. I used my phone to hold down one end and stop the roll rewinding and my wallet on the other. Then I examined it minutely.

Yes. There was a pinhole. Several. In fact there were pinholes close to all four corners. And across the plastic I saw a number of small black crosses.

But to complete the proof of my hypothesis, could I find where the map and plastic had been pinned?

I took a drawing pin of my own from the rucksack and tried to pin it into the desk. But it wasn't possible to push it in. The top of the desk was very hard indeed.

Maybe Alex had used a wall? But I tried; they were too hard as well. I glanced round once more and saw the wooden door.

I had to take my sheepskin coat off the hook before I could see it properly. And there they were. A pattern of pinholes, making the shape of a rectangle.

I got a tape measure from my rucksack and measured the dimensions. Went back to check the sizes on the plastic. Yeah! They were an exact match. I could even tell which way the plastic had been laid: it was landscape rather than portrait.

Now all I needed was to find which map the plastic related to. And hence identify the two dozen or more positions which Alex had been so keen to locate.

CHAPTER 28 Thurs February 16th Fiona at KLM

By late morning I had decided it was time to visit Phil and Fiona over in the KLM laboratory.

Overlaying the clear plastic sheet onto my Explorer map had been a complete waste of time – if indeed it was the correct map I was using. One key fact was missing, namely, where exactly the plastic should be located relative to the map.

I had spent ages trying to deduce a connection, using the pin positions on the office door. I could more or less match the pinholes on the door to the holes in the plastic. But the Explorer map, or whatever map it was supposed to lay on top of, could have been placed anywhere.

I had tried to think what the locations might tell me, once I knew where they were. It was a reasonable guess that they'd be off the beaten track. But that didn't help at all. Meant the matching map might go anywhere.

Very frustrating. All I needed was two known locations to tie the plastic precisely to a map. But how ever would I find those?

At that point a fresh idea had arisen. Might the plastic overlay, somehow, be linked to some of Alex's successful clay tip locations? Then came the thought: if they'd been successful, had led to samples, they must be known to the scientists over in the laboratory.

'Sorry to come at such short notice,' I began. 'But I'm on an urgent piece of work for Simon Cooke.'

'I'm afraid Phil's off site today,' said Fiona. 'Can I help?'

I considered. Maybe a geological perspective on location would be more useful to me than chemical analysis.

'Yes please. But it might take us some time.'

'Why don't we stroll down to the Charcoal Grill, then? It won't be busy; gives us more privacy than chatting in the laboratory.'

It was almost lunch time anyway. I wasn't hard to persuade. I hadn't forgotten the tasty meal I'd had there the week before.

'So what's this piece of work for Simon?' asked Fiona, once we'd reached the Grill, been seated and placed our orders.

'It's trying to find out what's happened to Alex. If he doesn't come back by the end of next week, Simon says he will report his absence to the police.'

She nodded. 'Not a bad idea. He's been gone for two or three weeks already.'

I recalled another part of my commission. 'Have you any insights on Alex? I'm trying to pull together our KLM collective knowledge – that's in case we need to take it the police.'

Fiona looked unexpectedly troubled. 'Not anything I'm eager to share, Mark.'

We'd been assigned a table beside the wall. I glanced around. There was no-one in earshot. This was as private as you could hope.

'I'm a newcomer round here, Fiona. Simon doesn't want any publicity. But if I'm going to be much help to anyone then I do need to know the stories. I wouldn't share anything you told me with anyone, not without your explicit permission. I won't even take notes.' I assumed my most sympathetic look. Would it work?

There was a pause as Fiona plucked up her courage.

'Alex's key task for KLM is the opening step. Finding promising clay tips that we'd be allowed to sample, as part of a pilot study.

'Of course,' she continued, 'each of these tips has to be sensibly chosen. Every pilot study costs money and ties up scarce resources. There are hundreds of possibilities; and we can't afford to try them all. So we need to ask, where was the clay pit located? Is there any solid geological reason to think the tip might contain lithium?'

'So you have to go with him to visit each candidate site, to help with the assessment?'

Fiona nodded. But she'd lost her usual self-confidence. I decided to give her some gentle encouragement.

'So did something happen one time, when you were out with Alex?'

Fiona looked at me then gave a sob. It looked like she was about to cry. I kept silent.

'It was one of the earliest trials,' she said. 'I hadn't been here long. Alex and I had to walk right round the tip, check it looked solid from all angles. And see the terrain behind it. I wanted to give him a geological perspective.'

She took a deep breath. 'We had reached the point where we were well away from the road, completely out of sight. Then, without warning, he went for me.'

If I hadn't heard a similar story from Naomi, I would have been even more shocked. But this was distressing enough.

'Fiona, you poor, poor woman. I'm so very sorry.'

But now she'd started Fiona wanted to finish the tale.

'Like most female students, I'd been on a good self-defence course at uni. Since then I always kept a perfume spray in my kagoule pocket. As he came for me, I pulled it out, fired it and hit him in the face from a range of two feet. Then, while his hands were covering his face and he was howling with pain, I ran like hell back to my car.'

Fortunately, our meals arrived at that point, giving us both a chance to calm down. I asked for ketchup to go with the gammon steaks.

Once we were talking again, I thought I'd be brave and ask a clarifying question. 'I presume you didn't report what had happened?'

She sighed. 'Mark, I was new to KLM and Alex was the old hand. It would be my word against his. Apart from Alex's weaknesses I thought the opportunities here were fantastic. I didn't want to give up, I wanted to make a difference. But I made bloody sure I was never alone with again.'

There was silence as we both tucked into our meals.

'Thank you for telling me all this, Fiona. It helps build up a fuller picture of Alex.'

She looked at me. 'I don't know why on earth I was prepared to tell that story to you, when I'd kept it to myself for so long. You're unusually empathetic. But that can't have been what you wanted to talk to me about?'

'Not exactly. Though it was about tracking Alex's movements; and all the places we know he was hoping to win for KLM to exploit.

'What bothers me, you see, is his most recent movements. I can't find anyone in KLM who has heard a word from him for nearly three weeks. That's a long time. It's almost as if he's gone to ground.'

'Best place for him,' she muttered.

We continued to eat while I worked out a way to progress my enquiry.

'Do you have any record, back in the laboratory, of the spoil tips you've been trialling?'

'Of course. Including the dates first visited and the dates we started sampling. I'm a scientist, Mark, not a rough and ready

China Clay manager.'

I tiptoed towards my key question. 'Do you, by chance, have any maps with these locations on?'

She looked up and nodded. 'Sure. What are you thinking of?'

'What I'm wondering, Fiona, is can I find a pattern on Alex's searching? He can't just have gone about visiting South Cornwall tips at random. There must have been some sort of system in his searching.'

Fiona ate more of her gammon before replying.

'From what he did to me, Mark, I find it hard to credit Alex with any systematic skills at all. But it's possible. If you like I can get out the active spoil tip map when we get back, trace all the places he's known to have been active. Then I can run off a list of the places and their starting dates. You can take it away, try to find a pattern.'

'The dates might be too far back to be useful. But it might help to know if he was working, say, North to South or East to West. Thank you. That could be a big help.'

When we got back to KLM, Fiona produced the map she was using to record the spoil tips visited. But it wasn't an Explorer map or even a smaller scale Pathfinder. It was a geological map. No common geographical features like roads or named towns. It comprised sub-regions, made up of all sorts of shapes and colours.

'Why haven't you used a conventional map?'

'I'm a geologist, Mark, hired to provide geological insights. This is the easiest map for the purpose.'

I could make no sense of it at all. 'What's the scale, Fiona?'

'One inch to the mile. The British Geographical Society, BGS, used that scale on their first geological maps in Britain:

that was Cornwall and Devon in 1832.

'The one-inch map was standard in those days. The surveyor was instructed to "affix geological colonies to standard maps of Devonshire". It's looked much the same ever since.'

'Is there any chance I could borrow it? Say just for the afternoon?'

She smiled. 'It's my only copy, so don't lose it. But please do let me know what you find.'

I put my latex gloves on again when I reached my office. The clear plastic sheet was probably the best source I would ever have of Alex's fingerprints, I needed to handle it with care and put it in an evidence bag when I could.

I laid Fiona's geological map on the desk. Fortunately she had marked the spoil tips of interest to KLM in solid black ink.

Then I seized the plastic sheet by the outer edge. Was there any way I could make the two sets of crosses overlap?

It was very difficult. The multi-coloured map below made it very hard to pick out the crosses.

But I wasn't going to be thwarted. Ten minutes later I returned from the main office with a large sheet of tracing paper. Very carefully I laid it on top of Fiona's map and traced all the crosses.

Then I removed the map and instead laid the plastic on top of the tracing paper. Could I make them match?

It took a while but I got it to work. The traced crosses lay beneath the plastic ones. There was no doubt, now, what Alex's clear plastic related to. A moment of triumph after a long and intense day.

CHAPTER 29 Thurs February 16th- 17th Mapping the trail

It was a good job I wasn't having my sing-along rehearsal with Naomi this evening. I needed time and space to think.

Once I was in my room and had changed out of my suit, I carefully put on more protective latex gloves and spread the tracing paper across my desk. Then, more gingerly, I laid the clear plastic on top.

I also got out my St Austell Explorer Map – a much larger scale. And Fiona's list of the location names of all the special clay spoil tips that KLM had taken an interest in.

The challenge was to tie these sources together.

I'd already superposed the clear plastic on the tracing paper once, back in the office. With some trial and error I repeated the process. But this time I took a clamp from my tool bag, slid the tracing paper and plastic gently towards the edge of the desk then clamped the two together. Now I could examine their combined message at my leisure.

My next action was to take Fiona's tip list and find the listed locations on my Explorer map. I even abandoned my old map to the cause, scrawling on it using a yellow highlighter to circle locations once I'd found them. Not many of the names appeared on the map, of course. There were plenty marked simply as "Tip (dis)", with no clue as to which clay pit they came from.

Sometimes I was looking for a hamlet or farm to match a name on Fiona's list. Even so, I couldn't find them all.

But could I now match the shape – the constellation – of the known tips on my Explorer map to the similar but smaller pattern on the tracing paper and clear plastic?

It took a while to get the two starting maps to the same orientation. Finally I found one way that made the patterns similar. Now I could lay the relevant folds of the Explorer map on the desk, alongside the clear plastic; I didn't need to go as far east as Looe or as far north as the A30.

After which I could search more narrowly for matching tips.

As I looked more closely it occurred to me that there were more crosses marked on the clear plastic than there were on the tracing paper below. Odd. What were the extra ones about?

I made myself a mug of coffee to feed my brain. Then it came to me, were they the position locators I'd been pining for earlier?

Two of them were, anyway. One cross was in the same position as the railway junction at Par. The other was further north, I guessed the road junction at the tiny village of Sweetshouse. These were both precise locations that would help tie different maps together.

Now I could make better sense of it all. I gradually found all the places on Fiona's list. Then I used an orange highlighter to circle my (estimated) locations of all the remaining crosses. There were about a dozen.

The only thing that came to mind was that these might be Alex's planned locations. One of these might even be where he was now. Or where he'd been pushed under a tractor?

Perhaps he'd tried to molest one woman too many and got his comeuppance from the woman's husband? Was one of these locations a crime scene?

I could see no alternative but to try to visit each of the no-tip locations. Was that the basis for another cycle ride on Saturday?

On Friday morning, I decided I would travel in by car so I could visit Alex's home address in St Austell.

I drove down to find Naomi at Luxulyan station and explained my plan. 'Don't worry, I'll be around this evening. Hey, would you like me to bring in some fish and chips? Give us more time to sing.'

She agreed and told me the best place to buy some. Then I drove in to St Austell.

Rachel had given me Alex's address: it was a flat, not far from the town centre. I parked and headed for it. Mind, I saw as I got there that I could have parked in his street.

His address was the upper floor of a pair of flats. No doorbell. I knocked hard but nothing happened. Was this a good use of my time? I hammered one more time.

I was about to walk away when I heard someone coming to the door. Alex's downstairs neighbour, a retired gentleman.

I gave him my name, then asked about Alex Price. 'He's a colleague of mine. I wanted to check he was OK.'

'He does live here but he's not at home. If he was, I'd have heard him moving about upstairs. Mind, he comes and goes. You know, I haven't heard him for several weeks.'

'Are you sure he's not lying ill upstairs?'

The neighbour considered. Then he peered out past me, onto the road. 'His battered Land Rover's not there. That's his usual means of transport. He parks it over the road.' He sniffed. 'Never cleans it, either.'

'He's mostly out visiting old clay pits,' I said. 'They're not the cleanest of places. But he is doing some useful work.'

I gave him my KLM business card. 'That's where we both work. If you do see him, would you mind giving me a call? He's been out of contact for rather a long time.'

As I walked back in the centre, I noticed a WH Smith's and wondered if I could get buy a one-inch map of the area.

'No chance,' the young man behind the counter told me. 'The Explorer maps are all we stock. They're far more useful.'

I bought a new, up-to-date copy whilst I had the chance. On my way out I noticed they sold thirty-cm wide rolls of clear plastic. Part of the schools equipment range.

Once back in Bugle I went straight over to see Fiona in the laboratory.

'Still on you own?' I asked, slightly surprised.

'Phil's on leave. It's the half term break, you see. He has two kids in school - needs to keep an eye on them. There's nowhere much to take them at this time of year. Too cold for swimming.'

'Can you spare me half an hour, then? I'd like to tell you where I've got to with maps.'

Fiona was obviously not that hard pressed. She was also eager to learn the latest.

'How about an early lunch?'

'I'm afraid I can't lunch at the Charcoal Grill today,' I said. 'I'm eating out this evening.' I didn't tell her who I'd be with.

'There's one coffee shop in Bugle. It's never that busy. Why don't we go there?'

I'd realised on the drive to Bugle that if I was going to share at all, I had to take Fiona into my confidence. After all, she'd shared something personal with me. It wasn't wise to do everything on my own.

'I have some exhibits which I don't want to take out of my rucksack. Not in a café, anyway. So I'll explain first, then if it sounds useful we can go back to your office and look at them after lunch.'

Fiona agreed and we set off for the café. We each bought a baguette to go with our coffees and grabbed a table near the back. I reckoned it was private enough.

'You know I'm camping in Alex's office?' She nodded. 'Well, I decided yesterday to treat it like a potential crime scene. At the very least I wanted to have his fingerprints and DNA.'

'In this day and age,' said Fiona, 'that ought to be taken whenever you start a new job: and also your next-of-kin.'

'Alex's office was almost empty. But to cut a long story short, I found a false back to one of the desk drawers. Behind was a roll of clear plastic. That was why I came for your BGS map of clay tips. I wanted to compare the two.'

Fiona sipped her coffee but said nothing. I continued.

'After lots of trial and error, I found that there were crosses on the clear plastic that often coincided with the clay tips you had marked on your BGS map. So one important question that raised for me was, how had Alex obtained them?'

Fiona stared at her baguette as she pondered. 'It goes without saying that I would never invite Alex into my side of the laboratory. Mind, he came in sometimes to find Phil. He was the nearest Alex had to a friend in KLM. They'd quite often go for a pint after work.'

'The crucial thing, Fiona, is whether he ever saw your BGS map?'

She considered. 'I'd sometimes take it on KLM awaydays. It was a way of talking to the rest of staff about the local geology. I even made use of the crosses showing some of the tips we were investigating.'

'So it wasn't exactly secret. All Alex would need, really, was one time when you had the BGS map out in your office but you weren't there – gone to the loo, for instance.'

She frowned. 'He'd also need some clear plastic, to copy the key markings.'

I nodded. 'Yes. But I was in St Austell earlier. They sell rolls of the stuff, exactly the same size, in WH Smiths.'

'Ah. You mean, he could keep one of those in his jacket pocket until the opportunity came along.' Fiona shrugged. 'I can't prove that didn't happen. I do go to the loo occasionally.'

I ate some of my baguette before moving on to another question.

'One thing still puzzles me. There are some marks on the plastic that I can't find on your BGS map. I can't account for them at all.'

Fiona frowned and considered but looked completely stumped.

'Are any of the "tips of interest" later discarded?' I wondered.

'Hardly ever. But even if they are, I've no way of removing a cross from my map. It's indelible ink, a statement of where we've been looking as much as anything else. Knowing that helps guide our sampling regime. At each of those points we've collected a huge amount of data.'

She couldn't say any more, we continued our lunch in silence.

I was all for sharing my findings with Fiona. Less keen to voice all my ideas.

So I didn't tell her my idea that the other crosses might be places where Alex had also visited; or intended to do so. I hoped to collect more evidence on that on my cycle ride tomorrow.

CHAPTER 30 Fri February 17th - Sat 18th The search

Friday evening: at last, a chance to unwind. I'd managed to find the recommended fish and chip shop, bought a meal for two, left my car at the King's Arms and walked over to Naomi's. For a while at least I could forget about Alex Price.

She was certainly pleased to see me. Looked like she wanted to give me a hug – or was that just my imagination?

'Right,' she said. 'I'll put the cod and chips in the oven for a few minutes, make sure it's really hot. What shall we drink?'

'While I was in St Austell today, I bought a bottle of Chardonnay,' I told her. 'Thought we could celebrate the end of the week.'

'Great.' She produced two wine glasses and poured us each a drink. 'Cheers.'

Maybe, in my detective mode I was becoming slightly more observant? Naomi looked ever so perky; attractive with her cropped dark hair and chunky glasses – a bit like comedian Sue Perkins. Then I realised she was looking at me too.

'You know, Mark, I've kept clear of men ever since the traumas of Wheal Richard. Didn't want to risk anyone close to me. You won't believe it, but you're the first man I've had back here for a meal.'

I laughed. 'And here's me providing all the food. How long before we eat?'

We sat side by side on the settee with our drinks, moved to the table a few minutes later. Two piping hot plates of fish and chips were brought out of the oven. They looked and smelled delicious.

As we started to eat Naomi was in a reflective mood.

'I've thought quite a lot about why I was willing to share my Wheal Richard ordeal with you, Mark. I've never done so with anyone else.'

'Glad you did, Naomi. It gives me a much clearer image of Alex.'

She mused. 'I had an intuition that there was a difficult back story in your life too. You were unexpectedly empathetic.'

I tried to shrug off her half-expressed query. 'It's a long story. You don't really want to know. Not tonight, anyway.'

But an inquisitive woman is hard to push away, especially when she looks at you across the table with appealing brown eyes.

In the end I caved. For the rest of the meal, as we munched the battered cod and chunky chips, I shared at least part of my own gloomy past.

I told her about the dreadful plane crash in Iran and how I was the only survivor. Then my experience nursing a lost memory in a remote Iranian hospital; and, later, being interrogated by local police. And finally how my memory had come back, ever so slowly, after a long lag.

Her eyes grew larger and larger. 'Mark, you've suffered much more than I have. I shouldn't feel sorry for myself at all.'

I reached across the table to give her hand a squeeze. 'Naomi, we're all damaged people in one way or another. I think the trick is not to let it destroy you.'

There was silence for a moment.

'This is all far too solemn for a Friday evening,' I declared. 'Why don't we have a sing?'

So we did. It might have been a warped imagination but I felt we were singing together better than we had ever done before. I could sense when Naomi would hold a final note for longer, or when she would add a spontaneous descant to my chorus. And she seemed to feel much the same as me (though I never tried a descant).

There was plenty of material there for the next two or three karaoke evenings.

By ten o'clock our voices were growing hoarse and we felt we'd done enough. 'So what's the plan for tomorrow?' asked my new special friend.

There was a pause. I'd thought generally about visiting the crosses; and I'd thought separately about a cycle ride with Naomi; but I hadn't put the two together. I'd have to say something.

'Please don't ask me to say more than I need,' I urged, 'but I think I may have found a clue to the places Alex has been visiting. Via a map he used to trace on, that I've copied to my Explorer map. They're all in a broad arc north of St Austell. I'd like us to try and visit them. Do they actually correspond to properties? And if so, has Alex been there?'

Naomi blinked hard. 'You're not exactly Mr Conventional, Mark. So you're taking me on a mystery tour; but one where you don't even know the proper meaning of the mystery?'

Then she giggled. 'Sounds great. I'm intrigued. I'd like to know what's happened to Alex too. But if he has fallen down a mine shaft, I confess I won't be the one rushing to rescue him.'

We set out at ten next morning. Like last week, Naomi was dressed for a heat wave, I was more ready for the "beast from the east". You can guess who turned out to be right. It was mid-February.

The first port of call was a blob close to a farm named

Tremethan.

'A pity your blob's not a bit smaller,' said Naomi judiciously.

I protested. 'The map I was starting from was on a smaller scale. It's all a bit hit and miss. But can you see anything hereabouts?'

We couldn't do that on two wheels. We locked our bikes together against a farmer's gate and wandered up and down, peering over the occasional hedge. We were in rolling countryside, there was a collection of solar panels, a modern intrusion on a distant field. Hey, might they hold the key? That seemed extremely doubtful.

'Trouble is,' I sighed, 'this is like a game of outdoor Hunt the Slipper, when we're not even sure we're after a slipper. The crosses were added to a map containing other crosses. They were ones that marked clay spoil tips of interest to KLM. Alex's crosses must mark somewhere equally specific.'

Naomi was an enthusiastic girl – a former Girl Guide, I'd deduced from the woggle on the mantelpiece – but I sensed even her natural curiosity was starting to wilt. Action was required.

'Let's go and look for the next one, Naomi. There might be something more obvious. Give us a clue what we're looking for.'

We walked slowly back to our bikes. As she unlocked them, I peered at my map. 'We'll head next for an area called Little Trevellion.'

It was only a couple of miles, the hills on the way were gentle. We rode till we reached the centre of my blob and dismounted.

I feared the worst. Behind the hedges were a field on one side and a wood on the other. Was this going to be another lost cause?

It was the sharp-eyed Naomi that spotted it. A tiny cottage on the far side of the wood. If it wasn't the depth of winter, with no leaves on the trees, you'd never have seen it. We left our bikes and took a little-used footpath through the wood.

The wooden garden gate carried the name "Last Chance.' Mind, it might not have been chosen by the current occupant.

There was no doorbell so I hammered hard on the door.

We heard some noise from inside, then the door slowly opened. An elderly man stood there. He was obviously cold, despite a thick sweater, but looked friendly enough.

'Good morning,' I said. 'My name's Mark and this is Naomi. We work for a mining company called KLM.'

A look of panic passed across his face. 'Mining?'

Naomi took over. 'It's all right sir, we don't want to spoil your peace and dig a mine here. It's just that we're looking for a colleague. He disappeared three weeks ago, we're trying to revisit all the places he might have come to.'

'Oh, well. Would you like to come in for a minute?' We followed him inside and sat across an old wooden table in his beamed kitchen.

'There was someone here, two or three weeks back.' He frowned. 'Sorry, I can't remember the name.'

'Was it Alex – Alex Price?'

His face lit up. 'You know, I think it was. I made a little joke about being priceless. He didn't seem to get it.'

'He's not much noted for his sense of humour,' said Naomi. 'Can you remember what he was after?'

I held my breath. This was the crucial question.

'He had a host of general questions. How long had I lived here and so on. Then he came to my wife. I told him, she died twenty years ago. It was from a stroke, actually. The thing is, Naomi, we don't have a phone here. I had to walk quite a way before I could get hold of the hospital. Then the ambulance got lost, didn't get here for another hour. By then it was much too late.' He looked upset.

'I'm so sorry,' I said.

'Mr Price had no idea of sympathy,' said the man. 'He didn't stay long after that. Left me to my misery. At least you two are friendly enough. Would you like a mug of coffee?'

It took us a while to extract ourselves. The poor man must have been very lonely. Eventually we told him we had other places to search and left him to potter on alone.

'Poor old man,' said Naomi, when we'd got back to our bikes.

'Yes,' I agreed. 'But it confirms that Alex did visit the crosses. And only a few weeks ago. Maybe the next one will tell us more.'

The next blob was on Bokiddick Downs. No building marked on the map, but the last place hadn't been marked either.

We cycled over, once more left our bikes by a farmer's gate. It was a marshy area, I didn't fancy wading through it, so we set ourselves to walk round the marsh edge. Which was how we came across the next location.

It was another farmhouse, just off the road. Looked in good condition, the roof was sound, anyway. So we repeated our pattern.

This was a more upmarket farm: it had a doorbell. A cheery looking man came to the door.

'I'm Mark Renfrew and this is Naomi.'

'Aye. And I'm Joe Dingley from Bingley.' We gathered, from his accent as much as his words, that he was a refugee from Yorkshire.

'We're trying to track a colleague of ours,' I began. 'By the name of Alex Price.'

'He hasn't been seen for several weeks,' added Naomi.

'You're on t' right track, lass,' the farmer responded. 'There was someone of that name 'ere. Mebbe three weeks ago. Mind, he didn't stop long. Don't think he liked the accent.'

We didn't stay long either. But we were certainly on the trail.

We found dwellings at three more of the locations and got quite proficient at presenting ourselves as concerned colleagues while we tried to glean what it was that Alex was after, and why he'd chosen these particular sites.

But it was tiring work. Not physically, we weren't cycling very far, but there was an increasing mental stress as we tried to solve the mystery.

Eventually we headed for a light lunch in Lostwithiel: hot chocolate and toasted sandwiches.

'Are there many more?' asked Naomi, as we started to munch. She was looking weary. 'I'm not sure we're learning much now.'

I opened the map one more time. 'Just one. Mind, it might just be an edge-of-map marker. And it's right at the top of a hill.'

But to her credit, Naomi was a completer-finisher. 'Come on then, we might as well do 'em all.'

And that was how we got to "Last Fling".

The building – it wasn't much like a farm – stood by the roadside, on a road out of Lostwithiel that led eventually to Par. It wasn't far from where we'd cycled the week before. We didn't have to look far for this one, there was nothing to block our view. There was also a splendid hilltop view across to Lostwithiel and beyond.

'That's Restormel Castle,' said Naomi, pointing to a venerable stone building in the distance. 'Perhaps we could go there one day.'

'Not today,' I said firmly. 'Remember, we've got karaoke to cope with this evening.'

I knocked. A middle-aged man, dressed in casual clothes, came to the door and we introduce ourselves once more.

'You're very welcome,' he replied. 'I'm Oliver Frobisher. How can I help you?'

'We're chasing after a colleague from KLM called Alex Price. Has he been here at all?'

I could see we'd struck a chord. 'You know, I think he might have. Two or three weeks ago? In a muddy old Land Rover?'

'That sound like Alex. I don't want to sound impertinent, Mr Frobisher, but can you tell us anything about what he was after?'

'He's disappeared from work, you see,' added Naomi. 'And we're all getting increasingly worried.'

'Mm. You'd best come inside. Would you both like a mug of tea?'

As he filled up the kettle, I glanced out of the kitchen window. It was a fine-looking farmhouse. With more buildings out the back, clustered around a tidy yard. There was something extra which I couldn't recognise at the far end.

'Is this place very old?' I asked.

'Century before last,' he replied. 'But we've always looked after it well – especially the well itself, of course. That goes down a long way.

'Alex was interested in our ancestry – especially my wife Debbie. I'm from Devon but she was brought up here. He got her family tree going back for five generations before he'd finished.'

I tried a wild punt. 'And did he want to search round the farm?'

'He would have liked to, but I told him there was no need. I'd cleared the loft to put in new loft insulation. All the outbuildings are pretty empty. He looked a bit disappointed when he drove away. But he said he might be back.'

'If you do see him again, I'd be very grateful if you could give me a call.' I handed over my card, which he glanced at.

'KLM Security Manager, eh. I bet Alex going missing is enough of a headache to be going on with. I'll certainly let you know if I think of anything.'

As we walked away I said, reflectively: 'You know, Naomi, I wish we'd had chance to look a bit harder at his well. It's an odd thing to have right on top of a hill.'

PART 5

February 13th - 19th

Extrapolation

CHAPTER 31 Tues February 14th Fowey

It was on St Valentine's Day that George Gilbert moved in with Emma Eastham.

No romance was involved. Emma was impatient to hear from her friend about copper mining around these parts – from Fowey to well beyond Par – in the nineteenth century. She had a second room in her rented apartment at Coombe Farm and persuaded George to join her.

'Look, George. The jog into Fowey every morning will give you some exercise – and the jog back even more. In the evenings you can bring me up to date on the business Joseph Treffry spent his life wedded to. Then we can work out how best to present it.'

For her part, George was becoming tired by the pace of life at the Ship Inn. Home cooking wouldn't come amiss. The traffic survey was running itself. Her role had evolved to collecting the results of interviews conducted among locals, refining the questions asked and widening the reply options offered.

She could do most of that away from the town. She was only fifteen minutes away if a phone call alerted her to trouble, could meet her young associates each day over lunch – a meal which she (and eventually the Council) would pay for.

She was still getting to know her new friend Peter Jakes. But she didn't want to talk to him about traffic surveys. She hoped he might invite her to his home in Polkerris.

'Well, Emma. How far have you got with Joseph Treffry?' It

was the start of a farmhouse supper. She was awaiting her portion of sweet and sour chicken.

As she dished out the meal, Emma recounted her adventures so far. The meeting with Susannah at Treffry's mansion at Place; the widening of her plans to include Charles Rashleigh; the visit to the harbour and pub in Charlestown; and the encounter with the drama group in St Austell.

'The harbour gives a terrific backdrop to talk about Rashleigh. He built the whole place, you know, and it's hardly changed since. The StormBox actors gave several ways of enacting the row between Treffry and Rashleigh over mining access to the port in Fowey. Fortunately there's no written record of what was said, so I'm free to speculate.'

'I never thought I'd hear a historian being thankful for ignorance,' said George with a giggle.

In her turn, George outlined her progress so far on the traffic survey, including the recruitment of local sixth formers and the tale of the flattened building beside the car park.

'It had a name: The Tavern. But it was all knocked down last week, so you can't see it anymore.'

She went on to describe how she had been taken inside the Tavern by one of her students, the night before. 'It was scary, Emma. I had to clamber over a ten-foot boundary wall in the middle of the night. Wilson had been before, reported a cellar doorway with a strong padlock. But when we got there the padlock that was supposed to bar the way in was missing.'

'Wow. So what did you do?'

George grinned. 'There was no choice, really. We had to keep searching. I was glad Wilson was there too, mind. I might not have gone down on my own.'

There was a pause. 'Come on, George. Don't keep me in suspense. What did you find?'

George paused for dramatic effect then went on. 'All we found was a few small wooden chests. All very old. They must have been locked at one time. But someone had smashed 'em open.'

She shook her head. 'We checked 'em all. I'm afraid each one was empty. It was a dead end.'

There was a thoughtful silence as they ate more of the meal. Emma was the first to speak.

'Ignorance about the details of an old row is one thing, George. Knowing something's been lifted from an old chest but having no clue what it was is something else. Come on, you're teasing me. There were more clues - surely?'

George gave a sigh. 'Not that I could see. Aren't historians supposed to make a great deal out of very little?'

She helped herself to more sweet and sour sauce as the historian wrestled with a smaller helping of a greater truth.

'You say, George, this place used to be a tavern? That's odd in itself: why leave something valuable in a pub cellar? If it was gold coins, say, you'd take them at the time; or at least when the Tavern closed?

She thought on. 'That suggests to me it wasn't always a tavern. D'you know its history? It might have changed hands after 1860. I'll try the Land Registry website tomorrow.'

Emma had planned pancakes for dessert. 'It is, after all, Shrove Tuesday. Let's feast on an interest we have in common. What can you tell me about Cornish mining in the 1800s?'

George took a pancake, heaped blackcurrant jam on it, rolled it into a wrap and took a bite.

'I'm still burrowing away,' she began, 'but traffic has taken more time than I'd expected. I tried to get an overall picture. If you had access to a mine, copper was certainly something to go for in the nineteenth century. It was early in the industrial revolution, huge advances were being made, many uses for new materials. Copper was a malleable metal and Cornwall was the place to find it.'

'Yes.' Emma nodded. 'I haven't found out yet how Treffry obtained his mines. In the end they were collectively called Par Consols. He didn't inherit full ownership but maybe his family had shares? I'll have to ask Susannah next time I see her.'

'On thing I learned, Emma, was that the world price for copper varied substantially. It went up whenever there was a war and down again in peacetime. Not easy if you ran a copper mine.'

'So it would go up during the Napoleonic Wars?'

'And also, after Treffry's death, in the Crimean War. It was probably most difficult for the smaller mines.'

'Maybe that's how Treffry got hold of them? Bought them when they came onto the market? OK, that's something I'll dig into.'

George dug into a second pancake. 'Another question for your television audience is why Treffry was so spectacularly successful. According to Wikipedia, Par Consols were "the most productive copper mines in Cornwall". That's quite an accolade. So what were his secrets?'

Emma nodded. 'Just the sort of thing I need help on.'

'I haven't got too far yet. He was obviously bright. Engineering at Oxford was a good start: made him systematic, collecting data, analysing the alternatives. That would give him a lead over local mine-owners, continuing the ways of their predecessors. He'd be one of the first to grab new ideas.'

'Hey, George. That goes with an idea from working with the drama group about Treffry's row with Rashleigh. The biggest thing Treffry might have gained from the debate was the notion of building your own harbour.

'One of Treffry's lasting achievements was in generating Par Harbour. That's less photogenic than Charlestown but it's still operating today. I'm going to see it tomorrow.'

'It's a commercial port, Emma. How did you manage that?'

'The subtle power of the BBC. I mentioned the idea to my producer and she pulled various strings.'

CHAPTER 32 Wed February 15th Coombe Farm

Wednesday, her first day in residence at Coombe Farm, gave George a chance to work on findings from the survey so far. Peter was on duty in Fowey. She joined him and the team for lunch and enjoyed the communal chatter.

'You OK, George?' asked Wilson discreetly.

'No worse for our adventure. I've got a historian looking into the Tavern's history. She reckons those chests must have been even older.'

His eyes widened. 'Let me know how it goes.'

In the afternoon the mathematician returned to Coombe Farm by a longer route, past the ruin of St Catherine's Castle, along the cliffs and then back up to the farm. She went back to traffic model building with renewed vigour.

Late in the afternoon Emma rejoined her.

'Par Harbour's an interesting place, George. It's very busy. Commercial boats being loaded or unloaded all day. I've got some good pictures. It's livelier than Charlestown Harbour, anyway. Trouble is, it's nothing like the port Treffry created in the 1820s. Hopeless as a backdrop for a historical drama. The Operations Manager who showed me round was disappointed when I said that.'

George laughed. 'He was hoping for a slot on television.'

'"He", George? Women do have top jobs these days, you know. But she also gave me something more on Treffry. Apparently, he discussed the idea of the harbour with Isambard

Kingdom Brunel, the engineer. Brunel told him it wouldn't work. But Treffry backed his own judgement, went ahead anyway.

'So it was a huge personal success, against conventional wisdom. I'm intending to find out if the two men met again. It might make another subject for my actors to get their teeth into.'

George felt slightly discomfited at her earlier stereotyping but smiled. 'Maybe you'll have more luck with the Par Consol mines tomorrow? If you can find anyone to show you – man or woman. It's my turn on duty in Fowey, I'm afraid, or I'd come with you.'

The name reminded Emma that she had promised to make inquiries from the Land Registry about the Tavern. That took an energetic hour on her laptop. George wondered if she had special access as an academic historian.

'I've got something,' she announced, looking pleased with herself.

'Is it time for tea? I could do with a mug, anyway.'

They sat in the lounge to share. 'Come on, Emma, what've you learned?'

'Well. The building you were skulking about in two nights ago changed its name to the Tavern in 1863. Before that it was a bank. "Fowey Consolidated". I don't know when that started – the Land Registry only began in 1862 – but the two oldest banks in Cornwall opened in Truro in 1771, catering for miners. So the Consolidated might have run from the early 1800s.'

'D'you think Joseph Treffry had a hand in it?'

Emma sipped her tea before replying. 'Well, he was living in Fowey by 1809. At Place. It'd be a long ride with his mines' takings if he had to travel over to Truro.'

'Hey. Would he have seen a bank in Oxford as a student?'

The historian nodded; she'd already checked this. 'He

would. The Old Bank Hotel on Oxford High Street was a draper's shop in 1775 that had become a bank by 1794. Well before Treffry's time there.

'He'd miss that foretaste of civilisation when he came back to Fowey. He might not have had the skills to start a local bank, but I'm sure he'd have supported it. Maybe he was a major shareholder?'

George had a further thought. 'The name "Consolidated" is close to the collective name "Consols" that he gave to his Par mines. Might that suggest a direct link between them?'

There was a short pause. Second mugs of tea were poured.

'There's another question about the Consolidated Bank. Why would it close again? 1863, you said.'

'Mm. Not long after the Crimean War.'

'Not that long since Treffry died either.' George had noted the key dates in the magnate's life, recalled he'd died in 1850.

Emma mused on. 'Maybe without Treffry's business flowing through the bank – or if the copper mines were struggling to make a profit after the Crimean War – the bank's income dried up. It might end up being sold at a knock-down price and the building turned into a pub.'

'Whatever happened, Emma, there'd be no gold left in the cellar. No-one's that stupid. But might there be some of Treffry's papers?'

Her idea grew legs. 'They'd be a lot easier to carry away in small bundles over several visits than all together in a chest. The chests were heavy; I could hardly lift one at all. Especially given there was only one way out of that cellar: up a steep ladder.'

Emma considered. 'I'm planning to see Susannah again later this week. I've already got some of Treffry's journals but I can ask her if there are any more. Or more critically, if she's aware of any documents that are missing.'

'It's very frustrating,' she concluded. 'The documents must have some perceived value. Someone took quite a lot of effort to remove them. Will we ever know what they were?'

CHAPTER 33 Thurs February 16th Par Consols

'D'you know what you're doing today, Emma?' asked George, as they started their porridge.

'I'm visiting some of Treffry's mines. It's taken me long enough to pin down their locations. I started with the names of the mines that became Par Consols: Wheal Treasure, Wheal Fortune and Wheal Chance. Later Lanescot Mine. Then I looked for them on a map from 1860, while they were still operating.'

'Where on earth did you find that?'

The historian smiled. 'The National Museum of Scotland has a website: all the maps ever produced by Ordnance Survey. It'll even let you superpose one on top of another, so you can translate old locations to present-day maps. I've marked them on my Explorer Map. They're a few miles north of Par.'

'And d'you know where the mine buildings are located?'

Emma shook her head. 'Not exactly. For starters, they're spread out. Even knowing where they were supposed to be in 1860 often doesn't correspond to particular buildings today. Buildings don't last forever. All I can do is drive round and visit every spot marked "Shaft (dis)", hope to find something that still makes sense. I want a good background view to talk to.

George considered. 'I hope you'll find one or two, Emma. It'll be hard work producing a tv programme about a Cornish mining supremo without something to demonstrate his efforts.'

'We've always got the man's viaduct, of course. Well above the Par valley.'

But George wasn't giving her cheap comfort. 'Trouble is, you'll need narrative to link the viaduct to the mines. Or at least to Par harbour.'

She considered. 'It'd be a lot easier if your man had built railway lines like Isambard Kingdom Brunel. It's hard to remember, when you look at a map showing the Great Western line from Plymouth to Penzance weaving across it: that wasn't there till years after Treffry's death.'

Emma sighed. 'Today I just want to narrow down the options.' She looked pleadingly at her friend. 'Might you be free to come with me on Saturday, see where I've got to?'

George had to agree. She couldn't refuse a direct call for help. Emma needed serious encouragement.

'It's hard work, you see,' concluded Emma, 'producing a well-illustrated programme on a man who lived two hundred years ago. Even if he was an engineer that built things. Harder than I'd imagined. Right, I'd better be off.'

George set off a short while later. She jogged down the holloway that led into Readymoney Cove then along to the town centre. As she passed her students, she handed out her latest analysis from their questionnaire answers so far and suggested how they might be augmented.

She continued jogging to the Bodinnick ferry to see Wilson and Tommy and told them about their latest thinking on the Tavern cellar.

'The Land Registry has it as the Consolidated Bank in the 1800s. We wondered if that linked it to the Par Consols and hence to Joseph Treffry. My historian friend Emma thinks the chests might have contained some of his later papers.'

She remembered where Wilson was heading if his exams went well and tried to earth her comments. 'Treffry was at

Oxford, you know: Exeter College. Studying engineering. No wonder he was good at managing mines.'

To George's surprise, it turned out Wilson was a budding geologist.

'Cornwall has an interesting geology, George,' he said. Cornish granite has a higher vertical temperature gradient than anywhere else in the UK.'

Then came a further thought. 'If Treffry was numerate, did he collect data on mine temperatures? Did it get hotter as you went down equally fast in all of them? Where did it get hottest fastest?'

George was surprised by his questions but was not out of her depth; she had thought about this sort of topic before.

'You know, Wilson, that's the sort of thing a geothermal energy firm, hoping to pump up hot water from the depths, would give their back teeth for.'

Wilson smiled. She'd given him an open goal. 'So d'you think, George, that these papers in the cellar had been left because they were just full of mine temperature data – data which no-one at the time thought had any lasting value?'

George looked at him in amazement. 'I've not the faintest idea. But it's a smarter idea than anything Emma and I've come up with. The notion that the papers had been abandoned down there for a reason is clever but very plausible. Well done!'

Tommy had been listening to their conversation in silence. But he was following the thread. 'Trouble is, guys, the papers are no longer down there. So will we ever know?'

Tommy's question echoed round George's mind as she continued round her students. The only way they would know for sure was if the person who took the papers was caught. Which was a matter for the police. There might be fingerprints on the chests

– though she recalled, neither she nor Wilson had worn gloves. Should she call Inspector Frances Cober? But as someone who had broken into the Tavern cellar illegally herself, she was hardly in a good position to complain.

Her best hope was if the nature of the missing documents could be gleaned from the material they still had. Either Treffry's journals back in Coombe Farm which Emma had been lent via the BBC, or possibly more evidence from Place. She would need to make sure Emma understood the problem clearly before she visited Susannah tomorrow.

Emma returned to Coombe Farm in late afternoon, looking rather disconsolate. George read her mood, made them both a pot of tea, then encouraged her to sit down and tell her story.

'It's hopeless,' her friend began. 'I've driven round a dozen shafts north of Par, all marked as disused or discontinued. They might as well have been labelled "disappeared".'

George peered at the Explorer map which Emma had laid out on the coffee table. 'Maybe that's what (dis) stands for?'

Emma snorted. 'If they'd disappeared, George, there would be no mark on the map at all. There was something. But it was hardly impressive. A few holes in the ground. You wouldn't think this was the hub of Cornish copper mining in the nineteenth century.'

She drank some tea before continuing.

'The only impressive thing I've found today is Treffry's viaduct up near Luxulyan. A hundred feet up and six hundred feet across. I've taken plenty of pictures there. Even got one with the Newquay train as it ran underneath. I read all the tourist notices as well.

'Was this an early railway line?'

Emma shook her head. 'Too early. Treffry was into horse-drawn trams. In one direction the track ran into Luxulyan, the other way was a gentle slope down to the Par valley.'

George looked on the map. 'But I can't see any mine in Luxulyan. What on earth was it collecting?'

'No, it wasn't collecting. It was a forerunner of the line to Newquay. He got it as far as Bugle. Treffry had the vision for a line right across the county, from Par and all his copper mines to the Cornish north coast. It's quite a vision for 1830: the man certainly thought big. But he died before it was finished.'

George considered for a moment. 'It's a strategic response to the challenge of selling his copper ore. All of it needed to go for smelting in South Wales – they had no copper but plenty of coal. If the boat trip was only across from Newquay to Swansea that would be much easier than having to sail round Land's End.'

CHAPTER 34 Fri February 17th Place

On Friday Susannah was looking forward to seeing Emma again. The encounter would even extend over lunch. How much progress might the historian have made in the past week?

Once more the women began their conversation with coffee in the Place lounge.

'I'm quite a lot further on with Charles Rashleigh,' Emma began. She told Susannah about her visit to Charlestown Harbour and her later encounter with the St Austell drama group. 'I reckon it was quite likely that it was Rashleigh who inspired Treffry to build a harbour of his own. So I've spent a whole day in Par Harbour.'

'Wow. Well done, Emma. I've never been in there.'

'Trouble is, it's completely changed since Treffry's day. It's a modern commercial port. I'll struggle to relate it back to Treffry's pioneering. I'm struggling even more, though, on Treffry's mining adventures. I spent yesterday trying to find any worthwhile remains of Par Consols on the ground. Every marked shaft on my Explorer map was completely abandoned.'

She stopped to see if Susannah had anything useful to add but there was only silence. More prompting was needed.

'I wondered if there were any more Treffry papers left here about his activities?'

'You've got his journals?'

'Those are fine for his early years – from Oxford up to 1830. But in the 1830s Par Consols were reputed to be the most productive copper mines in Cornwall. It would be really good to share with BBC viewers some of the man's secrets. How did he do so well? What makes one set of mines more efficient than all the rest? It couldn't just be luck with the geology, surely?'

Susannah paused for a moment. Her instinct for family protection battled against a desire to be helpful to a new friend.

'Why don't I show you the old Place study, Emma. You might make more sense of the documents in there than the family ever have.'

The study was upstairs and had been used by generations of Treffrys. Emma reminded herself that it wasn't Joseph's sole domain; the family had lived here for centuries. It included a desk that was old enough for Shakespeare close to one wall, and a huge antique bookshelf, with all kinds of books, from reference volumes to Jane Austen, against the other. Between them was a window looking out across the estate, which probably hadn't been opened for decades.

But Joseph was the first Treffry to have gone to Oxford; and to have had the chance to develop any taste for academic writings. Half of one shelf of the tall bookcase was occupied with papers from the early nineteenth century. These were concerned mostly with systematic mining methods, as studied by universities across Europe. It was a good job Emma's academic familiarity allowed her to skim them quickly; there would be enough there to source a whole PhD.

But what she really wanted was not what Joseph read but what he did.

Maybe he had marked the ideas that he could try in Par Consols? Or pencilled questions alongside key passages?

Emma seized the bundle of papers and pulled them out for a closer inspection.

But it was a fruitless trawl. Treffry had obviously been well-taught by the dons at Oxford: "never scrawl on published papers". They'd been carefully read, though. The occasional page was crumpled or even dog-eared.

It was after half an hour's frustrating browsing, when a disappointed Emma went to put them back, that she made an observation. There was something tucked away on the shelf behind them.

A fat, leather-bound notebook. Full of Treffry's own scrawls. She recognised the handwriting from his journals.

No time to read it now. It was almost lunch time. Emma seized Treffry's notebook and hastened downstairs.

Susannah had some home-made soup almost ready to consume. The table was laid, with cheese, baguettes and fruit to follow.

'One question that came up from the drama group,' said Emma, plunging in as they started their soup, 'is whether Joseph Treffry had any particular lady friends? Or even one or two selected female servants that he would take with him when he needed a companion?'

Susannah didn't reply so she hastened on. 'I could find no mention of anyone in his journals.'

They both supped more soup as the question hovered.

'There was no mention of a wife or descendants in his will, Emma, so I don't think he ever married. I doubt you'll find anything written down about an affair. People were much more private about their lives two hundred years ago. The media was far more pliable.'

Emma remained silent, hoping her new friend might add more.

'We never had many staff inside the house,' Susannah mused. 'Plenty of gardeners, of course, but they were all men, working on the estate.'

Another pause. Then she went on. 'I've no rumours to share, I'm afraid. Nothing's been handed down. But the most likely family to consort with round here would have been the Rashleighs, over in Menabilly.'

More encouragement might help her ideas. 'I believe Charles was the tenth child of his generation?'

Susannah nodded. 'That's right. He had three older sisters.'

'Trouble is, Charles was already thirty-five years older than Joseph. His older sisters would be far too old for a handsome young man from Oxford.'

'But there'd be another generation. Surely there'd be someone?'

'I can investigate,' promised Emma. 'Thanks for the idea, anyway. By the way, this soup is really delicious.'

For a while they ate, simply enjoying one another's company. But Emma wanted to make the most of the opportunity.

'Have you any idea where Joseph Treffry banked?'

Susannah smiled. 'That level of detail hasn't made the family archives, I'm afraid.'

Perhaps it was time to share a little of the Fowey Consolidated.

'You know the building that's being knocked down, next to Fowey's car park?'

'You mean, the old Tavern?'

'That's right. Well, I looked it up via the Land Registry. It was once the Consolidated Bank. The first bank in Fowey.'

Now Susannah was quick to respond. 'Joseph strongly supported local ventures. In his will he left half his wealth to the local church in Fowey. I'm sure he would have encouraged a bank here, been a major shareholder. Better than risking sending someone over to Truro every month. No internet banking in those days.'

Emma reckoned that was as far as she was going to get. They moved onto the cheese.

'There's one more point than that's come up in my searching. Apparently, Joseph once had an argument with Isambard Kingdom Brunel over his proposed harbour in Par. Are there any more contacts between them held in the family memory? Or is there anyone else famous that he's known to have conversed with? It'd all help give my programme a wider appeal, you see.'

Susannah helped herself to some Cathedral Mature Cheddar before replying.

'Brunel was close to being a contemporary. I'm sure they'd have had one or two debates about the railway line from Lostwithiel to Truro. That wasn't built till the 1850s, you know.' She munched some of the cheese and then went on, 'Would you consider Queen Victoria famous enough? She came by boat to visit Fowey in 1846, with Prince Albert. They landed on what's now called the Albert Pier. The pair had just been to visit Guernsey. I think it was her first visit to Cornwall – I mean, the Queen was only in her mid-twenties.'

'And you're sure Treffry met her?'

'He welcomed her to Fowey; or maybe, even, Par Consols. Would that be a famous enough contact for you?

CHAPTER 35 Fri February 17th Fowey & Coombe Farm

Friday was the final day of the Fowey Traffic Survey. Peter Jakes was on duty but George wanted to be around as well, to say thank you individually to her young helpers. She might one day be glad of their help again.

She went carefully round every pair of students, making sure she had noted their own observations on what they'd seen over the week. And their ideas on what might be changed.

There was plenty she had never thought of. The possibility of a cycle park at the top of the town, along the lines of the "Boris Bikes" in London, was raised. Would that make a fun twist for visiting families in high season? Would it enhance Fowey's popularity over other coastal towns? The scheme would need a more gently sloping cycle path back to the top of the hill than was achieved by the main road; but how hard was that to fashion?

Another idea was a free "park and walk" car park on the edge of the town. Or maybe, like Port Isaac, they could close the town to all cars except for local residents? Plenty more for George to work on once the main survey was completed.

Lunch in the town centre café for the whole team was a riotous occasion. It also gave Peter a few minutes to talk quietly with George.

'George, would you like to come for supper in Polkerris, to-morrow evening?'

'I'd love to, Peter. As long as we don't talk about surveys.

The only thing is, I moved in this week with my historian friend, Emma. She's working on a programme for the BBC on Joseph Treffry. Staying up at Coombe Farm.'

'Bring her as well, George. I'd love to meet her.'

George stood up to address the team before they went back to their last afternoon's surveying.

'You've been a great team. I'd like to say thank you properly. So I'm inviting you all to a cream tea at the Ship Inn. Five o'clock today.'

She gathered from their reactions that it was a popular invitation.

The Ship Inn was happy to oblige and provided a private room rear for the occasion. There'd been no great boost to tourist numbers in Fowey during the holiday week.

George phoned Emma to see if she would like to join them for the tea. There was always the chance the students could add to her knowledge of the Treffry family.

To her surprise Isobel was also there. Wilson had invited her and she'd cycled in from Golant. The pair quickly latched on to Emma. Was Wilson passing on some geological insights?

Or were the pair quizzing her on the contents of the cellar below the old Tavern?

George moved from table to table, listening to the chatter and adding an occasional comment of her own. She found herself committing to come back to the school to present the results of the survey. It was good to be wanted. Perhaps she could do more of these student liaisons across Cornwall? She could certainly add practical insights to the academic teaching.

Once she reached the table with Wilson, Isobel and Emma, George found that Wilson had dragged them from details of a dark cellar into a conversation about variation in underground temperatures.

'Because of its turbulent geology, Cornwall has a much higher underground temperature gradient than the rest of the country,' declared the young man. 'The average rise across the UK is a gain of 26°C per kilometre of increased depth; in Cornwall it's 40°C, even more in some places. It was highest, I think, where the mines were the most productive.'

'Trouble is, you'd need to dig the mine before you had the data.' George knew prospecting wasn't that simple.

'How d'you mean?' asked Isobel.

'We can measure all sorts of things today that we could never do before. Satellite phones, for example, allow us to pinpoint exactly where we are. Even give us an elevation. But even today, with all these instruments, you can't measure temperature at a particular depth unless you have a mine or bore hole that gives you access down there.' George had thought long and hard about data capture.

A pause as the problem was considered.

'Right. So how long have there been thermometers?' asked Isobel.

'Celsius was an inventor in the eighteenth century,' observed Emma. 'He came up with the idea of degrees centigrade. The instruments would certainly be around in Treffry's day.'

'And Treffry was at Oxford,' recalled George, glancing across at Wilson. 'He'd be into measurement. I'm sure he would have used them down his mines to track temperatures.'

'Did each mine have just the one shaft?' asked Isobel.

Emma could help here. 'I spent all yesterday visiting them. Most Par Consols had several shafts. It's a lot safer that way, of course.'

Isobel continued to follow the thread.

'So you would have regular readings from different depths

from two adjacent shafts,' she observed thoughtfully. 'In that case, could you estimate the temperatures at the places between the two?'

'You could. And even beyond,' replied George. 'You'd have to allow for differences in shaft elevation, of course. It'd be a rough and ready calculation. But it would suggest the best direction to progress along: where should you sink the next shaft?'

Emma and George didn't need a massive meal once they were back at Coombe Farm. The cream tea had been filling.

As they relaxed over another pot of tea, Emma told her friend the various things she had learned from Susannah at Place.

'She had no juicy rumours about Treffry or his links to any local girls. She suggested that if he was looking for a companion, he would most likely have taken someone from the wider Rashleigh family. They are the other renowned family in Fowey.'

George pondered the Rashleigh's family tree. 'You mean, one of Charles Rashleigh's nieces?'

'Yes. I suppose they would be.'

'That wouldn't have gone down well with Charles, Emma. Make their age difference seem even worse. No wonder he refused Treffry permission to take copper ore across his land.'

'Maybe.' Emma got up to pour their mugs of tea. What else had she learned?

'Susannah also told me about Treffry's meeting with Brunel. I'm going to find out if the two met again. If they did, that'd be a meeting of engineering giants. I could get the drama group to work on that.'

She drank some tea. 'I also told her about the Consolidated Bank. She thought that if the Consolidated started in Fowey, Treffry would certainly have backed it. He approved of local enterprise.'

Finally, she moved on to how she found the hidden notebook behind a bundle of academic papers. 'Susannah said I could borrow it for a few days, but she'd want it back.' She handed it across to George.

George was keen to make sense of the new tabulated data which appeared on many of the pages. The trouble was the book was almost unreadable without her friend's help.

'Can you decipher it for me, please?'

Emma seized it back and browsed for a few moments. 'A lot of it is technical details on Par Consols. The broad location of each shaft, the way the steam engines were deployed to stop them flooding and the direction of each tunnel which led away from the shaft. Also the way the copper ore was taken away down to Par Harbour. That involved both a tram ride and a trip on the Par Canal – he built that too, you know.'

'Can you make any sense of the tables of numbers?'

Emma browsed for even longer.

'Treffry didn't bother to mark the heading on each column.'

'Maybe because they were all the same? Is there more detail on the first one?'

Emma flipped back the pages.

'You know, there is. For each given shaft, these are all observed temperatures at different depths. Values recorded every week. Hey, isn't that the kind of thing we were talking about this afternoon?'

CHAPTER 36 Sat February 18th Par Consols

Saturday morning. George had already undertaken to go round the nearby disused Par Consols shafts with Emma, make sure she wasn't missing anything. Now, though, there was an extra motivation.

George wasn't just helping her friend look for the most striking camera angles on Treffry's extensive empire. She would use her phone to pinpoint each shaft's exact location, including its altitude. It wasn't worth doing any more with the temperature data in Treffry's hidden notebook until they were sure of each shaft's location.

The National grid reference system was introduced in 1936; it didn't exist in Treffry's day. In his notebook he had used the original names of the mines which were now grouped together as Par Consols, then added N, E, S or W to distinguish individual shafts.

Now the women had to work from Emma's download of the 1860s one-inch Ordnance Survey map which she had found on the internet, to categorise the shafts by their original names.

Lanescot was a small hilltop village on the modern Explorer map, so it was relatively easy to group together its nearby shafts.

Penpillick, a small hamlet, was another name which Emma had seen in Treffry's journals. That was also close to a couple of shafts. The village of Porcupine had another.

It took longer to narrow down Wheal Treasure, Wheal Fortune and Wheal Chance. They were sprawls on the 1860 map.

Some of the shafts marked on the Explorer map were well away from any road and involved tramping over muddy fields. Was this shaft Wheal Treasure South or Wheal Chance East? Sometimes they couldn't be certain.

One thing which George noticed, which Emma hadn't picked up before, was how close each shaft was to being absolutely vertical. They went straight down as far as the eye could see. George would take a small stone, reach out as far as she could over the hole and drop it. Time and again they heard no sound of it hitting a side.

'That supports our notion that Treffry was a precise and tidy man. Not slapdash in any way. A professional engineer.'

The Wheal Chance shafts were quite high up. From a few places they could see a long way, across the vale and up the wooded Par Valley. Then they heard the noise of a train, chugging steadily up the valley below.

George glanced at her map. 'That's not the main Great Western line to Truro. It's the one heading from Par, village by village, over to Newquay.

'Emma, it would be worth taking a camera crew for a trip on that train. It wasn't there in Treffry's time, but it was a route he was hoping to pioneer. You could explain that as you travelled: Newquay was closer to the copper-ore smelters in Swansea. It illustrates his vision. Getting the copper ore out of the ground was only the start of a long journey to help it yield a profit.

'You'd need to be ready for it, but you might also get an interesting angle from below of Treffry's famous viaduct. That's not far from here. It's hidden in those trees.'

By late morning they had visited every marked shaft and assigned each one to one or other of the shafts listed in Treffry's notebook.

They returned to Coombe Farm for lunch. George also needed desk space to work on.

As a starting point, the mathematician assumed that Treffry would have no access to accurate altitude data. He would simply be measuring the depth of each shaft from its point of access. He could do that with a long tape measure.

She took a spreadsheet and marked separate columns for each shaft, arranging them in geographical order so they ran from south to north.

Next, she looked more carefully at the data in Treffry's notebook. Many measurements had been taken for each location, perhaps over many years. But the values didn't vary much. They became steadier as they went deeper. Outside temperature had no effect for any depths below 25 metres.

Then she entered the average mid-winter temperature at each measured depth for the shaft, on the various rows below.

She carefully repeated the process for each of the other shafts. Then stopped for a break and a mug of coffee.

After that she examined the spreadsheet carefully. The temperatures rose steadily for each shaft as the hole got deeper.

They also seemed to be rising at a faster rate on the shafts located further north.

George recalled Isobel's question the day before: could shaft temperature data be extrapolated over two or more shafts? Might Joseph Treffry have had the same idea?

If you were going to sink another shaft, on the data she had before her – which, she remembered, Treffry had even copied laboriously into his notebook – where might you sink it?

Was it remotely possible that there were any more copper mine shafts on the hills nearby, which he had chosen directly? Was there even another mine – maybe a highly productive mine

- which had never made it onto the maps of the time?

What a breakthrough if she and Emma were able to find it. It would be a fantastic boost for the television programme.

It would be interesting, thought George, to feed the data into a three-dimensional mathematic model to fit the best estimate of temperature contours. That was the sort of thing that might be invaluable to a modern mining engineer, help him to plan for geothermal bore holes or even lithium mining. It was hard to imagine there was a more thorough collection of temperature data anywhere else in Cornwall.

But of course Treffry was working with pencil and paper, he didn't even have a calculator. Where might he have chosen?

George sought a large sheet of plain paper from her friend and drew ten-kilometre squares across it. Then she used the squares to identify grid-reference for each shaft they had visited that morning.

Very faintly she started drawing lines between the shafts which extended beyond the area they had visited. It ended up a complete mess. Treffry must have done better than that.

Now she picked out the lines which joined adjacent shafts where the temperature gain from one to the other had changed most rapidly. This was the best sign she had of increasing underground temperature.

This time she found that several of the lines roughly converged on a hilltop further north. A minor road ran along it which had started from Lostwithiel and ended up in Par. The nearest hamlet was called Milltown.

But that might fit. Presumably this road had been some sort of track two hundred years ago? If you were going to sink a brand new mine, you might as well start it close to a road of some sort. It would be easier to take the ore away - assuming you found any.

George spent another couple of hours fiddling around with different ideas. But the location she had found first kept coming up. She couldn't be certain that she was repeating Treffry's calculations. But the place might just be worth a visit.

CHAPTER 37 Sat February 18th Polkerris

George had once more put on her mid-blue dress for the meal with Peter Jakes. This time she also wore her chunky necklace. It was the only smart gear she had in Fowey. Emma had a wider choice and put on a cherry blouse and a cream skirt. The pair made a colourful combination.

George drove them up the lane to the edge of Fowey and then round a minor road to Polkerris. She gave Emma a smattering of Peter's back story as they drove.

His bungalow looked out over the St Austell Bay. He'd be able to look out on to Par harbour or Charlestown.

'Welcome, ladies,' he said, as he opened the door. He was wearing a Norwegian sweater. 'I'm pleased to meet you, Emma. I'm Peter, I teach sixth form maths in Fowey. That was how George and I met.'

He led them into the lounge. The large bay window would have offered a splendid view across the Bay if it hadn't been a cloudy, starless night. They could just make out the lights of St Austell.

'What would you like to drink? Tea or coffee, or a glass of wine?' White wine was the preferred choice.

Emma wondered if the evening was going to soar; she was the extra guest so set out to make herself known.

'I come from Truro,' she began. 'I'm in the Cornish History Unit. Has George told you? I'm in Fowey preparing a programme for the BBC about Joseph Treffry.'

'She's a Cornish variant of Lucy Worsley,' explained

George.

It took Peter a second to make the connection, then he smiled. 'I do like Ms Worsley's histories. Will you also have a few actors?'

'I'm hoping to. I've been to see StormBox in St Austell. They're keen to help me. The problem is, there is less written about Treffry than about the Royals which Lucy presents. It's a good story but a struggle to turn it into gripping television.'

'Treffry's an interesting character,' replied Peter. 'We studied him at primary school, here in Fowey. That's a long time ago. Mind, our teacher still lives in Fowey. I could introduce you to her if you liked?'

Emma nodded. 'That would be great, Peter. The only local expert I've spent much time with so far is Susannah Treffry.'

'Susannah! I was at school with her. She's a sharp cookie. Make sure you handle her wisely. If she's on your side she'll interview really well, enliven your programme. Add a touch of Cornish class.'

They continued talking on Fowey experts for a few minutes, then Peter noticed the time.

'The meal should be ready by half seven. Would you excuse me? I'm not very practiced at cooking for guests.'

George and Emma had no idea on what was to come when they were led into the dining room. Peter had obviously worked hard on making a good impression but it was not an effortless performance.

'We'll begin with honeydew melon with a cherry and ginger. I'm sorry, I should have asked about allergies: is that OK? Then I've got slow-cooked venison for the main course, with roast potatoes and vegetables.'

A sudden anxiety assailed him. 'I hope you're not vegetarian or anything, Emma? I know George isn't, she tucked into lamb's shank a week ago.'

'Peter, that sounds delicious. What a pleasure to be invited out. Thank you.'

There was a pause as they started their melons.

'I hope you don't feel too left out, Emma,' murmured George, as Peter disappeared in the kitchen to fetch the main items. Emma suddenly realised how much she'd been monopolising the conversation. Was there a topic they all had a stake in?

Peter returned with the venison casserole. Two more trips brought hot plates and roast vegetables.

'Please, help yourselves ladies.'

'Why don't you serve us the venison, Peter?' suggested George. 'This is as good as the Fisherman's Arms.'

He beamed and they started on the main course.

'Peter, d'you know anything about relations between the Treffrys and the Rashleighs?' asked Emma.

He mused. 'They are not exactly rivals, just opposite ends of the upper social class. Not as close as you might expect. The Rashleighs have always dabbled in politics. Lots of them became the town's Member of Parliament over the centuries, spent half their time in London. They were strongly Royalist in the Civil War.'

'Whereas the Treffry's . . .?'

'Were – are – more down to earth. Just kept their heads down. But they've got the more impressive Manor, as you'll have seen. They are probably a lot wealthier. Having a successful entrepreneur like Joseph in the family must have helped.'

Emma shook her head. 'I've not managed to get to Menabilly yet. Even though it's not far from where I'm staying in Coombe Farm.'

He smiled. 'I pass it on my regular walk around Gribbin Head. You could join me if you liked.'

'Peter, is there any more venison?' asked George. She was feeling ever so slightly isolated.

'So what have you both been doing today?' asked Peter, as they reached the lull between courses. He hadn't yet revealed what dessert was waiting in the kitchen.

'We tried to go to some of Treffry's mine shafts: Par Consols. But there's nothing to see now. Just holes in the ground. That's what I mean about Treffry not being photogenic.'

George seized her chance. 'Then I tried relating them to the notebook which Emma found in Treffry's study, over in Place.'

'Oh yes. It was hidden behind lots of academic papers from the nineteenth century. Susannah let me borrow it.'

'That sounds intriguing,' observed Peter. 'Replaying its discovery, after a couple of centuries, would surely make good television viewing? What was in it?'

George was itching to say more. 'There were masses of temperature data from down each shaft, at various depths –'

'– even I could see it was getting warmer as you went down.'

'So I've spent the afternoon trying to extrapolate the data. In which direction was the gradient steepest? If Treffry was using all this data to guess the best place to sink a fresh mine, where might he have chosen?'

Peter appreciated the way George was making a complicated calculation sound very simple. He was also a mathematician and would have loved to spend longer on how Treffry might conduct three-dimensional geometry in pre-Victorian times. But he didn't want to leave out the historian.

'And can you tell me the location you identified?'

'It's well above Par, up towards Lostwithiel. Emma and I are hoping to go there tomorrow.'

'An undiscovered Treffry mine would certainly add to your television programme, Emma. Right, shall we have our dessert?'

A brown-sugar pavlova appeared, with a layer of double cream and a pattern of mixed berries.

'It's too much bother making this just for one, but with three of us we can make a dent in it. I hope you both like cream?'

The dessert was too scrumptious to allow conversation for a few minutes. Peter seemed to have a rather exaggerated view of portion size, but it would be impolite to complain.

'So, Treffry was a man of mystery after all,' Peter suggested. 'Might this be related to those findings you mentioned in the Tavern cellar?'

'I found that the Tavern used to be the Consolidated Bank. That must have begun in the early nineteenth century. Susannah told me Treffry had been a strong supporter of local enterprise. He might have opened the place himself.'

George was slightly fed up of her friend doing all the talking. 'So if there had been papers left in the cellar, Peter, they might well have been his.'

Peter paused for thought. 'So there might be a second mystery. Trouble is, the two are in conflict.'

'How d'you mean?'

'If someone had removed valuable Treffry papers from the cellar, they couldn't be the items that Emma found in his study. That must have been a different secret altogether.'

CHAPTER 38 Sun February 19th A well above Par

It was midnight before the two women returned to Coombe Farm. Somehow, they had started to tell Peter the tale of how they had first met, three years ago, near to the start of the Covid pandemic.

Once again Emma's various contributions, culminating in her solo trip to the cemetery on Land's End, and later the macabre discovery of her Unit's boss, dead in his own flat, took a significant chunk of the time. George's long habit of keeping quiet on her work findings played against her. But overall it made for a cheerful evening. They wouldn't be setting off anywhere early next morning.

'We can't use satnav for this one,' said George as they got into her car. 'No postcode. We don't know if there's anything there at all. We might end up tramping the surrounding fields. But I think it's worth a look. If Treffry did want to expand his activities, a better located new mine would be a clever way to do so.'

Emma nodded. 'Yes. The three mines he took over which became Par Consols were all in place before Treffry had even started. He could well have had an itch to start somewhere else. He had a strong sense of adventure, didn't he?'

'He certainly liked to leave his mark. You and I know that. But what you need, Emma, is visual evidence that will impress the viewers.'

It didn't take them long to drive into Fowey then out on the road towards Lostwithiel. It was a grey morning, low cloud and a gusty wind, but at least it wasn't raining.

Five miles along, at the top of a long hill, they came within sight of Lostwithiel. The road behind them was free of traffic and there was no problem in George driving along slowly.

'On my extrapolation, Emma, it should be somewhere around here.'

There was nothing that looked like an abandoned copper mine. All they could see was a lonely off-road farm house.

'Why don't we ask at the farm?' suggested Emma.

Being so isolated was possibly what made the owners more willing than usual to welcome visitors. George had pondered how on earth she could phrase their aims and why on earth they were here at all but Emma wasn't bothered. A remit from the BBC was a passport to all sorts of places in the UK.

Their knock was answered anyway. There was someone in.

'Good morning. I'm Emma Eastham, from Exeter University; this is my colleague, George Gilbert. Could you help us by answering a few questions? It's for a BBC programme I'm trying to make.'

The owner smiled. 'That sounds interesting. I'm Oliver and my wife is called Debbie. Would you like to come in for a few minutes? It's a cold day. I'm afraid we get plenty of wind up here.' They followed him into a sizeable kitchen.

'Debbie,' he called. 'We've got some more visitors.'

His wife appeared and the visitors introduced themselves. 'Would you both like some coffee?' she asked.

They seated themselves around the kitchen table as Debbie bustled to prepare the drinks, Emma musing on possible opening lines.

But to their surprise, once the drinks had arrived, it was the farmer who began the dialogue.

'You two are the third visitors we've had here recently. After months of not seeing anyone. Are you Alex Price groupies as well?'

'I'm sorry,' replied George. 'I have no idea what you're talking about. We're here about something else altogether.'

But Oliver wanted to be sure. He went to the mantelpiece and returned holding a business card. 'This was our last visitor. Yesterday. He came on a bike. D'you know him?'

George glanced at the card. "Mark Renfrew", it said. "Kernow Lithium Mining, Bugle; Security Manager". There was a mobile number, but it wasn't one she had ever used.

'Yes, I know Mark,' she replied, trying to hide her surprise. 'We used to share a house on the North Cornwall coast. A sturdy chap with unkempt hair, about my age. Was he on his own?'

This time Debbie was the one to answer. 'Oh no. He had a lady friend with him. Another cyclist, she was in full cycling gear - shorts and all the rest. I'm afraid she looked rather cold.'

'Well, what a coincidence. He's moved on a long way since we were last in touch. So who's Alex Price?'

Oliver was about to tell them it was none of their business but Debbie got in first; she was glad to talk to anyone.

'Alex is another employee of KLM. But he hasn't been seen in the office for several weeks. Mark and Naomi were hoping to find him. They were excited to find somewhere that he'd recently been.'

'Could you tell them anything more?'

'They wanted to cover the same ground with us as Alex had. Which, for some reason, was my family tree. Eventually we traced it back for about five generations. I couldn't understand why, I'm afraid.'

She paused for breath and Oliver broke in. 'I'm sure our

visitors don't want to know all about your predecessors, Debbie.'

He turned back to Emma. 'So what exactly do you two want? How might we help you? Take your time, we're not busy at present.'

Emma started. She explained how she came to be preparing a programme for the BBC on a nineteenth century entrepreneur called Joseph Treffry, who came from Fowey. 'He ran copper mines, you see. Allegedly the most productive ones in Cornwall. I've just spent several days wandering round the Par Consol shafts; they're all abandoned now, of course.'

George took over. 'During her research, Emma came across a Treffry notebook with masses of temperature data from each of these shafts. I'm a mathematician. So I used them to project the best place to sink a new mine, if you were wanting to get down to the hotter rocks more quickly. And my calculations suggested that the most promising place would be somewhere around here.'

She stopped and looked at Oliver and Debbie. Had she struck a chord?

'Debbie, could we have more coffee, please? I've a feeling this might take us some time.' The owner said no more till they were all settled again, with replenished mugs in front of them.

'Thank you. This is the most arresting visit I think Debbie and I have ever had. Even better than Alex Price. And completely out of the blue. But now you've spoken, it does start to ring several bells.

'The notion that this farm might one day have been a copper mine is completely new to us. But I've only been here for a decade. The previous owner was here for half a century. They didn't sell it to us as a mine either.'

Debbie broke in. 'In fact, the last owner only came to own it because he married the woman who already lived here. It was her family that had been here for generations.'

Oliver took over again. 'Over the last ten years we've thrown out a lot of old junk. The outhouses were full of stuff, most of it made no sense at all. It took dozens of trips to the tip in Lostwithiel to get rid of it. Then we rebuilt most of the buildings, they looked like they'd been here for centuries.'

There was a pause. Then Emma asked the key question. 'But is there anything left that looks like the remains of a copper mine?'

Oliver and Debbie looked at one another. 'There's always the old well, I suppose.'

PART 6

February 19th - 24th

Contention

CHAPTER 39 Sun February 19th - 22nd KLM

I couldn't do any more about the still-missing Alex Price for a few days. I was busy, moving into my flat in Luxulyan.

Naomi offered to help me move but I wanted to own the place for myself, decide where everything would best fit, before I shared anything with anybody. Though I reflected, there was another car-full of my possessions in the cottage in Treknow that I still needed to collect.

In any case, Naomi and I were both worn out by the search on our non-electric bikes, visiting the places marked on the clear plastic sheet the day before. I wasn't yet ready to restore direct contact with George. My old phone was switched off, hidden in my bedside drawer. Fortunately my former housemate wouldn't have my new office number.

I tottered into the KLM office on Monday morning. To my surprise Naomi was not on the train. Maybe she was exhausted too?

'No sign of Alex, I presume?' I asked, as I checked in.

Sandra gave one of her trademark smiles and shook her head. There was no sense of anxiety. Did no-one miss this man? Or had he tried to make a pass at all of them?

Saturday had at least given me several addresses where Alex had been seen in the last few weeks. I wandered round the office, seeing if any were familiar to other staff. But no-one could make sense of any of them.

Then I thought of Phil Williams, over in the lab. He was the only person I'd come across in KLM who was declared (if only by Fiona) to being Alex's friend.

No doubt he was busy on some research idea or other to detect even fainter traces of lithium. But he couldn't object to a brief face-to-face chat about a colleague. I caught him in the lab coffee break.

He, too, was baffled by the addresses I showed him. Fiona was around too and inspected my search map from a geological viewpoint.

'None of them are close to any China Clay spoil tips, Mark. Or even old mines. Did you pick up whether Alex was there on a weekday; or was it a private jaunt at a weekend?'

'Mm. I can't be sure. I had the impression they all came at weekends – not that long ago, mind.'

Fiona mused for a moment. 'I'd say, they would most likely be the addresses he was calling on, rather than broad locations. But what they might have in common – who he was searching for – is anyone's guess. You don't have any more places to try?'

I shook my head. Tried to replay as many of Saturday's brief doorstep conversations as I could. The trouble was my main focus had been on Alex Price and whether the owners had ever met him. Even that was uncertain when I started out. Then I remembered a name.

'There was a Mr Dingley from Bingley,' I recalled. 'A refugee from the barren north.'

Fiona smiled. 'With an accent to boot?' Pause. 'But was Alex put off by the Bingley or the Dingley?'

I frowned. 'Both, I should think. He was certainly a larger-than-life character. Hadn't been in Cornwall for long.'

'The name Dingley isn't common in this part of Cornwall, Mark. Might the St Austell Council be able to tell you more?'

It was an idea. I could go to St Austell after lunch. Then I decided it would be better if I used the time to fetch the rest of my possessions from George's cottage in Treknow. George might be at home, of course. But she was often away on one of her projects, so there was a good chance I'd miss her.

As I did. The cottage didn't look like it had been lived in for a couple of weeks. It no longer felt like my home: I was moving on. I spent an hour stuffing all that was definitely mine into my car. Then I wrote a short note to George. I explained that I was happy and well and had found a worthwhile new job. I would be in touch in due course, but I'd left my house keys behind; I wouldn't be needing them again.

Then, a little sadly, I set off back for Luxulyan. At least, now, I'd be able to cook for myself. I was gradually settling into my new identity.

On Tuesday morning I took the car and headed directly for the Council offices in St Austell.

Once I was there, I realised I wasn't quite sure who I should approach. But there was an information desk in the foyer and I joined the queue. It took a while to reach the earnest looking woman behind the counter. I'd been trying to clarify my question as I waited but it didn't sound that slick when I voiced it.

'Does the Council have a record of people called "Dingley" on its database?'

'It might do, sir. What d'you want to know?'

There was hard logic behind my question but you'd need half an hour to explain it convincingly. And there was a growing queue behind me.

'I've got a list of Dingleys,' I said. I want to know if I have the lot.'

'I'm afraid sir, we can't pass on the names of our customers to an outsider – that'd be against the law.'

'Could you tell me how many names you have?'

She shook her head. 'Can't, sir. Data protection, you know.'

I sighed and turned away. And at that point my luck turned. For I recognised someone in the queue behind me. A police officer I had once worked with in Truro, called Frances. More to the point, she recognised me.

'Hey, Marcus. What are you doing these days?'

'Frances. I'm fine. Just got a job as Security Manager with the Kernow Lithium Mining, based in Bugle.'

'Why don't we go for a coffee? I'm still finding my way round St Austell. I started as Inspector here yesterday.'

Frances and I had always got on well, though I knew her in a time when my memory was highly deficient. Hence the misuse of "Marcus". In those days I was Marcus Tredwell.

But was this an opportunity to share my anxieties with a serious police officer? It was the best I was likely to get.

'I joined KLM two weeks ago,' I began. Nobody but me seems to care, but a senior member of their staff, one Alex Price, is missing. He hasn't been in the office for weeks. I've taken it over until my own is ready.'

Frances eyes lit up. 'Keep talking, Marcus, or whatever you're now called.'

So I did. Told her of the clear plastic sheet hidden in Alex's desk, which I'd decoded into locations north of St Austell and visited last weekend. My strong suspicion that Alex had been there before me. Hence my attempt to get more data on the Dingleys from the Council, which had just failed.

'So have KLM reported this to the police?'

'I'm afraid not. Apparently Alex has been given license to roam. They've just asked me to investigate it privately.'

Frances nodded slowly. 'Well, I'm glad you've told me. One thing you could do would be to revisit all the locations, check that Dingley was always the key person Alex was after, and what that was linked to. Here's my card. I'd be very grateful if you kept me informed.'

CHAPTER 40 Sun February 19th The well above Par

It was Emma who insisted on inspecting the well which Oliver and Debbie had spoken of.

It was at the far end of the farmyard. Behind a sturdily locked fence. The Frobishers weren't going to allow in casual visitors, anyway.

All four had put on their coats before venturing outside. It was bitterly cold, the northerly wind was still howling across the hilltop.

Oliver produced a key, opened the gateway and they saw it. If it was a well it was an extremely wide one – the hole was three metres across, with a waist-high brick wall around it. It had a wooden cover.

'Is it possible to see down the well?' asked George.

It certainly wouldn't be easy to get the cover off. If they hadn't already struck a rapport with the Frobishers over coffee in the kitchen, it might never have happened.

'It's never been off since some mates and I put it on there,' said Oliver. 'I made the thing myself. It's never been inspected by anyone. My aim was simply to make sure no-one fell down the hole.'

The four positioned themselves at equal intervals around the cover and braced their feet. Then Oliver gave the order.

'Lift.'

It was heavy to raise up, awkward but not impossible. Slowly they kept either side of the well and walked the cover off the brickwork towards some waste ground further along. Then, gingerly, they walked back to the hole in the ground and peered down into the blackness.

'D'you remember, Oliver, there was an old ladder here when we first came? But you took it out, said it was "too much of a temptation".'

'So you've no idea how far down this goes?' asked George. 'Would you mind if we dropped a stone and listened for it hitting the bottom?'

'Ooh, this is exciting,' said Debbie. 'We've always assumed it was just a long-abandoned well. Quick, find a suitable stone.'

George found a round one nearby, then held it out as far as she could over the hole. 'Ready?'

Very gently, she let go and the stone disappeared down the hole. They listened and listened but heard nothing, even after ten seconds.

They looked at one another.

'Have I got that right?' mused George. 'It can't be three hundred metres deep, surely? Not if it's a well. Shall we try again?'

But they got the same result. The hole was vertical; and extremely deep.

'Let's go back inside and think about this,' said Emma. 'I wouldn't mind another coffee.'

'It looks more like the top of a mine shaft than a well,' observed George, as they settled back round the kitchen table. 'But we'd need to climb down some way to be sure.'

'You're not doing that,' said Oliver quickly. 'Far too dangerous.'

'Mm. One of you mentioned a ladder?' she persisted.

'There was one here,' responded Debbie. 'I don't know how far down it went. Oliver just climbed down the first few rungs, to the start of the next stretch. Then he unscrewed the top bit from the rest and climbed back up; we loosened the fastenings and pulled it out. I'm afraid we took it to the tip.'

There was a moment's silence. They felt tantalisingly close to a discovery.

'I did plenty of climbing and caving while I was a student,' mused George. 'I always keep a few climbing ropes and gear in the back of my car. What we'd need is a secure point at the top that I could tie on to. And a safety rope held by someone else on the top, at least till I got down to the rest of the ladder.'

'What then?' asked Debbie.

'I'd make a very careful check on the state of the ladder that's still there. If it's rusty or coming loose from the wall, then I would go no further. All I want is a preliminary look.'

There was a longer pause. She sounded almost convincing.

'I really don't want to take the risk,' muttered Oliver.

Emma had one last card to play. 'In terms of compensation, Oliver, if something did go wrong, this project is being funded by the BBC. They insure all staff on fieldwork. It'd be our responsibility, not yours.'

They haggled for some time but Debbie also was keen to know more: this could be a major find. In the end Oliver gave way.

George went to her car to fetch her climbing gear, including boots, cagoule, belt, scarf and gloves. On a second trip she brought various coils of climbing rope. Finally she came back with her caving helmet, which had a torchlight built in.

Meanwhile Oliver arranged his tractor in the farmyard so it pointed away from the hole. He checked it was standing on firm concrete, not on mud which might slide. And that the brakes were on. This would be the anchor point for the climb.

Then he disappeared into one of the outhouses and came

back with a ten-centimetre pulley wheel, mounted on a three-sided wooden base, which just fitted over the brick wall. The rope could be tied firmly to the tractor at one end and run over the pulley into the hole, with George on the other end.

'This was what I used before,' he admitted. 'Good job I never threw it away.'

'How long was the ladder that you scrapped?' asked George.

'About seven metres, I think,' said Debbie.

'You know, it occurs to me,' said Oliver, as he viewed the preparations. 'When you want to come back up, there's no need for you to clamber hand over hand up the rope. That's hard work – and dangerous. If you are tied on securely, I could drive the tractor very slowly away from the hole and pull you up.'

'That sounds great,' said George. 'You'd have to go very slowly though, especially when I was almost at the top.'

'Better still if I was the driver,' said Debbie. 'You always keep telling me I'm no speed hog. Then you'd be free to help George back over the wall.'

In the end all was ready. George shook hands with the other three and then perched herself on the wall, safety rope behind her with Oliver and his tractor on the other end.

'Not a good idea to look down,' she told herself firmly. It'd been a while since she had last gone climbing, but she'd kept herself fairly fit.

She gripped the main rope over her shoulder, then eased herself out over the hole and started abseiling down the shaft.

Slowly, step by step, she went down. It soon became a lot darker. It was reassuring to feel the safety rope being let out gently as she descended. Emma was perched at the top, coordinating actions, while Debbie sat on the opposite side with a different perspective.

Suddenly, George noticed a vertical ladder, fixed to the wall.

'I've reached the ladder,' she shouted.

'Well done,' shouted back Emma. 'Take as long as you want now.'

George eased herself round to the ladder. It looked firm enough, wouldn't move when she tried to shake it.

She rested both feet on rungs lower down. Then she used one of her carabiners to secure a safety belt from her harness onto the ladder. Time for a short break, taking the weight off her arms and legs.

'The ladder's in good condition,' she shouted up. 'I've got a safety belt on it now. I don't need the rope you're holding. I'm going to go down a bit further.'

This wasn't what anyone at the top was expecting, but there was no point in arguing down the shaft. George was the only one in a position to assess the risk. They had to trust her.

'There's no hurry, George,' yelled down Emma. 'We're all waiting for you.'

George moved the safety belt down to waist level, then she stepped down a few rungs. No problem so far. She was glad of the torch on her helmet. It was quite dark. Glancing up, she could still see the three faces watching her from the surface. She gave them a wave.

Then she went down more rungs, moving the safety belt attachment down with her. It wasn't a fast descent but it was safe enough.

How far did she need to go? The only question for today, really, was to establish if this was indeed a mine shaft. One tunnel exit from the shaft was all that she needed – that would never be part of a well.

She did a couple more shuffles down and noticed a new

ladder section. She'd gone another seven metres. At least it gave a way of estimating her depth.

The ladders remained firmly attached to the wall so she carried on. There was no real reason to stop - she wouldn't be passing this way again.

She was fourteen ladder-lengths down - almost a hundred metres - when she found the evidence she was after. A tunnel, two metres high, in the rock beside the ladder. She could step into it directly from the ladder. Proof at last! This could only have occurred in a mine.

She told herself she mustn't spend long in here. Her friends were waiting. But she wanted something tangible. George shone her torch up and down along the passage. It went in quite a long way and looked to have been hewn largely by hand-held tools. The walls were rough, though there were no sharp edges to cause accidents.

Then she spotted it. A thermometer resting on a ledge, high up on the wall. Now she could go back satisfied: she had found something. Swiftly, she put the instrument into her backpack and returned to the shaft entrance, fastened herself once more to the ladder.

There was something odd, though. A dull glow coming from further down the shaft. And then came a stupendous noise, rising in intensity. Terrifying. George shut her eyes and hung onto the ladder as tightly as she could. This was something well beyond anything she could have imagined.

CHAPTER 41 Sun February 19th Coombe Farm

Emma had insisted on driving them back to Coombe Farm. She could see that George was too shaken to drive anywhere.

'All we heard, crouching round the top of the shaft, was a roar that got louder and louder, then gradually died away. We were all very worried for you – especially Debbie. We had no idea what it was. If it was the legacy of a copper mine, that was surely closed long ago.'

'But didn't the Frobishers know? They'd lived there for ten years.'

'Oliver reckoned they must have been shielded from the noise by the shaft cover. It's a thick piece of wood, he said, well fitted, would have been highly sound proof. I'm sure the noise wasn't nearly as bad for us as it was for you.

Emma paused then continued. 'We don't know how often it was there to be heard. We were very relieved, though, when we heard you calling up to us, half an hour later. Oliver had even been starting to think about the fire brigade.'

'I'm glad he didn't. It was stressful enough being hauled up by that tractor, especially being pulled back over the wall. Debbie's idea of "slow" was far too fast for me. I was swinging about inside the shaft like the clapper on a bell as she pulled me up. I wouldn't have coped with extra questions as well.'

Emma nodded. 'We all had lots of questions but agreed this wasn't the time to voice them. You looked completely wiped out. So we've been invited back for coffee next Saturday morning. Gives us chance to share any follow-up deductions. Also to discuss how we might include the shaft, and the Frobishers, in my programme.'

George yawned. 'That sounds fine, Emma. Would you mind if I had a rest, I'm exhausted.'

The explorer was still dead to the world when they got back to Coombe Farm. Even when gently awakened she looked half asleep.

'George, go to bed for an hour. I'll give you a call when I've cooked us supper.'

When she was woken, George felt much better, there was more colour in her face.

'I thought we might treat ourselves to Hunter's Chicken,' said Emma. 'I've roasted a couple of potatoes to go with it. There'll be carrots and sprouts ready in a few minutes.'

'Emma, that sounds wonderful. Just what we need after the howling wind – or the black hole.'

Five minutes later they were starting their meal. There was plenty to reflect on.

'So you're certain it was a mine shaft, not simply a well?'

George smiled. 'I climbed down a hundred metres, got to a tunnel that led off the shaft. It was definitely man-made. There might be more of 'em, further down. But then came that dreadful roar. I'd just got back on the ladder; I clung on like a limpet. After the noise had gone, I started climbing back up. Slowly. I was very shaken.'

They ate more of their Sunday meal and considered her report.

'Since the shaft was roughly where I predicted from Treffry's notebook data, it must be one of his, don't you think?'

'I'd like to think so. We could be more forensic with the

Frobishers next weekend: were there any log books, say, in their farmhouse? Had they completely emptied the loft? Were there any old diaries?'

'Or even a cellar?' added George, remembering the Tavern. Then she remembered something else. 'Once we've eaten, Emma, I'll show you something else I found down there.'

At this, Emma declared that the pudding – a blackberry crumble – didn't need eating straight away. 'This is far more exciting.'

'It was this,' said George, as she opened her backpack. She brought out a thermometer, mounted on a wooded stand. 'I found it high up on a narrow shelf at the start of the tunnel.' She inspected it more carefully than she had in the dark tunnel. 'You know, I think it's still working.'

Emma grinned. 'It certainly supports the idea that the mine was developed by a systematic man. Pity we can't prove it was Treffry's.'

George turned it over and looked underneath. There was a six-digit number inked on: 370501. 'All we need to do now is to find this number in Treffry's private notebook. Ideally, followed by a set of temperature data.'

It sounded easy enough. The crumble could certainly wait. Emma fetched Treffry's notebook and they cleared the table. 'Why don't I start by creating our own index for the whole book?'

George had doubts. 'You'd need to start by pencilling a page number on every page. Would the Treffry household mind that?'

'I'm sure they wouldn't. Not if it helps us make sense of it. Remember, they've never seen this. Not for a century or two, anyway.'

Indexing took Emma an hour. It was hard to find logic in Treffry's recording or to know what subjects to index by. It was probably his ideas and plans in chronological order. Gradually, though, she spotted recurring themes. Fortunately the notebook came with a margin, allowing Emma to pencil in themes once spotted, and to note the occasional date when these occurred.

While she beavered away George went off for a leisurely bath that left her a lot more relaxed. When she got back Emma had just finished a complete second tranche of the whole notebook.

'Right, George. I can tell you all the pages with tables of number on them.'

'OK. I'll photo each of 'em on my phone, then print them off full-sized via my laptop. You just stick with making sense of his handwriting.'

For an hour the women sat at either end of the table. Emma had to admit there was more logic in the notebook than she had supposed. But it had been a private diary. It was always hard to expand someone else's memories.

George wrestled with pages of numbers; at least the man was consistent in how he wrote them.

Some of the pages showed temperatures she had used on Saturday, to extrapolate from the Par Consol mines they knew about. This time she concentrated on the rest. It was some relief to know these came towards the end of the notebook – suggesting she was looking at data collected later in Treffry's life.

Try as she might, she couldn't find any six-figure numbers. But did spot successive numbers in key positions, mostly in the thirties: maybe these were year values?

Then, in another corner, she spotted single digits, all between one and five. Maybe he simply numbered his mines, didn't bother with names? So was there a table linked to mine number five?

There was. And on the first row of data was a line beginning 01. Then a single number, 102, followed by a series of almost identical values. 102 could well be the depth of the tunnel in metres. This was surely enough to link the thermometer she'd found to Treffry.

'I think I've found it, Emma. This was the first tunnel in the fifth mine shaft, installed in 1837. I think we deserve that pudding now.'

As they enjoyed crumble and custard, they considered wider questions. It seemed this was Treffry's last mine. It had been carefully located to maximise his chance of hitting the hotter rocks. But why wasn't it as well known as the rest of the Par Consols? Why wasn't it on the maps of the time?'

'You've got to remember, George, Treffry had taken over all the other mines. They were already well known. This one was a site he had a chance to keep secret, at least for a short time.'

George mused. 'Perhaps it was a financial disaster? He could keep it quiet while carefully selected men, well paid to keep their mouths shut, were digging the shaft. All his hopes were dashed when it came to extraction and there was little of value. But he couldn't admit it. His reputation was as the great mining success of South Cornwall. He didn't want to lose that.'

Emma had an alternative scenario. 'Or maybe the mine was such a success that he didn't want to admit it? Didn't want to pay huge taxes on the mine's output? Would that even be possible?'

There was a pause. 'You've certainly more questions for your research this coming week, Emma.'

Later, as they enjoyed their mid-evening mugs of hot chocolate, they returned to the question of the mighty underground roar.

'It wasn't supernatural, Emma. Or a ghost. I don't believe that. It was the loudness that was the most off-putting. I honestly thought for a few seconds that I was a goner.'

Emma smiled. 'You got the effect much worse than we did. For us the noise rose steadily and then faded away again. It was as though . . . as though a battalion of tanks were passing through on manoeuvres.'

A thought struck George. 'Hold on a minute.' She went out to her backpack and returned holding a St Austell Explorer map.

She studied it for a moment, then smiled. 'You know, the Frobishers' mine is not quite where I'd thought. I'd say it's built right over a railway tunnel, one that carries the main line from Lostwithiel to Par – or even, I suppose, from Plymouth to Penzance. It's built right over the track of the Great Western Railway. Yes, that would explain it.'

Emma still looked puzzled.

'It wasn't a battalion of tanks below us, you see. It was an express train, pounding its way up or down the line. The shaft must drop pretty much on top of it. No wonder the noise was deafening.'

Emma shook her head. 'I don't believe it. The chance of two structures like that coinciding is negligible.'

'By accident, I agree. But suppose it was deliberate. Was the mine targeted to land on the line?'

Emma shook her head. 'Couldn't be that. The line wasn't operating until 1858. That's long after Treffry had died. The only way it could be done would be if the line was deliberately targeted to pass close to the mine. And I'm not sure that's even possible.'

'Nor am I,' admitted George. 'But I can go and have another

look. Gaze up the hillside from below. Is there some point on the railway line from which you can see the Frobisher's farm?'

She mused and then continued. 'Whilst I'm doing that though, there is one more historical line of inquiry that this might all depend on.'

'What's that?'

'I think you mentioned that Treffry and Isambard Kingdom Brunel met early in their careers. He was the designer of the Great Western Railway. Did the two ever meet again? If they did that could have been a very interesting meeting.'

CHAPTER 42 Mon February 20th Treffry and Brunel

On Monday morning Emma settled down to make a thorough study of Treffry's new-found notebook.

She was a social historian, fluent enough in early Victorian handwriting. The problem was more that Treffry had developed bits of shorthand for familiar places and names; and the only index to these had been inside his own head. He also wasn't fussy about making use of capital letters to distinguish proper names.

But she was on the staff of the Exeter Cornish History Outpost in Truro, ECHO; she didn't need to do all the unpacking alone. An hour later she had driven over to Truro, got photocopies of each page and shared them out among half a dozen PhD students.

'It's an exercise in making sense of a nineteenth century Cornish adventurer,' she explained. 'Between us we need it digitising.'

By late afternoon Emma had a modernised version of the original notebook on her computer and could start to tear it apart.

First, she made more sense of the dates. There weren't many written out in the notebook, but they were at least sequential. No reason to doubt, therefore, that the book had been written in chronological order.

Then she used her computer to look for date abbreviations - Jan to Dec and so on. That gave her few more fixed points.

Now she could break the document into time zones and study each in turn.

The notebook seemed to follow on from Treffry's earlier journals, which the BBC had obtained for her, and went as far as 1830. This, though, was a more condensed story of his later life. It was a professional notebook, capturing key ideas and contacts. If Treffry had ever met Isambard Kingdom Brunel again, the encounter would surely be noted in here.

But she searched both on forenames and surname; the name did not occur once. Perhaps the men never met at all?

It was far more likely, she told herself, that Brunel was in this book somewhere, using one of Treffry's private nicknames. She tried "iso", "king" and "kink" but without success. Brunel was a highly inventive engineer, the star of his generation. In his time he had straddled rail, bridges, tunnels; even designed the first iron-hull steam boats. The nickname wouldn't be derogatory.

A few minutes contemplation. Then she tried "bard". If anyone was the engineering equivalent of Shakespeare it must surely be Brunel. And she found the name did occur, several times, around 1839.

Now Emma could take the relevant section and start to give it forensic examination.

George had spent the morning working on the Fowey traffic study. In the afternoon she set out to examine the physical possibility, in the nineteenth century, of planning a railway route that ran almost underneath their newly discovered Last Fling mine.

She armed herself with binoculars. Was it possible to see the Frobishers' farmhouse from anywhere on the line of the railway? Given the maps of the time, that would be the only way a surveyor could hope to plan the required route.

Her map told her the steeper slope up to the farm was on the eastern side. There was a minor road running along the bottom which was also marked as the Saints Way footpath; it must be a very minor road indeed. But it would do.

Half an hour later George had driven to the spot where the road went under the railway, parked and clambered out. She wouldn't go onto the track – she had found for herself that there were regular trains racing along it – but she could climb up the embankment, stand beside the fence and stare up the hill.

And there it was. The Frobisher farm was a tiny blip on a flat horizon. It would be possible for a determined railway designer to take his route more or less directly below the already built mine high above. There was no diversion needed, virtually no extra cost at all. Building a short connecting passage between the two might be a novel way of achieving ventilation.

George reminded herself that she was looking back to the era of the steam train. Extracting smoke and steam was a lot more essential in those days.

Emma ran off a hard copy of her computerised version of the notebook before she returned to Fowey. There was plenty more material, all needing further thought.

George had already got a meal ready when she got back to Coombe Farm, one of the benefits of shared accommodation.

After supper they exchanged notes on their progress.

'So I've proved the idea is possible,' concluded George, 'and you've got hard evidence that the two men actually met in 1839.'

'I think I'd better go back to my drama team to invent the dialogue for that meeting,' said Emma. 'Treffry gives no details at all. But the dates seem to fit: the mine would be there by then, anyway. So what d'you think might have happened?'

There was silence for a moment. Then George began. 'How

about this? Treffry's mine hasn't produced the copper ore he'd hoped for. It's a catastrophe in the making. Then he meets Brunel, who is down in Cornwall planning the completion of the Great Western Railway.

'Now, the route from Plymouth to Truro is problematic because of all the hills and valleys in Cornwall. Much harder than, say, the route from London to Bristol, where there aren't many hills, apart from the Box Tunnel. Brunel has planned the route as far as Lostwithiel, then realises there's one more hill between there and St Austell. One more tunnel will be needed.'

She paused and Emma took over. 'Maybe Brunel and Treffry meet socially – though I'm not sure either of them was much of a party animal. Treffry admits to his fellow-engineer that his latest mine isn't doing well. They are both innovators. Maybe they ride on horseback to see the problems for themselves; and realise they almost coincide.'

An excited George took over once more. 'Then, somehow or other, they hit on the notion of using Treffry's mine as a ventilation shaft for Brunel's tunnel. Nothing in writing, but a gentlemen's agreement arose between them: when, eventually, the Great Western Railway was built, the mine would close and leave the shaft to provide the ventilation. No doubt some sort of recompense would also be agreed. A marvellous example of two engineers finding a practical way forward.'

'I must have this meeting on my programme,' said Emma, her eyes gleaming. 'I'll get the drama group to explore it on Wednesday.'

George continued to ruminate on her scenario. It would work well for the key participants. Not so well for the workers. 'We don't know anything about what happened to them, do we?'

Emma clapped her hand to her head, looking crestfallen.

'George, I might know something. I forgot to tell you yesterday. There was all the panic over the roar and how it had affected you.'

George shrugged. 'Go on then. I'm over it now.'

'Well, it was like this. There were three of us left at the top of the shaft; it was clear you'd be some time. We decided to take turns to stay on watch, the other two keeping warm in the kitchen.'

'Very sensible. That wind was bitter.'

'At one point Oliver was on watch and I was inside with Debbie. So I pushed her on what Alex had been searching for. He established her maiden name, she said, then he tried to help her build the family tree.'

'Didn't we already know that?'

'But this time, George, she told me her original name; and also the name Alex seemed most interested in.'

'I hope this is leading somewhere, Emma.'

'I think so. Debbie Frobisher used to be Debbie Dingley. And the ancestor of interest to Alex, five generations back, was one Joseph Dingley.'

George still wasn't with it. 'So who was he? The first mine manager or something?'

'Well, he might have been. But I've come across Joseph Dingley in a different context. He was the original footman who diddled Charles Rashleigh out of all his wealth as the pair of them built Charlestown Harbour.'

Half an hour later they were still going round the new information over further mugs of coffee. George began.

'We know Treffry had a row with Rashleigh about access. It's likely that Dingley was also at that meeting. He'd know far more about the figures than Rashleigh.'

'Treffry was thirty-five years younger than Rashleigh,' recalled Emma. 'So he could well have been a similar age to Dingley. He might have discerned different qualities in the footman.'

'All Rashleigh wanted was some mug to carry the hassle and burden.'

Emma nodded. 'That's right. And didn't care how he did it. Dingley could do whatever he liked, as long as the harbour got built. And eventually he paid the price – lost all his wealth. Local tradition blames Dingley for the whole swindle.'

'But I think you said the courts didn't. Most of the problem might have been down to Rashleigh. Treffry might have discerned the same thing too.'

'Dingley was a capable man,' added Emma. 'Versatile, with plenty of energy and initiative.'

George nodded. 'He'd make a good manager. That's as long as you were clear on his boundaries and didn't give him unlimited access to funds. That might have suited Treffry fine. Especially if his mine was to be kept out of the limelight. They might both have a common interest in secrecy.'

CHAPTER 43 Wed February 22nd Connections

Both women had worked hard on their projects through Tuesday. Emma became more and more familiar with Treffry's style and shorthand idiosyncrasies. At least the man was consistent. Once an abbreviation was clarified in one or two locations, she could apply it to the rest of the amplified version, which gradually made more sense. She was still baffled, though, by many nicknames he was using.

By the end of the day George had finished pulling together various aspects of the traffic survey that had been conducted by her young associates; and come to some unexpected conclusions. She spent time on Tuesday evening bouncing them off Peter Jakes by phone; and arranged to go over to his cottage for further discussion the following evening.

After all, Emma would be out; her plans were to spend Wednesday evening with the drama team in St Austell.

On Wednesday, traffic study now well in hand, George decided to give some time to her one-time husband and recent housemate, Mark.

They might no longer be a married couple - he seemed to have walked out on her - but she still had some feelings for him.

George had made a note of the few words Oliver had spent on her former housemate the previous Saturday; now she looked at them more carefully.

There had been talk of a missing colleague - Alex. To her mind that sounded slightly sinister. It might have been excess diligence on Mark's part, but if someone had been missing for a couple of weeks, surely it should be reported to the police?

Even the mathematical George hadn't been able to remember the mobile phone number on the business card flashed before her eyes, but she had noted the business he was in: Kernow Lithium Mining, or KLM; based in Bugle. Mark was their Security Manager.

She felt pleased he'd found a role more suited to his capabilities but hurt that he hadn't bothered to tell her of his appointment.

Maybe, though, that was down to his new companion? – she hadn't caught the name. Cycling around with him in her shorts – even in a wintry February? Had he simply had a mid-life crisis, moved on to the legendary "younger model"? Was this search for Alex simply a ruse, so he could spend more time with his new friend?

George frowned at the thought. She surely wasn't becoming jealous? Probably this was a central task in his new company. But not one that needed effort on a Saturday, surely? He couldn't have been with the firm for more than a fortnight.

The thoughts went round and round, leaving her angry and confused. In the end she decided that she had to try and talk to him. No time like the present. She googled KLM on her phone.

It wasn't KLM the international Dutch airline, obviously. She tried being more precise: KLM, Bugle, UK. This time she got a short website and a contact number.

She forced herself to relax before making the call. A friendly voice answered. 'Kernow Lithium Mining. Can I help you?'

'Hello, my name is George Gilbert. I'm making an enquiry about one of your staff: Mark Renfrew. I think he's the Security Manager.'

'Mr Renfrew? I'm afraid he's not in today. Can someone

else help?' A few minutes later she was put through to one Rachel Tyler.

'My name is George Gilbert. I'm an old friend of Mark Renfrew.'

'Hello, George. Yes, Mark does work here. I don't think he's in the office today. Shall I get him to give you a ring?'

'He's already got my number, Rachel. I wanted to chat to him about Alex.'

There was a pause. 'D'you mean Alex Price? I'm afraid he's not here today, either.'

'Has Alex been missing for some time?'

'I'm not going to answer that, I'm afraid, George. But I'll tell Mark that you rang.'

As the call ended, George stared at her phone. So Alex was still missing. But the firm were saying nothing. It was all very peculiar. She hoped Mark would soon give her a ring.

In another room in Coombe Farm, Emma was having more success with the notebook. And had learned that Joseph Treffry had been appointed High Sheriff of Cornwall in 1839.

As far as she knew, Treffry had never shown the remotest interest in politics, national or local. But he was a prominent older businessman and highly successful. Recognition was long overdue.

It was an honorary appointment, unpaid, but it came with considerable clout. The High Sheriff was expected to find a worthwhile project and put resources into it.

Now Emma could make more sense of the details in Treffry's notebook. He was intending to restore some local ruin "in honour of QV". The young Victoria had become Queen just a couple of years earlier so that abbreviation was a no-brainer. Emma recalled Susannah telling her that Treffry would meet the Queen when she visited Fowey, but that was several years in the future. Were the two events even linked?

It was vital to her programme to work out where Sheriff Treffry had put his energies. It might at least provide an impressive backdrop for her talk.

But it was well-hidden. Treffry's notebook words seemed obscure at this point. Maybe he was too excited at being the Sheriff? Why couldn't he say what he was doing?

At one point he seemed to have developed a verbal stutter. He talked of "rest rest". Whatever might that mean?

Then Emma had a flash of insight. Might "rest" here not only mean restore, but also be the abbreviation for his project? She did a search on all instances of rest and examined them in turn. Now it started to make sense. But if she was right, it was highly ambitious.

For High Sheriff Joseph Treffry intended to restore the ruin of Restormel Castle.

CHAPTER 44 Thurs February 23rd Luxulyan

I hadn't seen much of Naomi all week. I'd been back to Tre-know collecting my belongings on Monday afternoon; and roaming round St Austell on Tuesday. While on Wednesday evening Naomi wasn't around because of her yoga class in St Austell.

But Thursday had become our regular mid-week meeting. A chance to practice our joint performance, ready for the King's Arms karaoke. She was already busy, cooking a simple supper, when I got to her flat.

I knew not to interfere. She was a much better cook than I would ever be. I got out my guitar and started picking out possible new songs for later duets. We hadn't done anything from Joan Baez on earlier evenings together – now that was a folk singer who'd spanned the decades. Though she'd be a hard act to follow.

So when the meal started it was our first real chance to reflect on the previous Saturday and our visits to the various Alex Price locations.

I explained my ideas on Dingley. How I'd been as far as the Council, trying to discover if there were many of that name living around St Austell. 'But I didn't get very far,' I admitted. 'And I've no clue as to why the name might be important to Alex.'

Naomi grinned. 'I think I can make a guess. It all came out of last night's yoga evening.'

I was intrigued. 'Tell me more. I don't know much about yoga, I'm afraid. You have to wrap your legs round your neck and such like, don't you?'

'And do the splits. I'll show you later if you like.' I assumed she was joking. She'd got me hooked now, though.

I managed to close off thoughts of Naomi in a leotard in all sorts of arousing postures and returned to her original comment.

'So what's your idea on Dingley then?'

'The yoga classes are in the St Austell Arts Centre. All sorts of meetings go on there, Centre visitors can drop in on any of them. I sometimes do that when the yoga's over – if I've got any energy left. One of the more interesting ones is the StormBox drama group.'

'I'd prefer that to the yoga,' I murmured.

'They perform at the Centre from time to time. When they're not rehearsing, like in February, they keep meeting. Last night they had a visitor from Truro, a historian. She wanted them to enact various encounters she sketched out. That was to help with a television programme she's been asked to develop.'

'My interest would depend on what the programme's about.' To be honest, I couldn't see where she was going.

'Oh, Mark, it was great. Lots of fun. They're a lively bunch. All ages and backgrounds. I might try and join them.'

'Let's stay focussed, Naomi. How did this throw any light on Dingley?'

Naomi ate more of her Spaghetti Bolognese before giving me an answer.

'Well. The programme is about the life of Joseph Treffry. He was a nineteenth century adventurer and copper mine owner from Fowey. But it also covers Charles Rashleigh, who developed Charlestown. Or rather, who hired the man that did: and his name was Joseph Dingley.'

There was a pause while I took all this in.

'Right. So we've identified one moderately famous Dingley, anyway. There must be more?'

'When the harbour was completed, there was a major scandal. Joseph Dingley ended up in court, charged with stealing Rashleigh's wealth from a chest in his bedroom: a hoard of gold coins.'

'This is more promising,' I commented. 'So Dingley went to jail?'

'No.' She smiled roguishly. 'The court found him not guilty. He disappeared from the scene. Rashleigh was left bankrupt and later died in poverty. The money was never found.'

'Wow.'

I mused for a few moments while Naomi fetched our dessert: chocolate brownies and ice cream. She was doing well once again.

'So you're suggesting a backstory that would make sense of Alex's behaviour,' I began. 'He's looking for the place Dingley retreated to with his ill-gotten gains.'

'It would explain all the locations we visited last Saturday,' she replied cautiously. 'But I think we can do even better.'

'You've got more? All out of StormBox?'

Naomi nodded. 'Last night there was even more work for the drama group. For it turns out, the lady from Truro told us, Joseph Treffry became High Sheriff of Cornwall in 1839. And the project he set himself was to restore Restormel Castle for the new Queen.'

I laughed. 'This is getting ridiculous. So all we have to do now, Naomi, is to visit the castle and look for Dingley's hoard? I said I wanted to visit the place one day. How about this coming Saturday?'

I was teasing – but then I saw she was still deadly serious.

'D'you want to know what the historian said or not?'

I nodded mutely.

'It turns out that Treffry later hired Dingley to manage his latest mine. No doubt under tighter control than Rashleigh had managed. No gold coins to pinch this time. The well those people mentioned on Saturday was really a mine shaft. That was Treffry's last venture. But it was a disaster, there was no copper there at all. That's probably why Treffry chose Restormel Castle as his new project. And the historian's guess – she's still looking for proof – was that he took the versatile Dingley along with him, to help supervise the restoration. She's hoping the Castle will make a dramatic background for her television programme.'

I tackled my brownie before venturing a reply.

'Remember, Naomi, we're on the trail of Alex Price. We haven't set out to recover Rashleigh's lost treasure. Now, you got this idea from a respectable historian. Is there any way that Alex Price could have obtained the same idea, but from a different source?'

There was silence as the question was considered.

'There is one possibility,' Naomi said, after a pause. 'Mind, it's only a theory. But it might be how it was done.'

'Go on.' I was feeling ashamed of my fumbling attempt to unpack all these deep secrets. I wasn't local enough. Naomi was far better at this than I was.

'I talked to someone in the drama group over coffee about recent events in Fowey. Apparently, an old building in the town centre has been flattened by developers. Turns out, it was once Treffry's own bank. But there had been documents in a chest in the cellar. Which have now gone. If Alex had taken them, they might have provided additional evidence on Treffry's arrangements at Restormel.'

I considered what we now knew. A strong narrative was

developing. 'OK, I agree. It would certainly be worth going to Restormel Castle and looking for ourselves. It's a national monument. I presume it stays open for the winter?'

'Have a look,' she said, handing me a brochure, 'I'll get us some coffee.'

When she returned with a tray of hot drinks, I broke the bad news. 'Says here that it'll open at Easter – that's not till the next month but one.'

Naomi gave another roguish smile. 'But the place has even worse security than KLM. There's no door on the castle at all. You just climb over the gate, you don't even need a ladder.'

I frowned. 'You say "just", Naomi. Does that mean you've been there before?'

She gave me a guilty look. 'I cycled over there in November. Hadn't realised it was shut, you see, until I got there. So I thought I'd have a look anyway. No problem on entry at all. We could go tomorrow night.'

I blinked. 'Why on earth should we go at night?'

'Well, we can't go Saturday night, can we. We're singing.'

'No, but . . .'

'The historian might be there by Saturday morning. Doing research on the place was her top priority. We don't want her to see us – or anyone else for that matter. Sooner the better, I'd say.'

'But if we go at night, will we see anything at all?'

'It's a doughnut ring castle, Mark, with a huge open space in the middle. We could just go round the path that runs round the top of the walls. I assume you do have a good torch?'

I didn't try too hard to resist. Naomi was very enthusiastic and I caught her mood. I wasn't going to turn down a night adventure with my new friend. This was more exciting than anything I'd ever done with George.

CHAPTER 45 Fri February 24th Coombe Farm

Emma had continued to grapple with the nuances of Treffry's notebook all through Thursday, goaded by some of the questions from the drama team. Plenty of the action now made sense but she was still struggling with the engineer's abbreviations.

Coming to it fresh on Friday, it occurred to her that Treffry might not always write about himself in the first person. He might use a third-person shorthand on selected encounters.

She went back to her list of unresolved words and examined it again. And there it was: "ref". Surely that would be a monicker close to his name – one that he could use of himself with pride. A ref held things together, made sure it all ran smoothly. She looked at all the places it was used: the interpretation made perfect sense every time.

Emma had spent the previous day analysing the new Treffry mine they had visited a few days before. She had found the point where ideas for it first appeared in his notebook; and seen diagrams, reminiscent of George's recent efforts, to predict the location of higher temperature rocks.

Coming at the list of unrecognised abbreviations once again, she wondered if any of them might be Joseph Dingley. Surely, he must feature in the book somewhere?

Emma found it a lot easier going from the full name to the nickname than trying to make the process work backwards. She knew quite a lot about him, of course. In the end she decided Dingley was most likely to be "glue" – things seemed to stick to him. But Treffry in his wisdom had reformed him, got him to stick new things together.

With this insight a lot more of the notebook made sense. "Glue" had worked in a Par Consol, then been appointed manager of the new Treffry mine in 1835. He was the one that had given it the name: "Last Fling". Maybe he longed to make the most of this unexpected twist to his career?

Sadly, she read on, Last Fling had not been successful. Even though Treffry had been one of the first to use the new safety fuse, developed in 1832. The fuse was dynamite, protected inside woven hemp, with a layer of tar on the outside. It made the use of explosives to blast out shafts and tunnels far safer.

Emma moved on to consider the visit of the young Queen Victoria to Fowey in 1846. There was plenty of material about the visit, the Royal family was well covered on the internet. If she could plan it right, this might make a memorable tableau for her programme.

As she had remarked to George over breakfast, 'This event could give the programme star quality. Everyone's heard of Queen Victoria.'

'Eastender viewers might link the name to the pub in Albert Square.'

'I don't think they tune in to BBC4,' she had retorted. But the conversation had inspired her to ring her producer, seeking permission to visit Restormel Castle this weekend.

She recalled that Susannah Treffry had told her categorically that Treffry had met the Queen on the only time she had visited Fowey. That would only be right: he was one of the most successful Cornishmen of his generation. But where had it happened?

She re-read Treffry's declared goal on taking the office of

High Sheriff: "restoring Restormel Castle". Now she used his decrypted notebook to work out what that might mean. She'd visited the Castle; it was hardly a residential dwelling.

It couldn't mean doing much to the walls. They were extremely old, built to withstand siege. It must mean removing the debris that had collected inside them over the centuries; and making sure every pathway was safe to walk on.

There was also the substantial matter of levelling the surrounding area; and creating a track up the hillside so a horse-drawn coach could visit it.

Not a huge job with trained staff and modern machinery but a major task in the 1840s.

It occurred to her that though it wasn't much like mining for copper, it had similarities to building a working harbour. A task that Dingley had completed for Rashleigh in Charlestown earlier in his career. That plus the forced closure of Last Fling would make Dingley an obvious choice to manage the Restormel restoration.

Now Emma read the passage in Treffry's notebook again. Something like this had happened. Restormel Castle was even visible from his copper mine. The location was close enough (perhaps a couple of miles?) that Dingley could commute from his manager's house at Last Fling.

Finally there came one more thought.

This work, with a dedicated team, could well have taken several years. So might it not have been Treffry's meeting place of choice for the Royal visitors in 1846? They could sail up the Fowey as far as Lostwithiel; then be driven on to the newly restored Royal Castle. What better place for the one-time High Sheriff of Cornwall to meet Queen Victoria and Prince Albert!

CHAPTER 46 Fri February 24th Traffic Survey

While Emma was delving into local history, George had boiled down findings on traffic in the town to a stark minimum. It would only be fair to share these with her young assistants at the Fimbarrus Academy while the topic was still fresh in their minds.

She managed to catch Peter Jakes, was invited to bring her results for a presentation straight after school. It would be good to get the students' reactions. They were as affected as anyone by traffic problems. Their comments might sharpen up the report she would eventually send to the St Austell Council.

While she'd got Peter on the phone, she contrived to invite him for a meal out, to say thank you for all his efforts. It turned out he was free this evening, accepted with scarcely a pause. She'd make a booking at the Fisherman's Arms in Golant once it was open.

While work pressure was off for an hour or two, it occurred to George that it would be good to find out how her friend Frances Cober was getting on in St Austell.

By chance she caught the police officer in a lull between meetings. 'All's well so far, George. Any chance of lunch together?' Two minutes later a rendezvous had been agreed.

George knew Frances would be more circumspect now she was in post, but she was used to reading between lines. It was important her friend felt supported. Frances could at least share details of prospective accommodation and other outside-work activities.

They met in a coffee shop in St Austell. 'I won't be able to do this once I'm on a case,' warned Frances. 'But this is only my first week. I'm taking a bit of time to settle.'

They ordered Caesar Salads. As they waited George reported the latest twists on the Tavern in Fowey. 'Turns out it used to be the Consolidated Bank, used by Joseph Treffry. We got as far as his final copper mine last Sunday. On a long hill overlooking Lostwithiel.' She was still talking as the lunches were brought.

But her words brought a moment of disquiet to Frances's face. 'D'you know, that's the second time this week I've been told about something odd, close to Lostwithiel.'

George was silent and started eating. She understood confidentiality, would never ask a police officer about her casework, even a close friend; but she wouldn't ignore anything she was told.

Frances mused as she started her salad. Then came an odd question. 'D'you remember, George, about that mystery in Truro?'

It was several years ago but George had good recall. 'Around the cathedral, you mean?'

'Yes. We had someone in to advise on security. He had a massive beard, I knew him as Marcus Tredwell. Well, he's lost his beard. And now he's working on lithium mining around St Austell. I had a coffee with him the other day.'

This was an unexpected, tough moment for George. For that man was Mark. She hadn't dared to broadcast the return of her long-lost husband to her friends before things had settled down between them. That had been a bumpy ride; and now, it seemed, he had bumped away.

There was a story there all right; but did it need to be told now? 'Oh yes,' she smiled. 'So he'd been to the mine too?'

Frances nodded. 'Everything he told me was "off the record". It's not yet an official case. I'm sharing it with you on that basis. But it sounded very odd.'

George had to respond now. 'You mean, about his missing colleague, Alex?' That was a key name and it opened a flood-gate.

'So you've heard it too? The thing is, he told me that his mining company, KLM, aren't keen to report it. So he's search-ing on his own. Which I warned him could be rather dangerous. I haven't heard anything from him, so I suppose he's alright.'

'I was worried for him too,' admitted George. 'I even rang KLM in Bugle to talk to him, but he wasn't there. The lady I did talk to, Rachel, admitted that Alex Price hadn't been around for a while either, but she wouldn't tell me anymore.'

Frances sighed. 'Until we've got solid evidence of something going on, it's hard for either of us to do more. It's not a job for the police to anticipate crime. I was fond of Marcus. We can only hope the evidence, if it comes, won't be a cold body.'

That evening George picked up Peter in Polkerris at seven o'clock and they headed for the Fisherman's Arms once again.

Her afternoon student feedback had gone well; the session had been very interactive. The ever-alert Wilson had been dis-cerningly critical, had asked if, in the scheme of things, traffic in Fowey was an issue requiring much attention. Were there not other matters with a greater call on the public purse? Making a realistic response to climate change was high on his agenda.

But he had asked the question with a smile and Isobel had given a counter proposal which had provoked wider debate. George could see the two were both well-ready for the wider world and a credit to the Academy – and to Peter Jakes.

There would be no talk of traffic this evening. The word "survey" was once again a banned word, with a forfeit attached.

'What forfeit do you have in mind, Peter?' It was only a playful question, but she wanted to see what he might say.

He paused, then a gleam came into his eye. 'Mm. How about we agree to discard something each time the word is used?'

'No way. I'm just in a dress. You've got a jacket, a cravat and a jumper on top of everything else.'

It would never happen. But it was a sign of a deepening relationship that they could joke like this at all.

They were shown to a table beside the window and given a menu.

'This meal is all on me, Peter. I want to say thank you for all your help these last few weeks. It would never have happened without you. It's a real lesson to me for future projects.'

'And we might never have met,' he replied. 'You've helped me so much to move on, you know, made me far more forward looking.'

He might have said more but their waitress arrived. It was Isobel once more, in her demure black dress.

'Still on duty?' asked George, with a grin.

'Tonight,' she replied. 'But I'm off tomorrow. I'm seeing Wilson in the afternoon.' She giggled. 'It's almost a date.'

'D'you know where you're going?'

'Haven't decided yet.'

'You could join Emma and me at Restormel Castle if you liked.'

'That's shut,' she said scornfully.

'Not if you're working for the BBC, it isn't. In fact, the pair of you could pose for us as Queen Victoria and Prince Albert.'

Isobel mused for a second. 'I'll suggest it to Wilson. Though he might have something better in mind. He's not much into royalty.'

'Has he climbed in Restormel Castle?'

Isobel looked doubtful. 'Dunno. I haven't. But that would mean bringing our climbing gear. Was Prince Albert a climbing man?'

'He might have been,' grinned George. 'I'd say the bigger question for you is, was Victoria? But I'm not suggesting you come in Victorian regalia. We'd only be exploring possibilities for television.'

'I'll suggest it to Wilson, anyway. Now what would you both like to eat this evening – madam?

The meal was another step forward in their relationship. They had a lot in common and were very comfortable together. George shared more of her previous life with Mark and Peter spoke openly and positively about his late wife, Annie.

Isobel saw them sharing happily and made no further attempt to intrude on their happiness. But she was a wise young woman, realised this was not an observation to be shared back at school. Not by her, at any rate.

As on the previous week they were among the last to leave. George was almost tempted to drop the word "survey" into their later conversation, to see what would happen.

But she decided to leave the gambit for a later occasion.

CHAPTER 47 Fri February 24th Journey to Restormel

I insisted on using my car on Friday evening. I certainly didn't fancy cycling to Restormel at night, didn't want Naomi getting any ideas. It was still very cold in the evenings.

We had agreed to keep our plan a secret, at least until we had come back and taken stock. What we were going to do must, strictly speaking, be illegal; and I was a Security Manager. It was my job that'd be on the line if there were any repercussions.

We were both to wear dark clothing and headgear for similar reasons. And gloves. I managed to persuade Naomi that, tonight, her cycling shorts would not do. We also took our cycling helmets - not ideal, for sure, but there might be low passages to navigate in the Castle. We had made sure both our phones were fully charged. We would leave any identifying items, like Naomi's driving license or my wallet, inside the car. We didn't want to leave any traces of ourselves in the Castle.

I took my backpack to carry our torches, water bottles, a packet of biscuits and a large bar of chocolate. I didn't know how long this would take.

We set out just after eleven; Luxulyan was at rest. Driving carefully, we reached Lostwithiel after twenty minutes and the base of the Restormel Castle hill ten minutes later. The sky was overcast and it was very dark. No streetlights out here, it was the back of beyond.

I drove up the winding lane to the car park at the top, which of course was empty. Then we walked up the footpath to the closed Castle entry kiosk. There was a locked gate beside it, but it was not hard to climb over. Now we were inside the grounds.

For some reason we were both whispering. Even though there was no-one there. I guess we were slightly overawed by the setting. The Castle had been here for centuries. It had been almost a ruin by the eighteenth century but been restored to something like its present splendour in the 1840s.

Though "splendour" was too grand a word. It was an impressive construction, certainly: a massive circle of thick stone walls, forty metres across and twenty metres high, with various rooms nestling inside. I'd read that there was a path that ran right round the top of the walls, with an occasional stairway down to rooms below. Plenty of protective walls but handrails were few and far between.

We approached the Castle across a flat meadow. There was a dry moat running all the way round the outside and a trail outside that, with an occasional bench for visitors.

'If there is anything hidden here, it won't just be lying outside,' I observed. I wasn't sure if we were looking for Dingley's hidden treasure or for any signs of Alex Price – who, we believed, had come here on a similar quest.

There was just one entrance into the Castle, a grassy gateway without gates or doors. We went in and looked at the high wall around us. There were steps to the top on either side of the entrance we had just used.

Presumably Alex had come here on his own? Probably also at night, for similar reasons to ourselves. If, say, he had tripped and fallen down a stairwell, been unable to climb back up, his body could be resting here until tourists found him some time after Easter.

From what Naomi had told me, and what I could see, there were no closed rooms in this Castle. If there had been an accident, a dead-end stairwell was the most likely location. We would just have to search each one in turn.

I turned to my companion. 'When we get to a staircase, Naomi, there'll be no point in us both going down it,' I suggested. 'We might get in each other's way. Why don't I go down and you keep watch at the top? I'll leave the backpack with you in case I have to do any scrambling. But please don't eat all the biscuits while I'm gone.'

As I'd guessed, Naomi wasn't that keen to find her way down the uneven steps of any inky black spiral staircase, even by torchlight, and accepted my proposal. 'I'll be OK to sit at the top and meditate,' she replied. 'Try to imagine what might have happened. So no hurry, Mark, you can take your time. But you must have a drink before you go down.'

We clambered carefully up the steps and onto the path at the top. We'd agreed not to switch on our torches until we had to. Our eyes had got used to the dark by now; we sensed the Castle's prominent position, overlooking the occasional light far below. In the far distance a few streetlights were still shining in Lostwithiel.

It was sinister, almost ghostly. The silence was suddenly disturbed by the hoot of an owl. Slowly, cautiously, we made our way round the Castle wall until we came to the first stairwell. There, as agreed, Naomi and I parted company.

Even for me, with all my experience of security work, the dark staircase felt oppressive. I switched on my torch. I was glad now of my cycle helmet – there were flat stones sticking out from the spiral above that I could easily have bumped my head on without it.

I wondered how tall Alex was: might something like that have happened to him? He probably wouldn't have had a crash helmet. I went down slowly, pointing the torch into every nook and cranny. But there was nothing out of the ordinary here at all.

It must have been twenty minutes before I got back to Naomi. She was seated with her back to the wall, looking very cold indeed. And rather frightened.

'Nothing down that one,' I told her, trying to sound jovial. 'But it's not the most cheerful of descents. I had to be very careful.'

'Mark, I think there's someone else in here,' she whispered.

I looked at here in surprise. 'Did you hear something?'

'There was some crunching and a whining noise, from the far side of the Castle.'

I considered. 'Could it have been a fox or something?'

'I guess so. But it spooked me.' She shuddered. 'I feel very scared.'

Her reaction surprised me. She'd always seemed a feisty girl. Maybe being in the pitch dark on her own had got to her? But I wasn't going to try talking her out of it.

'Would you like to go back and sit in the car?' I asked, offering her my keys. 'Put your torch on. I'll watch you walk along the top, over to the steps and down to the castle gateway. Once you're there you've just got to go back over the grass and down to the car. Make sure your phone is in your hand, though, ready to ring my number. And bellow if you see or hear anything. I'll come after you straight away.'

She thought for a moment, she didn't often chicken out. 'To be honest, Mark, I wouldn't mind doing that,' she said. 'I'll be safe enough in the car. But what about you?'

'I'll just go carefully down every staircase I come to, check if there's anything inside. I've got the hang of it now. It won't take me so long next time. Then I'll come back and join you at the car.'

She looked so scared. I crouched down and gave her a warm hug. 'Don't worry, Naomi. This place is frightening in the dark. Would it work better if we came here, say, early one morning?'

She shrugged. At this point she didn't care. 'Shall I take the backpack?' she asked.

'I'd better keep it, Naomi. D'you want a drink, though?'

She opened it and pulled out the water bottles again. 'That one's yours,' she said. We both gulped down a substantial drink, then I put them away.

'Right. You go now, I'll watch till you reach the doorway. Then I'll press on with the search.'

It was a simple plan, should have worked. I took off my cycling helmet and we exchanged a few more endearments and cuddles. There were some benefits of being in pitch darkness after all.

But as Naomi walked away, I started to feel dizzy. I tried so hard to keep watching her – or at least her bobbing torch – but the task got harder and harder. And I was feeling very strange. Fifteen minutes later, by the time her torch had got down to the Castle doorway, I had sunk to my knees.

A moment later I wobbled and lost my balance. Soon after that I was bouncing uncontrollably down the narrow staircase. Until I hit my unprotected head on a sticking out rock and knew no more.

CHAPTER 48 Sat February 25th Restormel Castle

George was glad that morning coffee with the Frobishers would not happen till eleven. It had been a very late night indeed.

Emma made sure she had all her findings for their visit to Restormel Castle before they left Fowey. The majestic building, with its royal connections, might well be the final reality pageant of the programme. George hadn't told her yet that there might be a young couple coming to join them, willing to play Victoria and Albert.

The women were made very welcome at the Frobisher's farmhouse. Once they were seated around the big table with their coffees, the conversation could begin.

Emma explained how she'd found Treffry's notebook hidden in his study. 'It was hard to get in to,' she began. 'Handwritten of course, with few dates and lots of abbreviations. But from what we'd learned and seen here a week ago, I knew what to look for. Treffry called himself "ref" and he called Dingley "glue".

There was a brief interruption. Debbie had to be persuaded to take this as a compliment, rather than an insult to her five-generations-back ancestor. Then Emma continued.

'He'd decided where to sink his new mine by looking at all the temperature-depth data from his other mines. It was here, in his view, that the rocks below should start to get hotter a lot quicker.'

'I'd repeated his calculations and got to nearly the same spot,' added George. 'That's how we found you.'

Emma pressed on. Oliver looked like he'd wanted George to go through the calculations; but they didn't need to do that today.

'Treffry had met Dingley via Charles Rashleigh, that's the man credited with Charlestown Harbour. Dingley had been a footman but he progressed to managing the harbour development and Treffry saw his potential. That was how he later came to be the manager here; and Debbie's family have been living here ever since.'

There was quite a lot of discussion at this point. Which was to be expected: Dingley was after all the key ancestor in their farmhouse.

'So what happened to Dingley, once the mine closed?' asked Oliver.

'That's a good question,' said Emma. 'You know Restormel Castle – you can see it from your farmyard?'

'Yes,' said Debbie, 'that's assuming it's a clear day.'

Emma smiled at the caveat. 'Well, that was Treffry's final project. He was High Sheriff of Cornwall by that stage. He closed the mine and took Dingley with him. Over the next few years Dingley managed the work to make the Castle visitable again. It was completed just in time for the Royal visit in 1846.'

Debbie was agog. 'You mean, my great, great, grandfather might have met Queen Victoria?'

'I can't be sure, Debbie, but I know Treffry did. George and I are going over there this afternoon to imagine how it might have happened.'

They left shortly afterwards, though Emma agreed to come back a week later. Another trip down the old mineshaft might need organising, this one with a professional camera crew. She hoped to interview both Frobishers on her programme. The challenge would be an interview where she knew far more than her subjects.

The next stop was lunch in Lostwithiel. It made for an enjoyable day out. Afterwards they had a short walk round the town, visiting the multi-arched ancient bridge over the River Fowey, next to the railway station.

'Course, the Great Western wasn't here when Victoria and Albert came,' said Emma. 'Or else the pair could have had an easier journey. Though when the river's as full as it is now there'd be no problem getting here by boat from Fowey.'

After lunch they headed up the narrow road towards Restormel Castle. It didn't go anywhere else, except the lodge and nursery below the Castle. This would have been the royal route as well.

They drove up the narrow lane to an empty car park close to the Castle.

'I presume Vic's coach could have made it up here?' asked George.

'I guess so. Easier than slogging on foot up the hillside, anyway.'

George smiled. 'So have you got the key, Emma?'

'To be honest, the message said to just climb over the gate. It's hardly top security. I guess they don't worry too much. There's not much to steal here.'

They followed the instructions and climbed over the gate. 'The vital thing, George, is to identify a suitable location for the welcoming. Not just next to this hut, anyway. We have to make the most of the Castle.'

They wandered across the meadow, the giant stone edifice of the Castle looming ahead of them.

'I'd say there are only two possibilities,' said George, as they drew close. 'One is just outside, in the gateway here, with the

Castle ahead of them –'

'– or else we go inside the doughnut. It'd be a lot easier to arrange a banquet in there. Food was a big thing in Victorian times. So what we really need is pictures of both options. If only we had a pair of young actors.'

But George had spotted bicycles through the entrance archway. 'I think that could be arranged.'

Even as she spoke, two young adults emerged through the archway: Isobel and Wilson.

'We decided to come,' Izzy said. 'Wilson hadn't any better ideas. How can we help?'

George made introductions then Emma took charge.

'What I'd like first is to imagine Victoria and Albert being welcomed just here, outside the Castle. 'I'll play Treffry the welcomer; you two play the royal couple and walk along towards me.

'George will video us from different angles. We'll try it a few times, then we'll have a look at the alternative.'

Everyone took the episode seriously, though when Wilson started addressing Izzy as "your majesty" there were smiles all round. Gradually, filmed from different angles, a pattern emerged.

Then they moved inside. George tried shooting from the centre of the Castle, behind "Treffry"; then from behind the couple as they came in; but neither was visually dramatic. They couldn't do justice to the huge Castle at the same time.

George showed them all both options, but staging the greeting in the gateway was clearly better.

'Right,' said George. 'That's our main business done. We might as well explore the Castle while we're here.'

'There might be somewhere that's even better,' added Emma.

George and Emma headed for the nearest steps to climb up to the top of the Castle wall; Izzy and Wilson went for the steps opposite.

'Young love,' murmured George as they looked across the Castle courtyard to the pair, walking slowly hand in hand round the other side.

It was inevitable that the couple would choose to explore one of the staircases that led down mysteriously inside the castle wall. No doubt Wilson was hoping to find a climbing challenge.

They were out of sight for some time. Then they reappeared, looking upset. Izzy's face was as white as a sheet, she might be about to be sick.

'Can you come over here,' she pleaded. 'Quickly.'

George and Emma hastened round the wall to join them.

'Whatever's the matter?' asked George.

'I think Izzy and I have found a body,' said Wilson.

PART 7

February 25th - March 1st

Resolution

CHAPTER 49 Sat February 24th Restormel Castle

'Before we do anything else, I'd like to see what you've seen for myself.' George had taken command of the situation now. She was the oldest one here and had been in one or two situations like this before.

She turned to the group. 'Izzy, stay with Emma, please. Both of you make your way back to the car; here are my keys. You'll be more comfortable down there. Wilson, show me, please, how you went down the stairwell. But try not to disturb anything as you go. This might turn out to be a crime scene.'

George didn't say more but she was fearing the worst. Frances had tried to warn Mark that searching for a missing person on his own was dangerous. But she wasn't going to start crying just yet.

'Izzy, could you lend George your cycling helmet, please?' said Wilson. 'And also the second torch.' The transfer was made.

He swallowed hard. It was going to be harder a second time. 'Right,' he declared. 'Time to go.'

He started making his way slowly down the stairwell. George followed him, a few steps behind. She was grateful for the iron handrail running down the spiral staircase and clung on to it tightly. Those steps were terribly uneven.

There was no light in the stairwell apart from their torches. How far down did it go? Was the body right at the bottom?

They continued feeling their way down. They had completed two spirals before Wilson whispered, 'We're almost here.'

He halted abruptly and George almost ran into him. Then he played his torch on the steps below. A man was lying there, head downwards and face to the ground, in a grotesque posture. One leg was bent upwards and the other was a peculiar shape, looked to be badly broken. Not a restful pose.

'He looks to be dead, I'm afraid, but we need to check that.' George knelt down, reached forward and touched his skin: it was icy cold. Then she felt for a pulse but there was nothing at all. Her only comfort was that the person wasn't Mark.

'Poor chap. It looks like he fell right down the stairwell. Perhaps he was drunk? If it was a deliberate suicide, he chose a very painful way to kill himself.'

'Are we going to try and lift him out, George?'

George shook her head. 'We'll leave that to the experts. We can go back up now. Then I'll ring the police.'

George had never had reason to consult the police in St Austell. But she knew one inspector there: she had her friend Frances's number in her phone. That would be far easier.

'Hi, Frances,' she began. 'It's George. I'm afraid I've found a dead body. It's down a stairwell in Restormel Castle.'

A short pause before Frances replied. 'Right. I'm at home, but I'll come over straight away. Can you wait there for me, please? It might take me half an hour to get to you.' The call ended.

George turned to Wilson. 'I've got an old friend who's a police officer. Frances Cober. Don't worry, she's very good with people. But she'll need to hear your story for herself. She won't be here for half an hour, I'm afraid.'

Wilson nodded. He'd seen enough crime stories on television to expect this kind of reaction. 'Can we keep Izzy out of this?'

George smiled at his unselfish concern. 'I'll do my best. This death happened some time ago. Days, certainly, maybe weeks. And you're both only here at my invitation, remember. You've every right to be here: BBC approval, no less. I've got the video of you performing as Prince Albert to prove it.'

'Would it be a good idea to check the other stairwells whilst we're waiting for your friend?'

She could see that Wilson was tense, needed to do something. 'As long as we do it together.'

Which was how the second body came to be found. But this time George knew who it was: it was her one-time husband, Mark.

Miraculously, he was still alive. Though far from conscious.

By the time they'd overcome their shock, checked for life and returned badly shaken to the top, George saw that twenty-five minutes had gone by. Should she ring for an ambulance straight away? A police inspector would have far more clout than her with Truro hospital. And Frances would know the injured man as well – though only as security man Marcus Tredwell.

Wilson wasn't up for climbing down any more stairwells. He'd found enough bodies for one day. They made their way to the Castle gateway, ready to meet Frances. This would need careful handling.

'I'll do the talking,' said George. Wilson was still in shock and happy to be a silent spectator.

Frances, not in uniform, came jogging along from the car park a couple of minutes later and greetings were made.

'Frances, this is Wilson. He and his friend Izzy were here helping my friend Emma and I to replay a moment of high drama. The women are now down in my car. When we'd finished acting, we all went for a wander round the top. The young ones went down one of the stairwells and found a body. I've checked, he's been dead for a while.

'But I'm afraid there's more. While we were waiting for you, we checked other stairwells. Your and my old friend, Marcus Tredwell, was collapsed halfway down one, still alive but in a coma. How quickly can we get him to hospital?'

Frances quickly grasped the most urgent challenge and pulled out her phone. She'd worked in Truro till recently, was well acquainted with the emergency staff at the hospital. Five minutes later an ambulance was on its way. The Health Service was still capable of high-speed action.

The call over, Frances turned to her immediate contacts. 'Right, George. Can you wait in the car park, please, and guide the ambulance crew up here when they arrive? Wilson, I need you to show me the collapsed man. And I might need your manly strength to help me and the ambulance staff to lift him out.'

Two hours later the ambulance had come and gone. The staff had struggled with the narrow winding stairwell; eventually, with Wilson's help, they got the collapsed man (Mark or Marcus) into a stretcher and then off to Truro hospital. George resolved to visit him later. Though it might take some time for him to recover consciousness.

A mortuary van had arrived too. With a similar effort, after photographs had been taken of the critical stairwell from all angles, the van had taken the dead man off to a mortuary in St Austell. It was certainly a suspicious death and warranted an immediate post mortem.

At this point the police had no idea who the dead man was,

though both George and Frances had their suspicions.

Frances had despatched all the non-professionals to buy hot drinks and refreshment in their lunchtime café in Lostwithiel. 'I'll come and talk to you once I'm done here.' George had all their names, anyway. She knew what was needed and wouldn't let anyone slip away.

Wilson had hoped to see a Scene of Crime Team in action, but Frances wasn't rushing to call them in. There was no hard evidence that any crime had been committed. The injured man might be able to tell them more once he'd regained consciousness; while the death, though similar, must have happened quite some time earlier. The first priority on him was to establish the dead man's identity.

For completeness the police officer walked carefully and cautiously around the top of the Castle walls but there was nothing of interest to be found. She made sure there was crime scene tape at the bottom of the stairs to inhibit any further access.

When Frances rejoined George, Emma and their young friends in Lostwithiel, there had obviously been a lot of talking between them. Both discoveries had been a shock. But they were resilient youngsters, not too badly affected.

The police officer heard Wilson and Izzy's tale for herself, noted the details and offered her sympathy. 'It must have been a dreadful shock for you both. Have you any thoughts on what might have happened?'

It was intended as a polite invitation to two helpful witnesses. But the response was far richer than she could ever have expected.

'Castle security is practically non-existent,' said Wilson. 'And the place is closed for the winter. Both men had boots and kagoules on. Even if they were there on a dark wet night they wouldn't easily have slipped. Unless their torch had stopped working or something?'

'But that wouldn't have happened twice,' continued Izzy. 'Is there any way you can check their blood for alcohol level?'

'I'm sure the dead man died many days ago,' said Frances. 'It'd be hard to detect anything in their blood from that far back.'

'You'd have some chance, though, with the one who's still alive,' added George. 'He must have been on the Castle wall very recently – perhaps even last night?'

A pause. Then came a further insight from the youngsters.

'You know, there was no car in the car park when we got here today,' said Izzy. 'He surely wouldn't have walked out this far, would he? Not if he had some tasks to do when he got here. So someone else must have moved his car after it happened.'

'Doesn't that mean he couldn't have been here on his own?' asked Wilson. 'In which case . . .'

'It couldn't have been an accident at all,' concluded Izzy. 'Let's hope the unconscious man wakes up soon.'

Frances had had similar thoughts as she supervised the removal of the bodies. She was only slightly discouraged to find that the two bright youngsters had followed along so quickly and independently. All she could do now was to encourage them.

'We know that the only road away from the Castle leads into Lostwithiel,' said the police inspector. 'If only we had the survivor's registration number, we could search for it on the local CCTV, see if and when it came here. And also, if it came back again.'

'As long as the camera's working,' mused Wilson. 'My family have lived in Lostwithiel for years. There are plenty of speed hogs rushing through the town that are never caught, I'm afraid.'

Frances would never have gone into this much detail of her own accord but had to respond to their ideas once voiced.

'There are various mechanisms, Wilson,' she replied. 'Flashing and filming a speeding motorist at night to get their car number requires deliberate human intervention at a police station. That's bound to be intermittent; we've only so many officers.'

She saw them nodding and then went on, 'But recording all the vehicles as they go past will happen automatically. You still need human intervention though, to check for a specific number plate. But my first task will be to make sure that last night's Lostwithiel traffic record is not overridden. That always happens after a few weeks.'

'We must hope they hadn't covered the car's registration plate before they set off,' said Izzy. 'But if they'd been involved in an attempted murder, they might not think of that.'

'They'd be more concerned to get away quickly,' added Wilson. 'Hey, can your CCTV cameras identify the car driver?'

George had been silent during the recent exchange, she'd had a different set of thoughts entirely. Which would require an unusual level of cooperation from her partners. That needed to be sorted now, before they'd had a chance to say anything to anyone.

'Can I change the subject a little,' she began. There were nods all round.

'It seems possible – to say the least – that Wilson and Izzy have helped us chance on a serious crime scene.' There were nods of agreement all round.

'But if we're smart, there's a consequence to that. Right now we have an advantage over the aggressor, whoever they are: there's no way they can know that we're hot on their trail. So might we possibly agree between us to keep it that way? At least for a couple of days. Not to say a single word to anyone.'

There was silence around the table.

'That's a big ask, George. But I can see what it might achieve. I'd be happy to stay stum. What about you, Izzy?'

'We want to catch whoever did this,' she said. 'If us staying quiet will do that, I'm happy to do so. But might you be able to share a little of the progress when it happens?'

George looked across to Frances. 'This is your call, I think.'

Frances reflected for a moment. 'The dead man died some time ago. The police can keep his death under wraps for a couple of days, while we try to identify him. We'll have his image once he's been tidied up by the pathologist. And we can contact the friends of all those recently reported missing.

'But it's possible he has some link to the surviving man. It's a big coincidence to have two such similar events in the same location, within a few days of one another. It'd be worth keeping that quiet for similar reasons. After all, he might regain consciousness in the next few days.

'It's not how policing is normally done. But we all want to catch whoever did this. In this case, secrecy from you all might be the best way to do so.'

CHAPTER 50 Sat February 25th Truro

The meeting in the Lostwithiel café had concluded soon afterwards. Emma had advised Izzy and Wilson to stay nothing to their friends about playing the young Victoria and Albert at Restormel Castle for the time being.

'You'll be able to say much more once the programme nears completion,' she told them. 'There's a chance I'll use you again when the BBC films it properly. In the meantime, the least you say the better. And whatever you do, don't put anything on social media.'

George had taken Emma back to Coombe Farm with her notes and ideas. She had plenty to work on now.

Frances had made sure there were no loose ends in St Austell police station. She formally registered the case with her superintendent; and the post mortem was set for Monday morning.

Then George had driven on from Fowey to St Austell. After which she and Frances had travelled together to Truro hospital.

On the way George divulged that Marcus's real name was Mark Gilbert; he was George's long-lost husband. 'It's a really long story, I promise I'll tell you once we've solved this case. But sadly,' she said, 'we found it impossible to put our marriage back together again after so long apart. I haven't seen or heard from him for nearly a month.

'So he might not want to see me at all,' she concluded.

'We'll need to abide by medical opinion,' asserted Frances. 'It was a terrific crack to his head. He's in Intensive Care, might not even survive.' It was a sobering thought for them both.

They reached Truro hospital half an hour later. Being with a police inspector did away with visiting hours restrictions and they were soon in Intensive Care.

'I was the one who found the man brought in from Restormel Castle,' George began. 'He might be my recent husband.'

'It would be good to give him a name,' said the senior nurse. 'I'm afraid he's still in a deep coma.'

'What are his chances?' asked Frances. 'I'm the inspector that arranged for him to be brought here.'

'He's got extensive injuries, I'm afraid. A broken leg, for a start. But we won't do anything at all until he regains consciousness. All we can do at this point is to hope.'

'Could I see him, please?' asked George. She and Frances were shown to a bed in the corner, with curtains drawn round it. The man was certainly Mark. But he was in a very bad way.

They gave the nurse their contact numbers and asked to be called, day or night, if he regained consciousness; or if he got much worse. But there was nothing more they could do here this evening.

'I think you and I deserve a decent meal,' said Frances as they came out of the hospital. 'It's been a long afternoon. Greek or Indian?'

They settled on an Indian restaurant in the town centre. It looked busy. But they could cope with a slow service tonight, they had plenty of talking to do.

'I'm sorry to say this, George, but I think we need to work out a plan of action on the assumption that Mark will be in a coma for ages. We can't keep everything quiet for long, though. So what leads have we got already?'

'It's definitely Mark; and we know he was based at KLM as security manager.'

'How long had he been in post?'

'Just a few weeks. I last saw him at the start of February.'

'He'd done well to annoy someone so badly in just three weeks that they wanted to bump him off. Was he often annoying?'

George grimaced. 'We'd had our differences recently. He'd had a rough ride, but he was trying to move forwards. I'm surprised he would blow up in just a few weeks, though.'

Frances frowned. 'OK. Let's leave Mark for a moment. What do we make of the dead man?'

There was a moment of silence as they considered.

'I'd say, Frances, that the other body was almost certainly Alex. We know that Mark was looking for him – you heard it from Mark himself and I heard it from the couple where Mark visited last week. KLM was also where they both worked. It's odds on, surely, that both assaults stemmed from something that happened in the company.'

'It's not certain. The events happened days or even weeks apart – we'll know better after Monday's post mortem. So why on earth would they both be assaulted in the same location?'

The waiter arrived before she could answer and took their orders. Both went for a Vindaloo curry with all the extras and plenty of water. And two halves of lager. There'd be more driving ahead later tonight.

George went back to Frances's question. 'One possibility is that the second attack was in the same location as the first because that attacker had found a method that worked.'

'I suppose so. From some points of view, Restormel was a good location. It was very remote; also, it was closed for the winter. All being well, there'd be no discovery at least until Easter.

By then, of course, Mark would also have died. It wouldn't have been easy, even for the best pathologist, to work out exactly when the deaths had happened.'

'Or even who they both were.'

'Though surely, George, someone at KLM would have raised an alarm before then? As Oscar Wilde almost said, "To lose one senior member of staff might be a misfortune; to lose two seems like carelessness".'

George smiled at the aphorism. 'Suppose for a minute that Alex was the main target. If there was only one body found in the Castle and KLM hadn't reported anything, would anyone else have made the connection? I mean, did Alex have a family or anything?'

It was a question neither could answer.

'The trouble is, George, we can't do very much without alerting KLM to what's happened. From what we do know it seems likely that the murderer at least has contacts there, even if they are not on the staff. You and I keeping silent for a day or two is one of our few special advantages.'

For a while they stopped talking and made some headway on their Vindaloo curries, which had just been brought. The sauce was really hot – a good job they had plenty of water to go with it.

George stopped eating a few minutes later. 'As the youngsters said earlier, it's almost certain that a vehicle would have had to be removed from the Castle car park after each assault. Mark had a fairly old Toyota. I can tell you it's number if you like.'

Frances smiled. 'I'm ahead of you, George. I've already got the numbers for both Mark Gilbert and Alex Price from the Driving Agency, the DVLA. The police still have one or two shortcuts, you know. As we speak one of my staff is poring over recent vehicle records in Lostwithiel, looking for any sighting of either vehicle.'

'I doubt he'll find anything. Hey Frances, if you had to get rid of a car around St Austell, where would you try?'

It was good to wrestle with a fresh problem for a while. They pondered as they continued their meal.

'Could you ditch it in the sea?' asked George.

'Trouble is, you wouldn't get it out very far unless you had a ferry boat. It would still be visible at the next low tide.' She paused. 'A better way to get rid of a car, if you wanted it gone for a long time, might be to sink it in a lake.'

'There are plenty of those around St Austell,' mused George. 'You'd need to choose a deep one, with some sort of track leading down to the water. And one that was well out of the way.'

'Not too far from Lostwithiel, of course. And not far from wherever the murderer lived. This would probably be happening at dead of night. They'd be walking home after it was dumped.'

'We'll look on the map properly when we've finished the meal,' proposed George. 'Let's enjoy that first.'

CHAPTER 51 Sun February 26th Luxulyan Quarry

It was mid-evening before they'd left the restaurant and driven back to St Austell. They'd agreed George was going to help next day on the search for Mark's car and Alex's Land Rover. For now that was their most tangible line of enquiry.

'Here's a thought, George,' said Frances. 'Why not stay overnight? I have a spare bedroom. Though I'm afraid it's a bit bare. I only moved in two weeks ago.'

George didn't need hotel-style accommodation and it would save time to stay here. Frances could offer her a spare toothbrush and pyjamas. She messaged Emma to say she had no news and would be staying with Frances till her role in the investigation was completed. But she thanked the historian for her hospitality and said they'd be in touch again soon.

'It's easy enough to pick out likely locations,' said George, as they pored over the Explorer map, holding their mugs of cocoa. 'But how will we search for a car that's hidden in the depths?'

'Ah. There are advantages in being a police inspector. We have a device at the St Austell station for scouring ponds and so on. It's quite expensive, called a "side scanning sonar". But it doesn't get used very often; I intend to borrow it tomorrow.'

It sounded plausible. 'But how do we take it across the water?'

'The police have got a small dinghy with an outboard motor, that fits on a trailer. I can tow it to a lake behind my car. Then the sonar is pulled along behind. It'll be a fun day out.'

Sunday was the start of another cold spell; there was a biting wind. "Fun" might not be the right word. George was glad she still had her kagoule and gloves with her. It would be cold in a dinghy on open water. Could the search be conducted whilst the boat was moving, she wondered; or did it simply provide a series of stationary depth values? How many readings were needed to pick out a vehicle on a bumpy lake bottom?

After an early breakfast they went first into the St Austell police station to pick up the boat and the sonar. The building was quiet – but it was only eight thirty in the morning. Frances explained that she'd already had a two-hour tutorial on the sonar from the resident expert during her induction to the station.

She had been assured that it was easy to operate, 'you'll soon get the hang of it.' She'd also been shown scans from earlier exercises. The device could give depth readings for about twenty-five metres on either side of the boat. They would need to rely on regular GPS readings from their phone, she said, to keep their sweeps systematic.

The only two locations they were certain of in this case were where the bodies were found, Restormel Castle; and where the two victims worked, Bugle. Imagining a line between the two, the only stretch of water close to it was the former Luxulyan Quarry, one mile north of Luxulyan.

But the lake might have appealed to the murderer as well. It was well off the beaten track. A very minor road ran around it, separated by woods from the water itself; but there was a track shown, that came off the road and ran through to the shore.

This would allow access for their dinghy trailer. It would also have allowed access for either victim's vehicle. It was as good a place as any to begin their search.

Frances drove them to the quarry. This was now an official police inquiry, albeit in a low key.

Her satnav helped them find the quarry and then the track to the lake shore. This was a concrete road: Frances checked but there were no signs of tyre tracks. There was no-one else around. It was too cold even for fishermen. The water had a blue tint, no doubt reflecting the copper salts that were common around these parts. It wouldn't be easy to see the bottom; or anything that was nestling down there.

It took them a while to launch the dinghy. Frances had to reverse her car and its trailer so the trailer was next to the water; then detach one from the other and haul the trailer and dinghy down the slipway to the water's edge. A good thing there were two of them. Eventually they got the dinghy into the water, the outboard motor started and the side scanning sonar ready to be towed behind. Both women slipped on life jackets and clambered aboard.

The first task was to get the hang of the sonar. George kept watch on the motor while Frances lowered the device into the water, then shone the device at the water in front of the boat's bow and pressed the firing button.

There was a short pause. Then the sonar display lit up. It showed a graph: distance from the boat on one axis, estimated depth of the lake bottom on the other.

'It gets deep pretty quickly,' observed George as she looked at the graph. 'Be a good omen if you were trying to hide a car.'

'It doesn't scan very far, though,' declared Frances. 'The lake's hundreds of metres across.' She sighed. 'It's going to take us all day to check this before we can be certain there's nothing here. And there are plenty more stretches of water round about. This could take weeks.'

There was a pause as they contemplated the enormity of the

task which the police faced.

'It's not that bad, Frances,' said George. 'Any car abandoned here wouldn't have got far across the lake.' She glanced around the old quarry. 'I can't see any other tracks onto the water, you'd have to start from here. Even if the car was driven into the water at speed and the wheels kept spinning as it sank, it wouldn't have gone far, surely?'

'Also, we know the line: continuing the slipway we came on.' Frances glanced across the lake and then back to the track. 'I reckon any car abandoned here has to be somewhere between where we are now and that gnarled tree on the other side.'

They set out across the lake, stopping every few metres to take sonar depth readings on either side. It was slow work. The sonar had to be hauled out of the water to give the readings; and there was often a hiccup.

Then, an hour later and fifty metres out from the shore, they found an anomaly.

'Hey. Look at this, George. There's a bump in the depth reading, over to the left.'

George looked. 'Try scanning again, pointing a bit more towards the bow; and then a bit more towards the stern.'

Slowly, with repeated scans, they narrowed the options. There was something rectangular sticking up, not that far away.

George made sure she'd got their GPS location from her phone. Then they raised anchor and moved closer to the mystery object.

They had certainly found something. The sonar readings showed it was reasonably square, rose a couple of metres above the surrounding level. It could well be a car. But was it one that they were after?

The object was several metres below them now, but the

murky water made it impossible to see any detail.

'I feared this might happen,' said Frances. She reached for her backpack and pulled out a towel. 'I didn't think it through. I've not brought my costume.'

George shuddered. The wind was still strong, but the need was stronger. 'If anyone's going to go down there, it had better be me.'

'I'm the police officer, George. This is what I'm paid for.'

'But it's probably my ex-husband's car. I know what to look for.' So speaking, George unzipped her kagoule and started peeling off her sweater.

'You can't go in like that, George.'

'No I can't. I want some dry clothes to come back for.' So saying, she took off the rest of her clothes and stood completely naked on the deck.

'What I mean, you idiot, is you needn't be naked. We've two wetsuits on board. The smaller one will fit you. Here.' She pulled it out the locker, helped George wriggle into it and zipped her in. It at least kept out the wind.

Slowly the mathematician eased herself over the dinghy side into the cold water. Even in a wetsuit it felt shockingly chilly.

A moment later she had taken a deep breath, let go and was swimming down towards the mystery object. It was vital to keep moving. She had perhaps a minute to investigate before she'd have to return to the surface.

As she swam further down, she saw it was a car: a fawn Toyota. That was what Mark had owned. It must be his.

The front passenger window was still open. She reached for the door frame and pulled herself down for a better look.

There was no body in the car. But there was something on the seat. She hadn't much breath left.

George stuck her head through the window and grabbed

whatever it was from the passenger seat.

For a horrible second she thought she'd got herself stuck. It would have been a sad ending to a busy life. Then she wriggled back out and headed for the surface.

Frances had been close to panic when George had gone for so long. It was well over a minute now.

Then a gasping dark head appeared above the surface, only two metres away. Frances seized the dinghy's boat hook and reached out towards her.

'Grab this, George. I'll pull you in.'

A moment later the swimmer had been pulled back on board. Frances helped her remove the wetsuit. Soon she was reaching for the towel, shivering uncontrollably. Frances helped to find her clothes and put them on. Finally, more or less fully dressed, she was able to speak. 'It is Mark's car. A fawn Toyota. And I picked up this from the passenger seat.'

Frances took an executive decision: finding one victim's car was enough to be going on with. It turned a possible accident into attempted murder. More important, now, was to get her friend warm. She'd been incredibly brave taking to the icy water, but she wouldn't want hypothermia as her reward.

'George, I'm going back to the shore.' She seized the outboard and turned the dinghy back towards the slipway. Helping put it back onto the trailer would exercise and warm them both.

'I'm going to drop you at my flat, George. Make yourself at home. I'll put the heating on. Have the deepest bath you fancy. But I suggest you don't make the water too hot.

'I'll be back as soon as I've dropped off the dinghy. Then we can have a proper look at your find.'

CHAPTER 52 Sun February 26th St Austell

It was an hour before Frances returned to her flat. George was properly dressed once more, looking warm and almost recovered from her swim. They decided to start their late afternoon review with a pot of tea.

'So what've you found, George?'

'It's a heavy-duty waterproof torch. Lying on the Toyota passenger seat. And I'm pretty sure it wasn't Mark's.'

'Trouble is, it's been in the lake for more than twenty-four hours. There won't be any DNA left now. That'll have washed off long ago.'

'But there might be fingerprints.'

'Even less likely, I'm afraid. I mean, we've been touching it ourselves.'

George shook her head. 'No, Frances. I don't mean the outside. I mean the batteries inside. It's a waterproof torch, I bet they're still dry. And I doubt that whoever owns the torch was wearing gloves when they put them in. It's a fiddly job.'

Frances nodded slowly. 'You might well be right. Well done. OK, so we might have got some hard evidence at last. All we need now is to know who to match them to.'

She poured out two mugs of tea, handed one to George and took the other.

'I've got two pieces of news, though.'

'Tell me.'

'When I took back the launch and sonar, I came across the station guru on underwater search and recovery. I told him where we'd been and what we'd found. I said I suspected there was a second vehicle in the lake, probably a Land Rover. Both vehicles almost certainly part of a crime I was just starting to investigate. So how quickly might he be able to haul out both cars, ready for forensic examination?'

'And he said?'

'He could do it this week. He'd make it his top priority tomorrow.' Frances looked elated. Being an inspector gave her real clout after all.

'While I was in the station,' she said, 'I checked how my team were doing on looking out for your Toyota on the cameras in Lostwithiel. So far, they've found it twice: moving once in each direction.'

'When?'

'The first sighting was just before midnight on Friday 24th, heading towards Restormel. The night before last.'

'So we've got a date for the event. And the second?'

'Two hours later, heading back again.'

'That figures. I don't suppose there were any pictures of the driver or passenger?'

'Nothing that would stand up as evidence in court. But the ones they have got do tell us a story.'

Frances grabbed her backpack and pulled out a brown envelope. It held two images from the Lostwithiel CCTV system.

'The first is on the way to the Castle. I reckon the driver is your ex-husband – the man we saw last night in a coma. The passenger looks female.'

'And the second, coming back?'

'This time I reckon it's the same woman driving. But now she's on her own.'

George sat back to finish her mug of tea and reflected.

'Frances, when Mark talked to you about his search for Alex, did he mention a woman helping with his inquiries?'

Her friend's brow wrinkled. She'd had so many conversations in her first week at work. 'I wasn't writing anything down, George. It was a chat in a café. But I don't think so.'

'I haven't seen a conscious Mark at all. But my witnesses a week ago, who had been visited earlier by Alex Price and who showed me Mark's business card, also mentioned a friend. Something about her "looking cold in cycling shorts".'

'Right. I don't suppose you have a number for them?'

'Not with me. But it's not too late to visit them, is it?'

Oliver and Debbie Frobisher were just settling down for afternoon tea when George turned up at their door, an unknown, taller woman beside her.

'I'm sorry to bother you on a Sunday afternoon –'

'Come in, both of you,' said Oliver. 'Would you like some tea?'

Frances wished that all police work was like this. She followed her friend inside and two mugs of tea were dispensed.

George began to give a reason for their visit. 'I think I mentioned yesterday that Emma and I were on our way to Restormel Castle. Well, while we were there, we came across Mark, that's the man from KLM that was here a week ago.'

'So you caught up with him at last?'

'Yes. But he'd fallen down a Castle stairwell, was badly injured. We got him to Truro Hospital, but I'm afraid he's still unconscious. Frances and I would like to contact the cycling friend that he had with him. Can you by any chance remember her name?'

Oliver shook his head. 'All I remember is her cycling shorts.'

Debbie snorted; then she did better. 'She was a very pretty

girl – reminded me of Sue Perkins. Mark introduced her as Naomi. I'm afraid he didn't tell us her surname. But I'm pretty sure she also worked at KLM.'

'Thank you. That's really helpful,' replied George. 'I'd be grateful if you didn't mention our visit to anyone for the time being – patient confidentiality, you know.'

'We won't say a word,' promised Debbie. 'But I hope Mark pulls through.'

CHAPTER 53 Mon February 27th Bugle Call

Back in St Austell, over a convenience meal, George and Frances had debated well into Sunday evening. After the find of Mark's Toyota in the lake, how long could they keep the gruesome discoveries in Restormel Castle a secret? Did they even need to do so?

It all hinged around KLM and on Mark himself. There had been no word of any improvement in his condition from Truro Hospital.

In the end Frances had rung the hospital: perhaps they'd missed a call while they were out searching Luxulyan Quarry? But the Intensive Care nurse had been very clear: there'd been no change at all. Mark was still clinging to life, but he was in a deep coma.

On Monday morning, Frances was due to attend the post mortem on the man they'd discovered first – they were not yet certain of his name.

George, though, was free to continue her inquiries on a freelance basis.

The biggest risk of visiting KLM right now would be to warn Mark's attempted killer that he was still in fact alive. Given that fact, it wouldn't be impossible to work out where he was being treated: Truro was the only major hospital in Cornwall. The safest option for the would-be killer, if they were determined to maintain their innocence, would be to go there and finish him off.

After all, on the evidence of the CCTV cameras in Lostwithiel, assailant and victim had travelled side by side to the Castle on Friday evening. Mark would know who she was.

Maybe the best way to protect him was for George, his ex-wife, to visit KLM herself and tell them that Mark was dead?

George considered the question for some time. It wasn't something the police would do. She herself might be in trouble later, though she could always claim she had been misunderstood. There was a useful maxim, "Seek forgiveness not permission." It might well apply here.

Could she, though, do even more than protect her ex-husband? She recalled the icy dip in the lake, her discovery of the torch and the likelihood that forensic evidence was now in the hands of the police.

It would be so much simpler if they could be certain that it matched Naomi's fingerprints. So how might those be obtained?

Then came an even better idea. Needing scarcely any deception at all.

George called KLM once more. This time asking to speak to Naomi. She didn't know the surname but with a bit of luck there'd only be one in the company.

A cautious-sounding woman came on the line. 'Hello?'

'Hi Naomi. My name's George. I think you and I have something in common.'

'And what's that?'

'We're both friends of Mark Renfrew. Has he ever mentioned me?'

There was a moment's pause. Clearly the news had come as a bolt from the blue. But would Naomi take the bait?

'I'm afraid he hasn't. Have you known him long, George?'

'We were married for many years. Recently we've gone our separate ways. We still talk on the phone from time to time. Is there any chance you and I could meet?'

George was hoping an off-balance Naomi wouldn't think about this too long; and she was correct.

'I work in Bugle, just north of St Austell. There's a quiet café in the middle of town. We could meet for coffee if you liked?'

George was there an hour later, fifteen minutes early, and claimed a table in the corner. The café wasn't busy on a Monday morning in any case.

She recognised Naomi as soon as she came to the door. She did look a bit like Sue Perkins. She gave a wave and the woman came over to join her.

'I'm George,' she said cheerfully. 'And you must be Naomi? Have a seat.'

Naomi was obviously uncertain what was going on but sat down anyway.

'Right,' said George. 'Would you like a slice of cake to go with your coffee? I'll have one if you do. They do look rather scrummy.'

The mechanics of placing their order eased the tension a little.

Naomi spoke for the first time. 'So Mark mentioned me to you, George. What did he say?'

George smiled. 'He told me you were very pretty. Looked like Sue Perkins on "QI" or "Just a Minute". But you were much more attractive.'

The ice was breaking. 'Don't know about that. But it's always nice to be appreciated. Did he tell you we sing together in the local karaoke?'

'I'll ask him about that the next time he rings. You've done a lot better than I ever did, Naomi. Well done.'

Their order arrived at that moment, relaxing the tension.

'Is he still OK?' asked George.

'He was when I last saw him,' she replied. She didn't expand further. 'It's good to meet you anyway.'

George smiled. 'And you. Hey is there any chance that we could take a selfie of us both here, sitting together? I could use it to give Mark a shock the next time I see him. Show him he can't move away from his past completely. We're all still talking to one another.'

She produced her smart phone, opened it and handed it over. 'Could you take it for me please? It always goes wrong when I do it.'

'Be glad to. I won't even tell Mark to expect it. Lady friends united.' She took photos of the pair from a number of angles before handing it back. George slipped the device carefully into her handbag.

'Thank you, Naomi. Would you like me to share a little of my life? Then perhaps you can tell me something about yours.'

An hour later George arrived at the police station in St Austell and asked to talk to Inspector Frances Cober.

'We could have a bite together if you liked,' said Frances.

'Fine. But could I leave this here, please. It's my phone.' She produced it like a rabbit from her handbag.

Frances was puzzled. 'Why can't you take it with you?'

'It's covered with Naomi's fingerprints. I got her taking lots of selfies while we had coffee together in Bugle. But don't worry, I kept Mark's injury secret. Can you get someone to compare them with the prints we found on the batteries, while we go for lunch?'

CHAPTER 54 Mon February 27th St Austell

Their Caesar Salads ordered, George and Frances took stock of where the Restormel case had got to.

Frances began. 'The post mortem I attended this morning was not very helpful. We're still not sure of the victim's identity, but for now we'll call him Alex. Nothing in his pockets to help us, anyway.

'The pathologist found no clear evidence of physical assault, though the body was starting to decompose. The smell was horrific. She said the death must have happened at least four weeks ago – maybe longer.

'If only one body had been found it'd be hard for the pathologist to guarantee it was a crime. Alex might just have slipped down the stairwell. But the chance of anything like that happening twice is nil.'

'Could she tell if Alex had been drugged?'

'The corpse was so far gone that you couldn't easily tell. You couldn't even get a decent picture of his face for the media. The only comfort is that she's got his DNA – if only we can find someone to match it to.'

Conveniently, their salads arriving gave them an opportunity to move on. They started eating, then Frances opened the debate.

'Let's assume Naomi's fingerprints will turn out to match those in the Toyota torch; and that she is our assailant. To take this further we need a story: how were the assaults at the Castle conducted?

George took up the challenge. 'We know from CCTV that the victim drove the assailant to the location. The two must have been on friendly terms. He must have been given what seemed a clear motive for going there, at night, in the middle of February.'

'He not only drove there, George, but he must have taken the steps up the Castle wall as well. He was far too heavy to be pulled up there.'

'Right. But then, it seems, he either slipped or collapsed. No electricity in the Castle to provide a shock, so perhaps it was something he ate or drank? If so, that must have been consumed voluntarily.'

'A poisoned water bottle, maybe?'

'Could be. Though now you mention it, nothing like that was found at the scene – in either case. And no phones either. That doesn't sound like Mark my former husband. He always had his phone with him.'

'Which probably means that the assailant watched the victim fall down the stairwell and then cleaned up afterwards. Removed his phone. And any other objects that might point towards what happened to him or hint at an identity.'

'But Frances, the Castle was closed. They might have got away with it. It was only because we had special permission via the BBC that we could be there at all. The place shouldn't open till the middle of April. What state would the bodies be in, if they weren't found for another six weeks?'

Frances sighed. 'In the case of the dead man, close to unrecognisable, I should think. And it'd be well beyond the date you'd get anything useful from the CCTV in Lostwithiel.'

There was a thoughtful silence as they continued their meal.

It was back in the police station that hard reality broke in on their well-constructed scenario.

'Done that comparison of the fingerprints, Jimmy?' asked Frances as she passed through the open plan office.

'Yes, guv. Tried to match them every way you could imagine.'

'And?'

'They are absolutely certainly not the same person at all.'

As Frances would observe to George later, back in her flat, 'The one thing all your efforts have proved – the swim in the icy lake and the selfies in Bugle – is that the assailant certainly was not Naomi.'

It was a real downer. They were back to square one.

CHAPTER 55 Tue February 28th Widening the Net

Frances had invited George to stay with her in St Austell until the case was concluded so she'd moved out of Fowey. She now had a few more options on what she could wear.

Over breakfast they discussed the need for secrecy. Frances was embarrassed at the status of the case: well-known inside the police station, consuming resources; but off the record beyond.

'OK then. How about if we still keep quiet on Mark,' suggested George, 'but go public on Alex?'

Frances nodded. 'At least as far as KLM. Hey, maybe that's the way to do it? "Not certain who the new found body is," I'll say, "but we need to eliminate the chance it's Alex." I could ask for his home address; but insist on privacy until we are certain. Have you heard any more from Truro?'

George shook her head. The nurse was still telling her to be patient. But Mark had been unconscious for an awfully long time.

Frances rang KLM after breakfast and booked to see Rachel, the senior manager on duty, at ten o'clock.

'I'm sorry to come at such short notice,' she said, 'but someone reported to me that you had lost one of your senior managers: Alex Price. Can I check first, is that true or has he returned?'

Rachel looked uncomfortable. 'I'm afraid it's true. Alex disappeared several weeks ago. He has a roving role here, he's our Acquisitions Manager. His job is to spy out clay spoil tips for lithium, and sometimes negotiate their acquisition. He's been a bit of a wild card, I'm afraid.'

'OK. What I'm about to say is confidential. I'd be very grateful if you kept it to yourself till I tell you otherwise.' She paused until Rachel had nodded her assent.

'The body of a middle-aged man was discovered over the weekend. We are trying to determine his identity. He might possibly be Mr Price. The body is decomposing and the best hope of identification is by DNA. We've now got that – the post mortem was yesterday – but we need something from Mr Price's flat to compare it with. So can you tell me, please, Alex's home address?'

Rachel went over the filing cabinet and returned with a sheet of addresses. 'I'll get this copied right away.'

Frances remained in her seat until Rachel returned. She was careful to touch the sheet as little as possible as she slipped it into her briefcase. She'd look at it later. But she had another question.

'If Alex has been missing for weeks, why didn't you report it to the police earlier?'

Rachel looked embarrassed. 'That was what Mark Renfrew, our security manager, said. We didn't worry for a long time, you see. Alex had always managed his own time and he worked best outside the office. And we didn't want disruption: we've valuable secrets here.'

Frances didn't respond directly. 'We'll need to come back to this if the body is that of Alex Price. In the meantime, Rachel, keep this conversation to yourself. Once we know the name, the relatives will have to be informed and so on. I'll get in touch once I'm able to say any more.'

Frances headed straight to the address she'd just been given, back in St Austell. Maybe a friendly neighbour might let her in.

There was. He admitted he hadn't seen Alex for weeks. He came round the flat with her as she looked for DNA-encrusted objects. The police officer left with a toothbrush, a flannel, and a hairbrush, in separate evidence bags. She hoped at least one would link Alex to the now decomposing body. Though making a firm DNA comparison would still take a couple of days.

While Frances was pursuing DNA, George decided to visit Luxulyan Quarry to watch the search for the second car. The underwater guru she'd met on Sunday was supervising operations. She didn't plan to strip off again. She'd been in that icy water long enough to last a lifetime.

The police dinghy was anchored where she and Frances had found the car. The first task was to recover Mark's Toyota. A recovery truck stood at the water's edge. A cable came out from it, across the lake and under the water, connected to the Toyota tow bar.

Then came a signal and a rumble. The drum on the recovery truck started, very slowly, to turn. This was going to be a slow process.

Not that slow, though. Twenty minutes later the car, gushing lake water on all sides, had reached the shore. It would go to the local forensic lab on a breakdown truck parked just up the lane.

Time now for the Land Rover. George watched with interest as the police dinghy continued the search operation the women had started on Sunday, along the same line. It didn't take long to succeed. Who was going to dive down to attach the tow rope? She was slightly disappointed: the man who did so was already wearing a wetsuit. What a wimp.

Half an hour later the second vehicle had been hauled ashore. Soon it would be joining the other for forensic analysis.

No doubt the police would have found the Toyota torch if it was still there – though would they have thought to check its batteries?

George drove on to Lostwithiel to see another piece of project action.

Last night, once they'd seen from the fingerprints that Naomi had not driven the Toyota away from Restormel, George and Frances had pondered how else she might have left the crime scene. The Castle was only a mile out of Lostwithiel. One option would be to walk into the town and hire a taxi to get back home.

Today a pair of officers were quizzing the taxi drivers in the town on the hires they'd made last Friday night. That was only four days ago. What made the search easier was that the police now had a clear photograph of Naomi, a clipped version of one of the selfies she had taken yesterday of herself and George.

George got there at the crucial moment; they'd just reached the key taxi driver.

'Yeah. I remember her,' he said. 'Thought at first it wuz Sue Perkins. Bit disappointed when it wasn't and all she wanted wuz to go to Luxulyan. Been hoping I'd get a hire at least as far as Plymouth.'

'Can you remember what time this was, sir?'

'It wuz my last call of the night. 'bout one in the morning, I reckon.'

'And can you recall where you dropped her?'

'Can't give you the number. But it was a block of flats. On the street between the pub and the station.'

'Right sir. Thank you very much. Very much indeed.'

George returned to the police station in St Austell to catch up with Frances. The jigsaw was coming together now. But had they got all the pieces?

Frances had a huge grin on her face when she found her in her office.

'Look at this, George.' She pushed across out two fuzzy photos.

'More CCTV pictures?'

'They are. That's Alex's Land Rover on its final journeys: Friday January 28th. Once I'd narrowed down his disappearance date to the weekend before Mark's interview at KLM - which you'd told me - I got my team to look at the Lostwithiel data again. They've just handed me these.'

George picked them up and examined them carefully.

'Better than the later ones, I think. A bit sharper. With two passengers in the car on each journey.'

'That's right. Go on.'

There were time stamps on each image. 'Going towards the Castle, there's a man - I assume it must be Alex - in the driving seat. With a woman I don't recognise beside him.'

She picked up the second photo again. 'On the way back there are two women. One's the same as we saw going, the other one looks a bit like Sue Perkins - maybe it's Naomi? So who's the mystery woman?'

Frances smiled. 'I believe it's the woman I met this morning at KLM. She's called Rachel and she's a senior manager.'

'A bit hard to be sure though, Frances. It's a fairly fuzzy photo.'

'Oh, I'm not relying on the picture, George. The thing is, she handed me Alex's home address on a clean sheet of paper. I checked it for fingerprints when I got back. They exactly match those you found inside the torch in Luxulyan Quarry. So your underwater swim had its reward after all.'

CHAPTER 56 Wed March 1st Spring

Frances despatched two police cars to Bugle next morning. One was to bring in Rachel Tyler and the other Naomi Fisher. She made sure the women were given no chance to talk to one another. Each was left to ponder what might be ahead, and how they should respond, in separate interview rooms. And whether or not to demand a lawyer.

Frances would conduct the interviews herself. She would alternate between the two rooms with her sergeant, Jimmy, alongside her. She'd done her best to bring him up to speed, though this was a complex case and he wasn't expected to say much. She was aware, too, that she was new to the station. Her reputation in St Austell would rest on how this case was handled.

Given the bizarre circumstances, she had asked George to watch each interview from behind the screen. George had found both bodies and knew the surviving victim intimately; she might have ideas to add. Frances intended to consult her between interviews.

The opening interview was with Naomi. This was the first time they'd met; how might Naomi respond?

The inspector introduced herself and explained that her questions and Naomi's answers would be recorded.

'I'm particularly interested in the events of last Friday evening,' she began. She was glad to see Naomi give a faint quiver.

'I've been looking at CCTV cameras in Lostwithiel. I'm pretty sure I saw you in the passenger seat of a car travelling through the town at about half past eleven. Was that you?'

Naomi squirmed. 'It might have been.'

'Ah. So you admit you were there around that time. Who was driving the car?'

She shuffled. 'I can't remember.'

'Come now, Naomi. We're talking five days ago, it's hardly the dim and distant past. Would it help if I told you that we've got the registration number for the car? It belonged to Mark Renfrew, the security manager at Kernow Lithium Mining. You work there too, I believe. So was it him?'

'I suppose it might have been.'

'Well, I've met Mark. Last week. I reckon the CCTV picture looks exactly like him. Are you suggesting he might have a double?'

Naomi looked overwhelmed at the evidence now collected. 'OK,' she said. 'It was Mark. He's only just joined KLM; we'd become friends. He lives in Luxulyan too.'

'So this was a date of some sort?'

'Mm. You could call it that, I suppose.'

'Going to Restormel Castle, were you?'

By now Naomi was unsure what else might be known. If she denied this, she would have to think of an alternative. But where else could you claim to be going, on a Friday night in Lostwithiel in February?

She sighed. 'We were. It was Mark's idea.'

'Was it? Bit cold for a romp, though. I was there on Saturday. There's no roof of course, just that path round the walls. So how did you two entertain yourselves?'

Naomi could sense she was being trapped but couldn't see a way out. 'We wanted to see the Castle at night. So we walked around the wall. It was almost like it was haunted – creepy.'

'I bet it was. The thing is, Naomi, I had to go there on

Saturday to recover Mark's body from the bottom of a Castle stairwell. Did that happen while you were with him?'

Naomi considered before answering. She didn't look too shocked. 'Mark was perfectly alright when I left him. We'd just had a bit of a disagreement.'

'So you left him alone on the top? Was he ill in some way? Had you gone for help?'

Frances had offered a way out but Naomi didn't take it, shook her head. 'We'd just fallen out big time. He told me to find my own way home.'

'So you walked to Lostwithiel, then took a taxi back to Luxulyan?'

Naomi looked surprised at how much the police officer already knew. 'Yes.'

'We've talked to the taxi driver, you see. He even remembers where he dropped you. "About one in the morning", he said.'

'I didn't notice the time, I'm afraid. I was too upset.'

Frances smiled. 'Alright, Naomi, let's take a short break. We'll continue in half an hour. We've by no means finished.'

Frances paused for a word with George before her second interview. 'I couldn't see an obvious way to disprove her story. Can you?'

She expected Rachel Tyler would be the harder case. She was, after all, a senior manager. Their strongest evidence was the fingerprints on the torch inside Mark's drowned car. But she would have to take the woman's prints officially before she could make much of that.

Frances switched on the recorder, introduced herself and her sergeant, then she began.

'I'm awaiting results on the DNA match for Alex Price,

Rachel. For the purpose of this interview I'm going to assume the body we found is his. Now you told me that Alex was "a bit of a wild card". Could you expand that for me, please.'

Rachel seemed relieved at the line of questioning. 'Certainly. Alex had had a rough upbringing, plenty of fights in his teenage years. And he had an eye for ladies. I had several complaints about his behaviour towards female staff. So it suited all of us – or at least, all of us ladies – that he was out of the office most of the time. Wandering distant clay tips was probably the best place for him.'

'Didn't you think of taking these cases to the police?'

Rachel looked scornful. She glanced at the police sergeant and then back to the inspector. 'For a nanosecond. Your lot aren't as bad as the Met but they're hardly empathetic. Alex was always very careful to make sure there were no witnesses. In each case it would be their word against his.'

'So if he had come to a sticky end, you wouldn't be heart-broken?'

'Sad but not distraught, Inspector. I never understood why Simon Cooke hired him.'

'OK. That's helpful, Rachel. D'you have any photos of Alex?'

Rachel responded angrily. 'I've got pinups of him round the office. What the hell d'you think?'

'My problem, you see, is that I've got pictures from a CCTV camera in Lostwithiel, taken on the evening of Friday January 27th. It's Alex's Land Rover all right, so I'd guess it's Alex driv-ing. But I can't be sure.'

Her words seemed to have disturbed Rachel. She was silent.

'The thing is,' Frances went on, 'someone who looks just like you sitting beside him. Could you confirm it was you?'

'Why on earth should it be me? In a car with him?'

There was a pause before Frances gave her answer.

'Unfortunately, Rachel, I can no longer ask him. He's dead. Came to a horrible end, upside down in a stairwell at the Castle. Both legs broken. Trouble is, he was so decomposed that the pathologist couldn't be sure what had killed him. It might have been the savage blow to the head as he fell down the spiral staircase. Or he might have suffered a slow, lingering death from starvation over the weeks ahead. We were very lucky, really, to find him when we did. By April he would have been a decomposed blob. Unrecognisable. But I guess that was the idea, wasn't it?'

Rachel was looking shaken now and took a moment to answer. 'I've no idea what you're talking about.'

'To be fair, I think you and Naomi suffered in the process too. After you killed Alex, you had to get rid of his Land Rover. I've another CCTV picture of you driving back through Lostwithiel, this one with Naomi beside you. Which made me ask myself, where would I hide a vehicle so it wouldn't easily be found?

Frances stopped but this time Rachel didn't respond at all. Frances continued.

'Yesterday, my staff trawled Luxulyan Quarry. They found two vehicles: Alex's Land Rover and Mark Renfrew's Toyota. Pulled both of 'em out of the water, they're busy searching them now. They want to find out who was driving them when they went into the lake.

'But you and I know that, Rachel, don't we? I bet that water was terribly cold. It was the end of January, two in the morning. I'm assuming you and Naomi had agreed some sort of a pact: you'd both do it all. Once you'd driven into the lake, you both had to wait till the Land Rover had almost filled to the top with water, then fight your way out through the car windows, twenty feet below the surface. That would be daunting enough.

'Once you'd reached the surface you had the swim back to the shore. After which, shivering like Eskimos, you had to make your way back to the road, then on to Luxulyan in your soaking clothes. Have you ever been that cold before?'

Rachel had been broken by Frances' detailed account and started sobbing. 'It was unbearable. We'd stripped down to our underwear before we drove into the lake, ready for the swim. Everything else was left in the Land Rover. Once we were ashore, we tried to make ourselves run, to warm ourselves up. But we'd made a mistake: we'd left our shoes in the car. We had to go bare footed over a mile of concrete track, then another mile over rough tarmac to the village. It was continual hell. Naomi swore she'd never do anything like it again.'

'And she didn't, did she?' asked Frances. 'Because next time, just last Friday in fact, you came to help her deal with Mark. The new security manager was getting far too close to the truth. You were prepared to go through that terrible ordeal a second time. Even if you were on your own.

'You're a brave woman, Rachel. I must commend you on that, if on nothing else.'

CHAPTER 57 Wed March 1st Case Cracked

'That's one of 'em halfway to a confession,' said the inspector, with a glint in her eye. She was having the promised chat with George before returning to deal once more with Naomi.

'Well done, Frances. You did very well.'

Frances shrugged. 'I watched you go so bravely into that freezing water on Sunday and then dive down to the car. That helped me depict the reconstruction to Rachel. It brought the ordeal back for her: it must have been very traumatic. That's what made her confess. But have you any ideas on Naomi?'

'Could you ask for her ideas on why might Mark have collapsed? And see what she says about water bottles?'

The inspector returned to continue the interview with Naomi a few minutes later and spoke their names into the voice recorder.

'Right, Naomi. We've got your opening account of last Friday night at Restormel Castle with Mark Renfrew. We'll come back to that. But I wanted to start with the earlier visit you made to the Castle.'

A flicker of alarm passed over the woman's face but she remained impassive.

'I'm talking, Naomi, about your visit with Alex Price in late January.'

'You speak as if you believe I was there too.'

'I know you were there, Naomi. I've seen the CCTV cameras. Rachel has already told me quite a lot about it. Now I'd like to hear your side.'

Frances judged that this line of inquiry was coming as a shock. Naomi had some defence ready for last Friday. But the events of January were a long time back. She took a while to respond, but Frances was happy to wait.

'Alex Price was a monster,' Naomi began. 'He assaulted me, years and years ago. We both worked at Wheal Richard Clay Pit, just before it closed. I was eighteen and completely innocent. He walked me to some faraway woods then tried to rape me. By some lucky chance I got away but it almost ruined my life.

'I hadn't been at KLM for long when I saw him again. But he didn't recognise me – I was much older, no doubt he'd ravaged many others in the meantime. So I went to Rachel and asked for a separate office, which I could keep locked; and I kept out of his way.

'Over time I realised he'd tried something with almost every woman in the company. One day last December Rachel called us all together for a long lunch in the Charcoal Grill – told the firm it was our Christmas meal. She declared we had to do something about Alex; and we all agreed. The question was what? He was stronger than any one of us: no-one wanted to suffer another assault.

'Then someone suggested drugs. We all agreed it was a great idea. I knew the drug scene in St Austell – not personally, but I was in the town for yoga every week. I offered to obtain GHB: it's a rape drug, said to act on a woman very quickly. I presumed it would have the same effect on a man.

'The next question was location. We didn't want his body found anywhere near the KLM offices. Someone said Restormel Castle was closed for the winter; and had several deep stairwells. He might not be found for months. But how would we get him there?

'It turned out I was the only woman in KLM he hadn't tried to molest recently. So it was agreed I was the best bait. Rachel said she would do the deed if I could lure him to the Castle. Between us we came up with a scheme about hidden treasure and Joseph Dingley.'

'I've heard of him,' said Frances. 'Didn't he diddle Charles Rashleigh?'

'That's right. Well. I used to work for the Council, still had friends there and knew how it worked. I asked them to tell me the addresses of all the Dingleys living around St Austell; I added Restormel to the end of the list. Then I put them in order, going steadily towards the Castle; and hid them at the back of Alex's desk drawer. Rachel said she'd make sure he found it and egged him on to visit them all: were any of them descended from Joseph Dingley?

'And Alex fell for it. Spent his Saturdays trailing round every Dingley north of St Austell - in the order on my list. Until, finally, he came to Restormel Castle. Rachel told him it might be where treasure was hidden. It was closed for the winter, she said, but Naomi knew a way in. So that was how we went there one dark January night: Rachel his guide sat at the front and I was in the back.

'We parked up the hill. I led them over the gate and up to the Castle. Alex was after his treasure but he also had hopes on me. He needed me to complete his set of KLM women.

'I led him up the steps and around the wall, with Rachel some way behind. She had a baseball bat with her now and didn't want Alex to see it. We came to a stairwell. 'Try this if you like,' I said. I meant the stairwell. But I started undoing my kagoule at the same time and of course he took the bait.

'A second later Alex had me on the ground and was clawing at my clothes. I tried to resist him but he was brutal. At that point Rachel appeared, hit him hard on the head and injected a needle into his neck. He howled in pain. Between us we managed to hold him down until the drug started to take effect.'

'And then?' asked Frances gently.

'We'd planned just to push him down the stairwell. But he might survive that. So we set on him with the baseball bat. Broke both his legs and half his ribs. We hit him hard and we hit him often. With a certain amount of relish, I must confess. This was revenge for all of us.

'Then, between the two of us, we dragged him down the stairs to the bottom of the well; and made sure there was nothing in his pockets to reveal his identity. Rachel said she'd make sure KLM didn't alert the police; if the man wasn't found till after Easter, he might be very hard to recognise.'

There was silence for a moment.

'Thank you for all that,' said Frances. 'But you might as well complete the story. We've found the Land Rover by the way, in Luxulyan Quarry.

Naomi was still for a moment. 'We'd planned where to dump it. I live near Luxulyan Quarry, knew it was hardly ever visited, the water's too contaminated for fish. We had both committed to take it there. But we hadn't thought through all the details. We'd stripped down to our underwear to make it easier to swim. But we'd no idea how hard it would be to get out of the window of a sunken vehicle as the water rushed in. Or how cold that water would be. Or even how far we'd be from land.'

Frances broke in. 'That's more or less what Rachel said.'

'What finally did it for me, Inspector, was Alex's bloody Land Rover. His front passenger window was jammed: it wouldn't open. The water pressure outside was too high for us to open any of the doors. Rachel got out of her window first. I had to wait till she was out, then fight my way in total darkness across the vehicle and round the steering wheel, before I could follow her. It was pure hell, I was absolutely certain I was going to drown.'

'I think you need a mug of tea,' said Frances. 'I'll send you one down. But there are still plenty of questions unanswered. I'll be back in an hour.'

CHAPTER 58 Wed March 1st Final Round

'We're getting there, George,' said Frances. 'On Alex, at any rate. And he's the one who's died. We can charge them both on what they've already admitted. Even if there are extenuating circumstances.'

Frances was enjoying a mug of coffee before the next round of interviews. She'd already chatted to her colleague Jimmy. But it was good to have some external judgement.

'There's still uncertainty on exactly what happened to Mark.'

'Yes. I don't buy the massive row with Naomi, it's just too convenient. And we've got to remember that Rachel was there again. Her fingerprints on the Toyota torch prove it. So what might have happened?'

A pause as they wrestled with possibilities.

'Neither man had any identification, Frances. D'you think they intended to put them both down the same stairwell? If they weren't found for a couple of months it'd be even harder to make sense of it all.'

'It'd be an easy mistake to make. Both stairwells were used to hide the bodies in the dead of night and several weeks apart. But how did it happen?'

George attempted an answer. 'They had a different motive for Mark. Not revenge this time, simply dealing with the perceived risk of exposure. They just needed Mark to be silenced. Maybe they simply didn't hit him hard enough?'

'Possibly. I'll probe a bit deeper next time.'

It was time to talk once more to Rachel. The recorder was started again.

'Right, Rachel. You've told us plenty about events in late January. I want to turn now to last Friday evening. You were there again?'

Rachel blinked. She'd thought all her troubles came with Alex.

'What d'you mean?'

'I have CCTV footage for the evening, from Lostwithiel. The driver this time was Mark Renfrew; it was his car. There was a female passenger, Naomi: she hasn't disputed that. On the way back there was only one person in the car, a female, but we know it wasn't Naomi: so was it you?'

Rachel considered for a moment then admitted defeat. 'It probably was.'

'You were at the Castle too, last Friday evening?'

'I'm afraid I was.'

'So what happened to Mark?'

'Naomi led him into the Castle and up the steps onto the wall. They went round together. At some point, near a stairwell, they both had some water. Mark went down the stairwell for some reason and returned twenty minutes later. There was some sort of argument and they had another drink. After that Naomi went on round the wall alone. But Mark seemed to collapse. I crept round and hit him over the head. Then tried to heave him down the stairwell.'

'Tried?'

'Yes. But he was too heavy for me. I phoned Naomi to come back and between us we pushed him down the stairs. We didn't go down to check, though; we thought it was where we'd previously pushed Alex. We just went back to the car.'

'And then you dropped Naomi in Luxulyan?'

'She couldn't face another night-time swim in Luxulyan Quarry. She had almost drowned the first time. Said she would just get a taxi home. So I had to do the rest alone.'

'Was the second time any easier, Rachel?'

'It was even scarier. This time, though, I left all my clothes on the bank before I drove in. So when I came out again, stark naked, I had something dry to put on. And this time I had shoes for my feet. But I swear, I'm never doing anything like it again.'

Later France returned to interview Naomi once more.

'I want to go back to last Friday with Mark. Rachel was there too, of course. She tells me that you and Mark stopped for a drink on the way round; and had another one after Mark's first trip down the stairwell.'

By now Naomi too had almost given up. The inspector had made it sound like Rachel had confessed everything. Her own story couldn't compete with a rival account.

'That's right.'

'These were drinks of water?'

'We weren't drinking vodka.'

'And you had them in identical water bottles?'

'I suppose we did.'

'So what had you added to Mark's bottle?'

'I'm not sure.'

'Come, come, Naomi. You've already admitted that you provided the GHB to deal with Alex. This was a repeat event. And after drinking the liquid, Rachel tells me that Mark started to collapse. So did you give him pure water – or was it drugged?'

Naomi was panicking now. 'I'd added GHB. But I didn't see him collapsing.'

She wasn't going to get away with that. 'Rachel says she had to call you back: Mark was too heavy to push down the stairwell on his own. So you did see him collapsed? And you did help push him down the well?'

Naomi nodded.

'For the tape, Naomi, please answer out loud.'

'Yes.'

'But you've told me that Mark was your friend. Didn't you feel at all guilty as you helped to finish him off?'

Now Naomi started crying. ''Course I did. I was becoming really fond of Mark. He was great fun. We enjoyed our cycling and it was beautiful singing together. But as Rachel kept pointing out to me, he was becoming just too curious about Alex. Sooner or later he was going to get to the truth. The final straw was when Fiona told Rachel that Simon Cooke was going to call in the police, if Alex hadn't reappeared by last weekend. We could see no other way out but to silence him.'

CHAPTER 59 Wed March 1st Reflections

George and Frances decided to treat themselves to a celebratory meal now the case was close to being resolved. George found a special Chinese banquet on sale in Tesco and was busy preparing it (or to be precise, reheating it) when her friend came home.

'Great,' said Frances, picking up one of the boxes. 'What sort of wine goes with this?' She fetched a bottle of Sauvignon from her sideboard and put it in the fridge.

She disappeared to change out of her uniform and have a shower, returned twenty minutes later. Soon they could begin to eat.

There was plenty of late news from the police station and reflections to accompany their meal.

'We've charged both Rachel Tyler and Naomi Fisher for the murder of Alex Price,' said Frances. 'And various pieces of key forensic data have arrived.

'The DNA match from the body to Alex's hairbrush came through this afternoon, so there'll be no issue with corpse identity.

'Forensics sent an interim report on the cars in the lake. They'd found two lots of women's clothing in the Land Rover, including shoes. But women don't label their clothes any more. And Forensics said there was no hope of extracting DNA because the clothes have been so long in the water.

'Finally, my team confirmed that the official fingerprints taken from Rachel after she was charged exactly matched those on the batteries inside the torch that you swam down to rescue from the Toyota. Hard evidence, if still needed, that she was involved in the second attack.'

George smiled. 'They all support the case that we've already made and confirm many of the confession details. Mercifully they don't contradict anything either.'

For a few moments they stopped talking to enjoy their Peking Duck.

'It may be only a starter but it's very filling,' murmured Frances.

'I wonder what goes into hoisin sauce?' asked her friend. 'It's an unusual taste.'

'Probably best you don't know.'

But their thoughts soon returned to the case.

'At least we can see now why KLM didn't pursue Alex's disappearance with the police,' said Frances. 'I remember Mark was seriously bothered about that when he and I talked last week. He thought it was administrative sloppiness. But if there was collusion among all the female staff to keep it quiet, it makes a lot more sense.'

'Haven't all of 'em broken the law, if they knew what was meant to happen to Alex and didn't speak out?'

'Possibly. But on the other hand, it wouldn't have happened at all if they had confidence to talk to the police when they were first molested. That's a serious issue for us police officers. I'm going to have to do a lot of work on that over the next few years. Alex shouldn't have been viciously murdered. But he should have gone to prison.'

There was a pause as they got the next courses out of the oven. Black bean sauce and sweet and sour chicken, with plenty of fried rice and several intriguing vegetables.

'I don't quite understand, Frances, about the plastic crosses that mapped onto a one-inch map. Why would Alex have bothered to do that?'

Frances considered. 'We don't know that Alex was super computer literate. He might have been more at home tracing locations on a map via a plastic sheet, rather than doing the whole thing digitally.

'Or perhaps the plastic sheet wasn't Alex's at all? Was it put in the drawer by Rachel or Naomi, to warn if Mark was getting too close? Then Mark not only found it but was clever enough to make sense of it. But after that he was too trusting of Naomi, let her lead him too far.'

'The amazing thing, Frances, is that though Mark was working in the same office as one of the killers, and was singing karaoke every week with the other, you and I managed to solve the whole thing without any direct input from him.'

'But George, I was helped by the chat I had with him last week. Without that we wouldn't have got anywhere. And we owed a lot to the CCTV cameras in Lostwithiel. If those hadn't been working, and working reliably over several weeks, we'd have hardly got started. It was your information on the date of Mark's interview with KLM that helped to narrow down the dates we needed to inspect on the Lostwithiel CCTV.'

There was a pause as they ate more of the banquet. Then George spoke again.

'As far as I know, Mark is still unconscious in Truro Intensive Care. Have you heard anything from them?'

'Not since this morning. The nurse keeps telling me to be patient. Aren't you more anxious? I mean, you were married once.'

'It's a very long story, Frances. I won't go into it tonight, this is an evening of celebration. But essentially, when he'd got the job with KLM, Mark walked out on me. I've lived without him often enough. He may be surprised, when he comes round, to realise what his friend Naomi was playing at.'

She smiled. 'But now, Frances, whatever happens to him, it's time for me to move on.'

Frances glanced at her glowing face and made an inspired guess. 'How's your traffic survey going by the way?'

'It's been an unusual piece of work, Frances, I doubt it'll change the world. The Council made up their mind before it even got started. It may still have interesting consequences though. Peter, the sixth form maths teacher who supervised the survey students, is a kind and inspiring man. He lost his wife through cancer five years ago.

'He and I got on really well, ate out together a couple of times over the week. I shouldn't be surprised, you know, if we see a lot more of one another in the days ahead.'

EPILOGUE

The BBC had advertised their new series, "Major Cornish Engineers", extensively. Honey blonde Emma Eastham, with her uplifting smile and gentle Cornish lilt, had featured in their trailers. Much to her surprise she had become a minor celebrity – the best anyone could hope for on BBC4. Now came the opening episode: the first scene was Restormel Castle. Emma was centre stage.

'This Castle has been here for almost a millennium. Its restoration was down to a leading Cornish engineer of the nineteenth century called Joseph Treffry. Somehow his name has got lost among heroes like Charles Rashleigh, the inventor of Charlestown – the harbour you'll have seen if you ever watched Poldark – and Isambard Kingdom Brunel and his Great Western Railway, with all its bridges and tunnels.

'Tonight I want to tell you about Joseph Austen Treffry. He was a near-contemporary of Brunel – lived from 1782 to 1850, during the industrial revolution. Like Brunel, Treffry was primarily an engineer, his passion was building things.

'Treffry developed Par Harbour. It's less spectacular than Charlestown, just along the coast. There's a reason for that: Par isn't just a home for old sailing boats, it's still in commercial use today. Each year it exports a million tons of locally mined kaolin, better known as China Clay, around the world.

'The engineer was behind the Treffry Viaduct. I'll show you it later, spanning the Par valley. A hundred feet up and six hundred feet across. But it wasn't part of a new railway. For there weren't railways in Cornwall in the 1830s. This viaduct was a double decker. The top deck carried horse drawn trams, the lower one transported water.

'Treffry's biggest achievement was to build up a set of local copper mines, the Par Consols. He made them productive: so productive, in fact, that in the 1830s they were the biggest copper producer in Cornwall.

'Joseph Treffry was a pioneer. He'd studied engineering at Oxford. Now he applied logic to the mine temperature data he had routinely collected. And used it to predict the best place to sink a new mine.

'Later we'll visit his final addition to the Par Consols, a mine called the "Last Fling". We only discovered this when making this programme. But mining's a tricky business; even the best of schemes can succumb to the vicissitudes of Cornish geology. It wasn't a commercial success. But he and Brunel combined to use it in another way entirely: one that's still relevant today.

'Treffry never married. He still cared a great deal about his family and his workforce. While making this programme we found one perceived "failure" that he made something of. That so-called failure helped him rescue this magnificent castle from pre-Victorian ruin. They met a young Queen Victoria and Prince Albert on this very spot.

'Others follow in Joseph Treffry's footsteps today. No longer mining for copper but prospecting for lithium – the key to batteries that we hope will help us cope with global warming. A worthy legacy from a fine man.'

Once the entire programme was over, Oliver Frobisher turned to his wife with a satisfied smile. 'You were great, Debbie. You put your great, great grandfather Joseph Dingley into a far better light than he's ever been seen before.'

'I've only one regret,' she replied. 'In all his career changes those missing gold coins from Charles Rashleigh went out of focus. It seems no-one cares about them anymore.'

Oliver smiled. 'You know, everyone who found their way to our farm – Alex Price and Mark Renfrew and George Gilbert – they all got caught up in the possibilities of our well. No-one bothered to ask us if we'd exhaustively searched the old cellar. Perhaps we should have another hunt down there tomorrow?'

AUTHOR'S NOTES

Like earlier Conundrums, this novel is a work of fiction starting from a medley of historical facts.

Joseph Treffry (1782-1850) was a prominent engineer and pioneer from Fowey. After leaving Oxford, he took over several failed copper mines north of Par and gave them a new lease of life as the "Par Consols". They were said to be the most productive copper mines in Cornwall.

To give the ore an export path to South Wales, he established Par Harbour – following the lead of Charles Rashleigh in nearby Charlestown.

Rashleigh's harbour is better known, not least to viewers of Poldark. It still looks much as it did in his day. In contrast, Par Harbour is in daily commercial use, exporting China Clay.

Rashleigh was diddled by his footman-turned-manager Joseph Dingley during construction of his harbour and died in poverty. Dingley was taken to court but found not guilty and disappeared.

The notion that he was later employed by Treffry is my invention. As is the sinking of a new Par Consol at "Last Fling".

Engineer Isambard Kingdom Brunel was a contemporary of Treffry. They certainly met. But their scheme to find a new use for the failed copper mine is my idea alone.

Restormel Castle, near Lostwithiel, is a historic monument now run by English Heritage. It was visited by Queen Victoria and Prince Albert in 1846. Treffry certainly welcomed them, but I put for the meeting in the Castle gateway.

There is an Arts Centre in St Austell, its drama group is called StormBox. I've not yet had a chance to see them in action. I hope they won't mind my borrowing their name.

There is a secondary school in Fowey but it doesn't have a sixth form. "Place", the long-term Treffry home in Fowey, is still occupied by the family.

Frances Cober appeared earlier in "Crown Dual" and "Unsettled Score". Emma Eastham first came in "Brush with Death".

As with my earlier books, I am grateful to friends and relatives for wise comments on early drafts, especially Simon and Karen Porter, Les Williams, Chris Scruby, my wife Marion and my daughter Lucy Smith. Dr Mike Pittam refined some medical details. Angela Bamping was a highly efficient copy editor. All errors, including those remaining, are mine.

If you have enjoyed this book, please tell your friends; and consider a one-line review on Amazon to encourage others to read it. If you have any detailed comments – or ideas for future conundrums – please contact me via the website below.

David Burnell *website: www.davidburnell.info*
May 2023

CORNISH CONUNDRUMS 1-10

Set in Padstow, Delabole, Looe; Trelill, Bude, Lands End; Lizard, Truro, Cleave Camp. *Brush with Death* is widespread.